MW01117969

Published by Evening Post Books, Charleston, South Carolina

Copyright © 2023 by Nancy Ritter

First edition

Editor: Elizabeth Hollerith

ISBN: 978-1-929647-85-9

To Robbin –
with such fond
memories of growing
up together.
love,
Nancy

Slack Tide

A Novel
by Nancy Ritter

For Tom

Oh, Quiet Tide
  a gift to me.
The wisdom that comes with the knowing
  that the cycle begins again.
The back and forth and back again
The in and out and in again
Water shares the rhythm of my breath
  a second chance
  a fresh start
  a return home
    in the soft surrender to each Quiet Tide.

– Carolyn Jirousek

one

I see the great vault of the heavens in my dog's eyes. Wink and I have stopped at a rest area off I-95, just over the South Carolina border. We're lying in the sun, lost in a drowse, as the early days of June sail towards summer and the earth begins to store the sun's heat. For just a moment, I close my eyes. When I open them again, Wink is staring at me, his muzzle inches from my face. That's when I see it: The perfect reflection of puffy, white clouds drifting across my boy's obsidian eyes.

In that instant, time stands still. It feels both fantastic and ominous, as if I'm teetering on the fulcrum between past and future. It's always available to us, of course, that precious moment of "now." But we humans rarely notice it, which is a shame because only in that liminal space, between the known past and the unknown future, do we find true peace.

A few hours later, Wink and I cross the Whale

Slack Tide

Branch of the Beaufort River. I lower all the windows and Wink lifts his nose to the prickle of salt-tinged air. He hangs his head out the window. The tide is out and the vast, pock-marked mudflats are plump with oyster beds that rise from the mud like little cities. I know Wink can smell the pluff mud with its stinky, mysterious scent that now will perfume his dreams.

When he pulls his head back in, he stares at me in the rearview mirror. I hold his gaze for a moment, quirk my eyebrows, and whisper.

"Almost home, boy."

And we are.

The drive from New Jersey to our new home in Beaufort, South Carolina, has taken two long days, but I'm overjoyed to have Jersey behind me. In the past six months, I faced compound calamities that nearly did me in. First, my mother died, then Ben left me. Three months later, I lost my job. Just when I'd sunk about as low as I could get, an unexpected severance check arrived. So, I put a down-payment on a small cottage in Beaufort's historic district and we headed south. South to an otherworldly, semitropical archipelago ruled by insects. South to a botanical kingdom where Spanish moss drapes giant oaks like a royal mantle, and the air is so soft, one feels *bathed* by it.

We stop briefly at our new cottage, but, after two days in the car, Wink and I are itching to get outside.

"Wink!" I call. "Come!"

And here he comes, galloping down the hall on five-inch legs, skidding across the polished floor, and plunking his fine little hiney neatly at my feet. He looks me square in the eye, serious as a surgeon.

Here it bears noting that Wink is the most Zen-like Jack Russell mix to ever walk the planet. Not that he's disinterested or reserved. Far from it. It's all in there, the tail-wagging, the Indy-500 racing in tight circles, and other happy-dog behaviors. But he keeps it suspended just below the surface because he knows it's superfluous to his primary mission, which is to determine what I want . . . and give it to me. He's stunningly focused.

I stare back with equal intensity, stone-still and expressionless. Oh, how I love to prolong these moments of communion.

"Here we are, boy," I murmur, encouraging him to stay in the zone. "Far from the madding crowd of New Jersey."

I raise the pitch of my voice a hair. What a tease I am.

"But first" — he cocks his head — "how about an inaugural walk in our new town?"

He wags his tail, tentatively at first. But when I grab his leash and begin to extol the wildlife discoveries that await us, his entire body quivers like a taut bow.

"The possum and the skinks, and, oh, Wink! The Carolina *squirrels*."

I haven't the faintest idea, of course, if Carolina squirrels are different from Jersey squirrels. But this is unlikely to matter to Wink who regards s-q-u-i-r-r-e-l-s as the most provocative lifeform ever.

At the end of the sidewalk, we turn right and head through the sun-shot landscape toward the river. Wink pees on a fallen palmetto frond and yelps when the razor-like edge grazes his belly. I assure him that he'll live.

We're just turning onto Wilmington Street when there's a low rumble from the north. Wink's body goes rigid as the sound intensifies and grows shrill. My boy fixes his glazed eyes on me as if it's the end of the world. I squat down and he cowers in the space between my legs and outstretched arms. When two fighter jets pass, low and directly overhead, the shock waves reverberate in my ears and chest. I know Wink is experiencing it, too. Then it's gone as quickly as it came.

I give my boy a good snuggle. We had passed the Marine Corps Air Station coming into town, and when the fighter pilots are training, Beaufort rocks and rolls. But I promise Wink he'll adjust because I know he will.

Then, there it is, dead ahead: The Beaufort River, laid out like a strand of pearls. Although it sits a mere 20 feet above sea level, this grassy promontory overlooking the river is called "the Bluff." Which, as someone who cut her baby-teeth on Washington State's Cascade and Olympic mountains, tickles me. But it is magisterial, the Bluff, because it is home to some of the largest Southern live oaks around. These behemoths, with their massive trunks and moss-festooned limbs, dominate the landscape all the way to town. It is astonishingly lovely.

Wink and I cross Bay Street and step onto the grass, a carpet of green velvet tailor-made for a dog's naked paws. And, oh, so many new smells, so many tree trunks to pee on. Wink looks up and says, Untether me! So, I take off his leash and off he goes, while I sit on the grass and watch my dog being a dog.

I think about my first time here. Fifteen years ago, my friend Anne and I were vacationing in Savannah and we asked folks about a possible day trip. Without hesitation, everyone recommended Beaufort, a little gem tucked between Charleston and Savannah in the South Carolina Lowcountry. Anne and I drove up for lunch, came around the Bellamy Curve, and I nearly forgot to breathe. It was like Eden springing from the great salt marshes. I've gazed over red-rock canyons in Utah and horizonless stretches of the Amazon. I've overlooked vistas in Italy and Turkey that would bring a nonbeliever to her knees. But never have I experienced a sense of place as profoundly as the first time I laid eyes on Beaufort.

Over half the county is water and, when the light is right, as it often is, the gigantic estuary twinkles like mica. The way this crazy-quilt of meandering tidal creeks refracts sunlight is unsurpassable magic. Like a mirror pressed into the deep-pile fields of Spartina grass, reflecting green in summer and golden-red in winter. And because the land is low and flat, the sky seems bloated. Sixty years I've lived and I've never seen a better sunset.

A few weeks ago, when I flew down to close on the cottage, I remarked on this to a man sitting on a bench overlooking the river.

"Oh, yes, dear," he responded, "our sky is landscape, too." The tenderness in his tone was unmistakable, suggesting that, to date, I'd only half-lived.

I catch a glimpse of Wink down near the water

and call to him. He comes to me at a gallop. I leash him up and we sit, side-by-side, looking out over the river. When the tide comes in, flooding like now, the river undulates against the tall grasses lining its banks. At the far shore, fields of Spartina grass seem to swallow the tidal channels whole. But in reality, these waterways simply meander another 15 miles to the Atlantic. From a plane, you can you see how the Lowcountry creeks snake and thread over the landscape, but from ground- and water-level, they simply vanish behind hillocks and grasses. These disappearing landscapes, and the secrets they hold, fascinate me.

And, Lordy, the pluff mud! Unless you've been to the Lowcountry, you're unlikely to have heard of it, but I am in love with pluff mud, both in reality and as metaphor. Twice a day, the tide comes in and covers the mud flats; twice a day, the tide goes out and exposes them. At low tide, the mud bakes in the subtropical swelter and releases a powerful odor. But I've never heard a local complain about the smell because this rich, gooey muck supports the Lowcountry's motherlode: The sacred triumvirate of shrimp, crab, and oyster.

A sound must have escaped my lips at this thought because my ever-vigilant Wink looks over and cocks his head in puzzlement. I stand and assume a second-position ballet pose, opening my arms wide to the mysterious network of streams and oxbows before us. The after-haze of the day's humidity is turning the sky a gauzy orange that hits me square in the solar plexus, taunting me to turn away from the kind of sunset one lives for. Wink begins to prance in place, so I unhook his leash and off he goes again, in a nose-to-the-ground zig-zag across the grassy Bluff.

"No squirrels, Wink!" I call.

Behind me, a voice barks, and I nearly jump out of my skin.

"*Twink*?! What kind of name is that for a boy? Is he gay?"

My initial impression is that the man is elderly. He's slightly hunched and has the elongated ears you see on some old men. But when he comes closer, I realize he's not much older than me. Maybe younger. His face is tanned and unlined and he's extremely handsome, if a bit unkempt. There's a week's-worth of stubble on his chin, his shirt is wrinkled, and his chinos are bald and bagged at the knees. He bears resemblance to an absent-minded professor who's spent a showerless day with his nose buried in a tome of poetry and, only now, in the cool of the waning day, has ventured outside.

"As a matter of fact—" I say, intending to correct Wink's name.

"I *knew* it!" he cries. "I simply *knew* a lovely homosexual canine would cross my path today. And here he is!"

What can I say? There is something utterly disarming about the man, a sweetness, or perhaps a vulnerability. He has a wound that can't be closed, I think. One can sense that in a person. But what truly catches my attention is his humming. It sounds like the deep-throated purr of a well-tuned engine, and he seems wholly unaware of it.

In any other situation, I'd stop to chat, but the movers are due soon, and what follows is a harmless little scrimmage that leaves both of us flustered. Just as the man bends to pet Wink, I reach down to re-hook his leash. I fear the gentleman misinterprets it as a reproach because he jumps back and grows shy, all previous bravado gone.

"Oh, my," he bleats. "I *do* so hope I didn't offend."

"Not at all, not at all," I say, but, by then, he's turned away and may not have heard me.

I look one last time at the western sky, which is now a smear of ochre and bubblegum-pink. I give Wink's leash the whisper of a tug and he begins trotting by my side. Within a few minutes, I've forgotten all about the man, except for a lingering air of sadness.

two

S ome of my friends think I bought my Beaufort cottage on a whim. True, it was just months after Ben ended our relationship and, while I don't disavow my impetuous nature, I know that it can also be my greatest asset. I feel most alive when I push the boundaries of my comfort zone, and living in the South would certainly do that. I have spent my entire life in rarified echo chambers: political and religious, professional and cultural. So, yes, living in the South would unmoor me for a while, but I welcomed that. Plus, I was desperate to feel anything besides Ben's betrayal.

So perhaps my decision was slightly impetuous, but the Lowcountry was not unknown to me. Since my first taste of the place, I was smitten and, over the years, visited when I could. If I was working on a lawsuit in Charleston or covering a story in Savannah, I'd finagle a way to get to Beaufort for a day or two.

Slack Tide

Once, the year before Ben and I met, I saw a National Geographic special on the Port Royal Sound watershed and immediately booked a kayak tour. Led by a renowned naturalist, we paddled backwater creeks and explored salt marshes, beaches and maritime forests. The region's biodiversity blew me away.

I also kept the Lowcountry spark alive through my reading, devouring every Pat Conroy novel the moment it was released. I read the work of other Southern writers, too — some Ron Rash, all of Ann Patchett and Jesmyn Ward, and, of course, the greats: Faulkner, Styron, and Wolfe. But it was Conroy's lyrical style and poet's sense of dark mystery that fueled my fascination with the Lowcountry.

So here I sit on the heart-of-pine floor in my new cottage. But for Wink's food and water bowls, the house is empty. The movers are due in an hour, and I am suffused with a sense of well-being as I watch the shadows of oak leaves play on my living room walls. In Jersey, I often searched for a big oak just to sit near and admire. A Laurel oak or Willow oak would do. But to now live under a canopy of the grandaddy of them all — a Southern live oak — be still my heart!

My love affair with Lowcountry trees began the moment I saw a forest of loblolly pine packed like giant toothpicks along I-95. Their very *names* delight me: Lacebark Elm, Bottlebrush, White Fringe. The variety of maples alone staggers me: Red and Swamp and Hammock, Trident and Three-Toothed, Japanese and Chinese. A single multi-trunked River Birch can fire my imagination for hours. After Ben ended us and I lost my job, the trees of the South called to me like a siren.

I hear Wink snuffling in one of the back bedrooms, searching for ghosts of Rodents Past. I follow his progress through the house by the click of his toenails on the floor. When they become sharp and staccato, I know he's in the bathroom, combing the baseboards and memorizing the fruity, resinous odors that have piled up over the years. This, I think, will be my new soundscape: Wink's nails on hardwood and tile. Ben and I lived in a house with wall-to-wall carpeting, where Wink's peregrinations were padded into silence, but now, I think, *now* . . . I will always know where my boy is, and I find that comforting beyond measure.

Ah, Ben. I think about the first time I saw the man. I was in the lobby of the law firm where I worked, talking to Lizzie, the receptionist. I heard the big glass doors open, but didn't turn. That is, I didn't turn until Lizzie's eyes widened in startlement and she gasped. An actual gasp. Not quite a gulp. More like a carnal puff through pursed lips.

I turned and saw an impossibly handsome man holding the lobby door open for two women. He was as beautiful as Omar Shariff, moustache and all. I'm generally not a fan of moustaches. They seem to possess a predatory, animal quality, menacing even, like the head of a dead fox on a fur stole that rises and falls ghoulishly on a woman's clavicle as she breathes. But I have none of these thoughts about Ben, for he is who this man turned out to be. His big black moustache reminded me of a furry little animal begging to be petted and cooed over. The shape of it was the perfect counterpoint to his eyes, which may have been the most soulful I'd ever seen.

Even now, I can picture the way he carried his trench coat, draped over an arm with louche perfection, the rich Pendleton lining peeking out. He turned and looked at me, held my eyes for a second too long, glanced at Lizzie, then slid those searching eyes back to me as easily as a hand over a thigh. A sideways pull of his lips, and I was a goner.

Well.

Eight years later, I sit on the floor of my new cottage and think, Life is nothing if not unexpected. Wink comes over, stretches long against my leg, and rests his chin on my thigh. In the next moment, there's a loud thunk from the rear of the house. It ricochets like a rifle shot. Wink takes off, hot on the intruder's heels, and as I scramble to my feet, I catch a blur of red disappear into the kitchen. A quick reconnaissance of the living room reveals nothing that can be cobbled into a weapon. Even my purse is still in the car. I think about escaping — I could be safely outside before whoever is burgling the place even knows I'm here — but I would never leave my dog. Wink is my rock, my ballast, particularly since Ben turned my world upside-down. I repeat: There's no damn way in hell I'd leave without my dog.

I resolve to be brave, fully recognizing that one woman's bravery is another woman's stupidity. But I have much to learn about small-town life in the South. Perhaps it's someone sneaking in with a welcome-to-the-neighborhood pecan pie? There's no time to consider this or any other possibility, however, because the intruder is quite suddenly rushing toward me under a storm of bottle-blonde hair. She's petite and pale-skinned and at the nether end of old age. Wink trots by her side.

"What do you think of *this*?" she squawks, wagging a piece of paper at me.

Now that she's closer, I see how tiny she is. I'm only 5-foot-two and she's at least six inches shorter. She glowers at me and her brows shoot up. Her message is loud and clear: My failure to appropriately respond to the question may very well constitute her last straw.

Perhaps if I were still in Jersey, I'd ask this crazed gnome of a woman to leave immediately. But, as I say, I have little understanding of Southern ways, and Wink has positioned himself at the woman's feet, declaring her to be harmless.

I take the piece of paper from her hand. It appears to be an undated letter. At the top, in big looping cursive, it says, "Dear Eloise." At the bottom, in the same flowery hand, "Love, Simon." But between salutation and sign-off, there is nothing. The letter, if indeed that's what it is, is blank. I turn it over and find nothing on the other side. I hand it back to her.

"Eloise?" I ask, tentatively.

"Well, of *course*, I'm Eloise!" she sniffs. "I'm not a damn *mail* thief!"

"Of course, you're not."

"Although I guess I *am* a trespasser, so t'wouldn't be far-fetched for you to think so."

My head is spinning.

"So?" she says, dipping her head at the piece of paper.

"I'm sorry, Eloise, but I haven't the slightest idea *what* to make of it."

Her face softens at the sound of her name. But her expression quickly turns to one of defeat and she may even be on the verge of tears. If my furniture were here, I'd invite her to sit. Maybe offer coffee. But I have nothing to offer. She hangs her head, and the paper, pinched between two fingers, dangles at her side.

"Oh, my dear," I say, reaching out to touch her arm. "Let's see. Can you give me some context?"

"Context?" she cries, riled up again. "Context?! Lordy, child, are you one of those fools who thinks Life can be explained by *context*?!"

Her words are harsh, but her tone is not. I look at Wink, still at the woman's feet. Wink is an amazingly intuitive creature, and he seems to be suggesting that Eloise needs protecting. But I'm not sure how to answer her question — or even if there *is* an answer. Does context, I wonder, open the door to understanding? I close my eyes, feel my bone-weariness, and tap my thigh. Wink moves to my side. Okay, then. Apparently, I have a modicum of control in this curious situation, if only over my dog.

It occurs to me that Eloise might be suffering some form of dementia, so I resolve to be kind, go slowly, do the right thing. But what *did* I make of a blank letter? Could it convey a thought, a feeling, a fact? I suspect it could, again depending on the context.

"May I ask who Simon is?"

She stands firm, crosses her arms, stares at me blankly. I glance at my watch.

"I'm so sorry, Eloise, but the movers will be here soon. I'm afraid I'll have to—"

"What're you gonna do with your dog? You takin' her to Zeke's?"

I'm startled, but grateful for the change of subject. Truthfully, I'd not thought about boarding Wink until I talked with one of my oldest friends last night. When Carol asked how it had gone that morning with the movers, I had to admit that Wink became extremely anxious seeing his favorite chair fed into the gaping maw of the moving van. Then, earlier today, Carol texted the names of three kennels in Beaufort. I recognize 'Zeke's' as one of them.

"Cuz I'm just *saying*," Eloise continues, "I'll take her — him? — you know, while the movers are here."

Wink looks at me, his eyes soft with infinite love. He's a trouper, my Wink, but there had been a bad thunderstorm last night at our hotel in Richmond. Thunder is Wink's absolute nemesis. His velvety ears were pulled back in fear, as I held his quivering body against mine. I tried to shield his eyes, a trick that sometimes can calm him, but didn't last night. Torrential rain and unabating thunder continued until well past midnight, and I doubt either of us got more than a few hours' sleep. Then, up at 5 a.m. and the long slog through the Carolinas nearly to the Georgia border. Now those strange, heavy-booted men would be back, stomping through a different house with their comings and goings, as a Lego-city of boxes rises around my boy? Suddenly, it strikes me as a good idea to board Wink for a few hours. But Eloise is a stranger and, truth be told, simply too odd to trust with Wink.

"Yes," I say. "As a matter of fact, I *am* taking him to Zeke's. Out on Boundary, isn't it?"

I'm winging it. Boundary Street, the main drag in and out of Beaufort, is as good a guess as any.

Eloise shrugs and, for a moment, she looks wounded, as if I've simultaneously rejected her friendship and maligned her reputation. I move toward her again, hoping to soothe her with a touch and steer her out the door. But she turns and scuttles towards the rear of the house.

"Known Zeke since he was a kid," she says over her shoulder. "On 21, just past the drive-in."

I call after her.

"Eloise, you can use the front door."

She turns.

"The back door will do me just fine, thank you."

Her hand is on the door knob when I catch up with her.

"I heard you were pretty, but you're not *that* pretty."

She looks at me, quizzically, as if expecting a response.

"You're right," I say. "I am *definitely* not that pretty."

As I'm locking the door behind her, my cell rings. The connection is bad, but I make out that the movers are delayed. All of my earthy possessions are stuck in a massive traffic jam on I-95, fifteen miles from the nearest exit. The soonest the van will arrive is 5 p.m., still an hour from now.

I Google Zeke's kennel. It's called Zeke's Paws Spa, and it's on Shug Lane, about a mile off Highway

21. There are a few other kennels in the area, but Zeke's has a couple of good Yelp reviews. I punch in the number.

"Paws Spa. Zeke here."

"Hello, Zeke. This is Cecilia Gilbert. I know we're getting towards the end of the day, but I'm just moving in — waiting for the movers, actually — and wonder if you might have room for my dog for a few hours?"

There's a long silence. The line crackles, and I make a mental note to investigate if there's another carrier I should switch to.

"Uh, sure. That'd be okay. We close at 6, but I ain't doin' nuffin' tonight, so I'll be around. When can you get her here?"

"Him," I say. "I can be there in 20 minutes."

I'm about to inquire about the price and offer assurances that Wink has all his shots, but the call disconnects. I'm sure, aren't I, that he didn't hang up without a goodbye or perfunctory 'See you soon'? More likely, my cell dropped the call, but I again remind myself that I have much to learn about Southern ways.

three

Zeke's Paws Spa is a doublewide trailer with fake shutters hanging askew. The fenced yard is not much more than a neglected field of unmown grass. Along the fence line, a jungle of weeds flourishes, and, in one corner, old tires are piled, higgledy-piggledy. There is an air of abandonment about the whole place.

I consider turning around, but resist the temptation to be judgmental. My friend Anne points to the fine line that separates nonjudging from buck-stupid naïve, and she is constantly encouraging me to pay more attention to my instinct. It's solid, she says, and always merits a second think-through. So, yes, I *do* think twice about Zeke's sketchy neighborhood, the rundown house and the scruffy yard, but I decide to at least meet the man.

The protective plate over the doorbell is missing. Exposed wires protrude like entrails. In my peripheral

18

vision, I see a window-blind move, but no one comes to the door. Eventually, I knock. This prompts a convulsion of barking from within, which, needless to say, gets Wink going. His tail wags like a metronome gone wild. He whines. He cavorts. He wants in.

A full minute passes before the door is opened by a large man. I would be hard-pressed to describe his demeanor. Not angry or indignant, precisely. Mirthless comes close to it. I extend my hand, but he simply waves me inside. I'm exhausted, overwhelmed and in new territory, which I could offer as an excuse for ignoring warning signs. And, of course, I *want* to believe everything will be okay.

"Come," he grunts, and we are immediately beset by four enormous canines. It's pandemonium with all the barking and butt-sniffing. Wink submits, while still standing his ground. But, at 20 pounds, he's little and these dogs are big. I worry about him being ganged-up on. I unleash him, so he can defend himself if necessary. But my worries are groundless. One of the pups takes off with the others in hot, yappy pursuit. Wink follows the pack, glances back at me, and his whole body cries, 'This is going to be *fun*!'

Zeke sits on a couch with tired cushions that look none-too-clean. He doesn't invite me to sit, which is fine by me. He scowls, apparently waiting for me to speak, so in my inimitable fashion, I begin over-sharing. I've just moved to Beaufort from New Jersey because a long-term relationship ended. I lost my job, my mother died. My back is giving me fits after the long drive and I hope to find a good physical therapist . . . does he know of one? Good grief. Fortunately, the dogs return before I hand over my social security number.

Zeke, who has yet to speak, chuckles and names the dogs as they tear past us. There's Lexi and Beau, Bentley and Carrie. This time, Wink is in the middle of the pack. He shoots me a look, but does not slow his pace. Then, a screen door slams and I hear excited, friendly barking from outside. Apparently, the dogs can come and go at will. I'm not sure why this reassures me, but it does.

Zeke stands.

"Well, Miz Gilbert, you best get a move on. Ha! Get it? *Move on* because you're moving *in*?"

I laugh to be pleasant. It's then I notice his front teeth are missing and both lower incisors are capped in gold foil. It's shocking and menacing, those preternaturally shiny tusks. Not something a dentist would do. More like a gang tattoo.

I face him, caught in a moment of indecision. Then, the movers text that they're 20 minutes away. I look out a window to the backyard and see Wink cavorting with four new friends. I tell Zeke I will pick Wink up by 8.

The next few hours are a blur. The movers, Darryl and Pete, get off to a bad start when the van's overhead is too high to back into the driveway without taking out a low-hanging limb of my oak. The men are clearly exhausted, having driven nonstop, and I can see they're impatient with my spiel about the sanctity of Lowcountry trees, where arborists and all manner of ordinances abound to protect these treasures. I stop short of a lecture on the penalties attached to damaging even a branch of one of these old souls, not to mention the approbation of one's neighbors in perpetuity.

Of course, they acquiesce, but that doesn't stop the kvetching about having to carry furniture and boxes an extra 30 feet. Halfway through the unloading, I take Darryl, the head grumbler, aside and assure him that the tip will recognize their extra effort. Although this curtails the commentary, we never do hit a groove where I can direct the placement of particular boxes in particular rooms. My bed ends up in one of the guest bedrooms and two living room side tables land in my bedroom, that kind of thing. But this doesn't really bother me because I'm in no hurry to set up house. No deadlines loom, so even as kitchen boxes stack up in the bathroom, I feel lighthearted, knowing that all that lies before me are the blank pages of sun-sotted, jasmine-scented days.

When the box count comes up one short and the boys are searching high-and-low, I use the time to decide on a good hiding place for one of Wink's squeaky toys. I experience a jolt of pure delight when I picture him, in just a few minutes, tearing through the house, while I goad on his search for his toy, in this case a well-worn fox with a missing ear. I tuck it behind the door of the room that will become my office.

By the time I sign an astonishing number of documents and pay Darryl and Pete, it's nearly 8 p.m. I try Zeke's, but it clicks over to voice mail, so I leave a message that I'm on my way.

On the 10-mile drive, I think about strange, little

Eloise and her blank letter from Simon. Who is he, I wonder? A husband who's flown the coop? Oh, dear. That's ungenerous of me. A brother, then? Perhaps, a friend?

Again, it takes forever for Zeke to answer the door. He appears startled to see me. I smell alcohol on his breath. He sways a bit and grips the door jam.

"Wink," I say.

"We'll go around," he grunts. "They're bedded out back."

He nudges past me. Is that a slight push of his shoulder against mine? I follow him around the side of the house, through a chain-link gate, to a small storage shed with a roll-up door. The entire unit couldn't have been more than 8 x 10 feet. Zeke bends, pulls hard on the handle, and says, "You brought cash?" At least, that's what I think he says, but the rattling as the door accordions up partially drowns out his words. I'm trying to wrap my brain around why the dogs would be shut up in a storage shed.

Out they bound. One, two, three, four dogs. None is Wink. I step forward and peer into the fusty darkness.

"Wink? Winky-boy! Come, boy."

I hail him softly. Nary a stir from within. I take another step forward, trip on something, and end up sprawled on my hands and knees. I feel lumpy ticking under my palms. Zeke reaches down and none-too-gently hauls me out.

"What the hell?" he mutters, but I don't know if he's referring to me or the apparent absence of my dog. He pulls out his cell, swears, and turns on the flashlight app. He roams the beam around the small shed, revealing a wall-to-wall mattress and a couple of water bowls. Clearly, Wink is not here.

In a single heartbeat, the world shifts off its axis. The air goes thin. All the oxygen is sucked out of me and I can't catch my breath. I'm standing at the edge of a chasm. It is deathly silent. My heart pounds and, for a moment, I go deaf. Then, sound rushes back in and I hear the surround-sound of cicadas and Zeke breathing behind me. I smell the sharp odor of sweat and stale tobacco.

Random thoughts bumper-car around in my skull: The ominous feelings I ignored when I dropped Wink off, the fact that he was housed, or *not* housed, in a windowless storage shed. I glare at Zeke. His expression is blank, but he gives off a hostile vibe. Or maybe it's fear? He doesn't hold my gaze for long, nor does he say a word in surprise or concern. Is he as dumbfounded as I about Wink's whereabouts?

I walk to the middle of the yard, navigating around tree roots that erupt from the grassless ground. The air is warm and smells foul and mysterious, like rotten leaves and the sharp punch of brine that comes off shrimp boats. As twilight lengthens, it takes a moment for my eyes to adjust, and when they do, I scan the perimeter of the fence line. In places, the chain link is bowed and sagging, and I see spots where Wink easily could have escaped. But why would he? He's not a bolter, but this is a strange place and he may have been disoriented after two days' captivity in the car. But Wink trusts me. He would not leave the last place he saw me. This, I know absolutely.

Slack Tide

As my mind catches up to my body's reaction to the shock, everything unspools in slow motion. Every movement, of Zeke, of the dogs in the yard, of my own body, becomes dreamlike. The knot on a tree trunk, the flutter of bat wings, is magnified and grotesque.

I swing around and turn to Zeke. Or, rather, turn *on* him.

"Where is my dog?"

I step back, as if he's dangerous. Or perhaps because I am. I hiss like a cobra, "Where'zzz. My. *Dog*."

Zeke leans against the shed, a thug slouched against a lamp post. And, his eyes, oh, his *eyes*. They're viperous, cold. I can't tell if he's frightened or ready to pounce at me. Is he challenging me to go berserk? Daring me to accuse him of negligence . . . or worse?

"I have no fucking *idea* what happened to your dog," he snarls. "You were right here when I opened the kennel. How could I *possibly* know anything?"

Of course, this makes no sense. Is he confused or is this a clever ruse? I want to know why my dog was entombed in this claustrophobic prison in the first place. As a former paralegal and reporter, I'm not shy about asking tough questions of a noncooperative interviewee, but I know better than to piss this guy off. At this point, he's my only connection to Wink.

"No, of course not. But when was the last time you saw him? Let's think back."

'Of *course* not?' '*Let's*?' I grit my teeth, sickened by my sham obeisance. The sting of bile rises in my throat. I want to grab this awful man by the shoulders and shake loose whatever shred of common sense and decency he has left. But I have never touched another

24

in anger and starting now, with this very large, half-drunk stranger would be unproductive. Not to mention, foolish. I have to stay focused.

I look over his shoulder to the western sky. A fingernail moon has risen. Clouds scud across the tender crescent and a shadow moves across Zeke's face. He shifts from one leg to the other and paws at his goatee in a show of deep contemplation. I don't believe a word that comes out of his mouth.

"Well, now, let me see. Your dog went in there with the others about an hour ago."

An *hour*? I'd only been gone two-and-a-half hours. Why weren't the dogs allowed to stay in the house or play in the yard? The sun set just minutes ago and there's still enough light to see Zeke's face. He pulls it into a grimace, whistles and the four dogs come loping behind him as he lurches toward the trailer.

I have no intention of waiting to see what he'll do next. I begin picking my way to the fence line. Much of the top railing is rusted and collapsed, leaving jagged spikes that remind me of Normandy Beach after D-Day. It's an angry, hostile space, and I understand why Wink might want to escape. Then, from behind me, two bright lights pierce the darkness. I hear voices as the beams approach in jerky arcs and see Zeke carrying a large flashlight and beside him, holding a smaller torch, a boy who I estimate to be in his mid-teens.

Zeke nods in the kid's direction.

Nephew Wade," he mumbles, then adds, a bit gratuitously, "Just arrived."

Zeke walks past me, head down. He steps over

a piece of collapsed fence and into the impenetrable forest beyond. Wade seems nervous. He fidgets and shoots me sidelong glances. I quick-step to walk beside him.

"Do you have any idea what could have happened to my dog, Wade?"

A harsh intake of air. The boy looks like he's been punched in the gut.

"Ma'am?"

"I mean, you probably wouldn't . . . I'm not suggesting . . . I mean, if you just arrived—"

"Zat what Uncle Z said?"

It's an odd response and renders me both suspicious and hopeful.

"Wade? *Do* you know something?"

"No, ma'am," he says, swallowing his words. He picks up his pace, leaving me behind. With no flashlight.

I maneuver gingerly around the yard. It's three-quarters of an acre, perhaps, and hemmed in to the north and east by dense forest. I move toward the westerly edge, but it's rough going and I stumble over protuberant roots. At one point, I trip on what feels like a furry rock, which prompts a startling rush of wings. I look up and see bats slicing through the stygian sky. Light from Wade's torch moves herky-jerky, like a disembodied figure with wonky eyes.

I chastise myself for not retrieving my cell flashlight sooner and wonder if this how it's going to be now — thinking too slowly, not trusting my instincts. I walk in the back door of the doublewide without knocking, thinking Zeke is still outside. Or not thinking, really. But he's sitting in the living room in the dark, and I nearly jump out of my skin when he speaks.

"Ain't gonna find him tonight. Dog's long gone."

I walk out the front door. Why isn't he looking for Wink? He creeps me out. *Everything* creeps me out: The isolated trailer, the dense, dark forest, the mad chorus of insects, more ominous somehow than insects in New Jersey.

I retrieve my cell and aim the flashlight down the dead-end road. The beam illuminates my immediate path, but is worthless beyond that. I follow the road to the west, the only direction I'd not been able to see from the backyard. It ends in salt marsh 100 feet or so beyond Zeke's trailer. I stand at the edge of the marsh and call. I listen. I call again. Wink. Here, boy. Come on, boy.

Although my instinct is to shout at the top of my lungs, I also want to listen. I wait for thrashing that might suggest he's stuck somewhere, for whimpering, for a single bark in call-and-response, for the familiar jingle of his dog tags. I have no idea what to make of Zeke sitting silently in the dark trailer, drunk and getting drunker. And Wade? He searches for, what, perhaps a half-hour and, during that time, he avoids me, wandering aimlessly, or so it seems to me, around the yard. At one point, I approach him. He looks cornered. His eyes dart here and there, as if he'd rather be anywhere but here.

"Do you have any ideas?" I ask.

"What ideas?"

I look him hard in the eyes.

"I *mean*, Wade, do you know where else we should look?"

I speak firmly. He cowers a bit as if he's trying to be smaller, as if he could simply shrink into nothingness and disappear. It is too dark to venture much further than 15 or 20 feet into the forest and I am just going over old ground. I consider trying to extricate more information from Zeke, who scares me *and* seems shut up tighter than a drum. Should I call the police? Return home and start again tomorrow? Or stand guard here, spend the night in my car? It's a mild June night and unlikely to fall below 65 degrees so, temperature-wise, Wink should be okay.

While I'm considering my options, Wade says, "I gotta go" and walks away. Apparently, he considers the search for Wink a lost cause, at least for tonight. Hoarse, terrified and exhausted beyond words, I'm beginning to agree.

four

I sit in my car, hands planted at 10 and 2, staring straight ahead. I get out of the car. Stand. Circle the car two, three times. Get back in. While I'm sitting there, Zeke's porch light goes off. He must know I'm here, and I find it completely bizarre. I get out of the car again and stand in front of his mailbox, trying to excavate details which, mere hours ago, were buried in the banal, but now may make the difference between life and death. Did Wink pee on the bushes flanking this mailbox before we went up to the trailer? Did he leave his scent and thus recognize the spot as the last place he saw me?

I walk to the end of the road and peer into the marsh. It's so quiet, and it feels wrong, this quiet. As if the whole forest is standing still. All I can hear is the sigh of the wind in the trees and I resent it. I shiver and think, This is what I've come to: hating trees for

being trees. And hating myself for hating trees for
being trees. In the next moment, I'm out of my body,
looking down at myself from above: I see a middle-
aged woman, alone, in the pitch-dark, on a dirt road in
rural South Carolina. Her body has gone from scared to
paralyzed. Her mind has warped into overdrive, and all
she can think about are trees and the plans she had,
until a couple of hours ago, to make Lowcountry trees
the center of her new life.

Oh, she would learn everything she could,
pushing her own neural network to learn about "forest
wisdom," the neural network of a forest. She'd learn
how trees communicate their needs and share their
immune systems. How, before they die, they send
nutrients to their neighbors, and, yes, how they travel.
As her knowledge grew, her perspective would change.
She'd leave behind her self-referential point of view
in regarding trees as vehicles for her own viewing
pleasure. She'd open herself to vital lessons: How
trees search for their kin and send warning signals to
seedlings when environmental change is afoot. Oh, her
knowledge would become vast, indeed. She'd care more.
Become a better person. Her humanity would expand.
She would help save the planet.

Instead, she sits alone in her car, mortified by
her colossal hubris. Her — *my* — narrow-mindedness
shames me. I wanted all the good and none of the bad.
In a single heartbeat, I go from hoping to "understand"
trees to wanting to chop down every damn one of
them so I can find Wink in this oppressive forest. Once
alluring, my beloved Lowcountry is suddenly terrifying.
Once revered, it is now filled with dangers I can barely

comprehend. Sharp-beaked owls with viciously curved talons to rip Wink to shreds. Breeding ground for mosquitos and no-see'ums and all manner of mites with pointed proboscises — or entire bodies — that can burrow into Wink's flesh or simply drive him insane with their frenzied, high-pitched wailing.

This shouldn't be happening, I think, this *couldn't* be happening. But it is.

I sit in my car, windows down, and listen. Then, I stand at the edge of the marsh, head cocked to hear more acutely. I pace up and down the road in front of Zeke's, stand at the edge of the forest. I venture in nine or ten feet until darkness envelopes me, listening for anything that moves. Sometime during the night, I fall asleep, then wake with a start and realize I've been dreaming about Ben. Every detail in the dream is just as the end happened, which can't be true, can it? Doesn't the precision of details suggest that I've been fully awake and simply perseverating, as I have been for months, on the story of our end? Regardless, it's here, in exquisite, excruciating detail: Wink and I walk in the back door of our house, a circa 1930, two-story clapboard with tons of character, including a wrap-around porch that has started to sag. I hang Wink's leash on a hook in the mud room and see Ben in the kitchen, slicing a tomato. The dishtowel we both fell in love with in Portugal is tucked in his chinos, and he seems mesmerized by the juice and seeds dribbling from the quartered tomato.

"Everything okay, Ben?"

"I'm so sorry, Cecilia," he says, eyes glued to the cutting board. "But it's over."

At first, the words don't register. More stunning, however, is what he says next.

"I'm sorry to add to your *annus horribulis*, CiCi."

I stand, mouth agape. It's cruel, referring to the death of my mother this way. Ben is not unkind by nature, but his wit is sharp and he's more than capable of wielding Latin like a cudgel. Eventually, I eke out three words.

"Say more, please?"

Please?

Yes, please. Please, as in I'm begging you. Please, as in I'm down on my goddamn knees. Please, as in nothing ends this simply, does it?

"Honey," I say, "what's happening?"

"It's too much, Cecilia. All of it. I can't handle the store and still love you."

"Oh, Ben."

I carry a chair from the dining room to the kitchen. Ben unties the dishtowel and it pulls his shirt tail out of his pants. He leans on the counter, looks at the floor and not at me, and I rush headlong, desperate to control the conversation.

"We knew the shop was a longshot, Ben."

He says nothing. Refuses to look me in the eye.

"I used our rent money for the first consignment, Cecilia." He pauses. "I think it's best you move out."

Are these sentences connected? What am I missing? Everything, apparently. Wink trots in from the living room, where he's been gnawing on a bone, and sits at my feet. Has he sensed a shift of energy in the house? Heard the flatness in Ben's voice? The panic in mine?

Ben squats and Wink goes to him.

"What a good dog," he says. "We'll be okay, boy."

My stomach lurches. *We?* Ben could not possibly be thinking—

"— of course, he'll stay with you, Cecilia. I wouldn't even think—"

I adopted Wink a year before Ben and I met. There's no way Ben could, or would, lay claim to him. I begin negotiating, pleading.

"What about a trial separation? I could rent a room from Holli for a couple of months. You could concentrate on the store and then see where we are?"

His eyes fill with pity, as if he's embarrassed by my grasping at straws. But to me it seems a reasonable proposal. Some space and distance might save our relationship and even help heal old wounds.

"No, CiCi. No. I've thought about a trial separation, but we'd just find ourselves back at the same place."

"Which is?"

"In different places."

"Wait! We'd find ourselves in different places, by which I assume you mean, the same place? The place where you don't love me anymore? Or, we'd find ourself in *different* places?"

"I can't do this, Ci. You twist me in knots with your incessant unpeeling until you get to that one hard, little nugget that you believe is my truth. But it *exhausts* me, Cecilia. I just can't do it anymore. You're the optimistic, ever-forgiving surgeon and I'm the broken patient you're determined to fix. But I don't

want to be operated on, don't you see? I don't want
my innards exposed by you or *anyone*, for that matter.
And you don't have the right to *demand* that I expose
said innards voluntarily, *enthusiastically*, like *you* do.
You know what makes you tick, Ci. And I'm glad for
you. Truly I am. I envy that you know how to be happy.
You may believe I'm deluding myself, but I assure you
I know what makes *me* tick. I simply don't need to
explore it as much as you. I'm sorry for that, really I
am, but you're too needy."

Needy? That was new.

"Needy how, Ben?"

"Needy of delving into the deepest, darkest part
of me. But, if there's one thing I know for sure, Cecilia,
it's this."

"What?"

"You would not *like* it in there. You think
exposing my darkest corners would make you happy,
but you're wrong. And it certainly wouldn't make
me happy. In the end, I wouldn't love you. I probably
wouldn't even *like* you. Which I do now. I like you, Cees,
I do. But after your surgeon's knife excises tumorous
portions of my psyche, I don't trust you to know how —
or even *want* — to put me back together."

"My head is spinning, Ben."

"Welcome to my world, Cecilia."

He inhales deeply and looks down at Wink.

"I'm truly sorry," he says.

Is he apologizing to me or to Wink? He leans his
head close to our dog, *my* dog, and mutters words that
I can't make out. Then, he looks up and again asks
me to move out. It would be easier, he's concluded, for

me to find another place. Why he believes this, I don't know. But the man would brook no discussion. The iron gate descended, closing off every part of himself. And so Wink and I move out.

Those are dark days. Through April and the seemingly endless nights of May, I stumble around in a fog, as cold winds off the Shark River seep into the cracks of the cheap, month-to-month apartment Wink and I rented. I continue to work, continue to walk Wink, continue to put one foot in front of the other. But I am nearly crippled by sadness. So acute is my misery that it often wakes me in the middle of the night, my face wet with tears. I become obsessed with unwinding the last year, convinced that if only I could reverse-engineer how Ben and I got to this point, we could fix it.

It is true we'd been going through a rough patch. When my mother died, I was addled by grief. But wasn't that normal? Even now, I become angry that Ben tried to make me feel that this was anything but normal. "Damn you, Ben!" I say out loud, banging my hand on the steering wheel as I pull myself back to the phantasmagoria I'm in now.

My dashboard clock reads 3:30 a.m. I get out of the car, lean against the rear bumper, listening, thinking. Perseverating. Getting pissed off all over again as I remember the long hours I worked at the *New Jersey Sentinel* to help finance Ben's life-long dream of opening an antique store. I often worked 12-hour days and arrived home beat down to my socks. Money was tight and, for months, Ben and I performed a financial high-wire act. I'm sure I'd not been easy to live with. When I get stressed like that, I tend to over-analyze things. So says Ben, and I don't disagree. A few days before he ended it, he asked me, in all seriousness, if there was even a *crease* in my psyche that I hadn't explored? Except he didn't really *ask*. At best, it was rhetorical. At worst, an accusation.

Yet, despite our challenges — the miscommunications, the long silences over dinner that neither of us could fill — I thought we were basically okay. I loved Ben profoundly for six years and believed we'd emerge even stronger from our year-long blitzkrieg. In fact, Ben had assured me of such, repeatedly, which is why I was so blindsided when he asked me to leave.

During those months, Wink was the anchoring force of my life. I rarely talked to friends. It wasn't healthy, but I simply could not muster the energy to be nursed and counseled. Wink may have been the only thing that saved me from complete paralysis. Often before dawn, I'd grab my boy, and we'd head to Sandy Hook, a barrier spit that juts into the Atlantic. With the outline of Lower Manhattan ghosting in the distance, Wink and I would walk the wrack line of that beautiful beach, scaling dunes to the interior of the island and wandering the scrubby-pine back-trails. Occasionally, I'd curl up in the leeward swale of a dune, which Wink found strange. What was his human doing, prostrate on a mound of pulverized rock in the middle of nowhere, shielding her eyes against wind-driven quartz lifted off the dune's surface? I was 60 years old and utterly bereft, not knowing how to pick myself up and start over. But Wink never judged and, soon enough,

I'd pull myself off the sand dune and continue our destination-less walk.

Then, just as I was beginning to feel steadier, a financial conglomerate with no interest in publishing bought my newspaper. In an all-staff meeting, the new owners offered wholly incredible assurances that, although organizational changes were inevitable, no one would lose their job. Clearly, they took us for fools. As managing editor, I lasted longer than most of my staff. I knew a lot about the operation: how to hold pitch meetings with reporters, build circulation and ad sales, the writing and the editing. But I felt like the worst kind of turncoat, collecting a paycheck while my team fell around me like soldiers.

Those were the darkest days. Days of shock, desperation and hopelessness, abject fear. I think of those days now and know one thing:

This is worse.

five

It's nearly 4 a.m. when I decide to go home. My plan is to return at a reasonable hour and press Zeke, then file a report at whatever animal shelter exists in Beaufort. I also want to go to the police.

Before I drive away, I pull my shirt over my head, wad it into a ball, and rub it almost feverishly across my armpits. When I place it in the dirt a couple of feet off the road, a sob catches in my throat. I pick the shirt up again, kiss it, set back down. A few minutes later, I'm inching down Shug Lane, clad above the waist in only a bra. I lift my nose to the air, wanting to smell everything — wood smoke, jasmine, the ammonia of sweat and urine. I want to smell Wink.

When I walk in the door of my new cottage, I'm overcome by a profound loneliness, like the sun has burned out or I've been cut open and all my organs

removed, leaving nothing but noxious air, though
Wink's absence is more than mere emptiness. It's more
than the silence, the vanished toenails on hardwood,
the tinkling of his tags. His absence is a hulking,
menacing presence, and I have no idea how I'm going
to traverse the eternity between now and dawn.

I consider pulling a mattress onto the back porch
for a couple of hours, so I can hear Wink if he comes
home. But I know I'll never sleep. Better to sit on the
front porch where Wink has twice entered the house,
when we first arrived and when we returned from
our walk. That, I reason, is the direction he'll likely
come from. I 'reason'? Really? As if it's possible that
Wink will find his way from Zeke's Paws Spa, ten miles
away. Does he even *know* this is his new home? We sat
in the empty house for all of an hour. We wandered
the neighborhood once. He had met no one. No, my
muddled brain responds, that's not true. He met Eloise,
our next-door neighbor, and the odd, sad man on the
Bluff. But surely, he'll re-appear at Zeke's and Zeke will
get in his car — does he *have* a car? — and bring him
home to me immediately.

I sit in a rocking chair on the front porch.
The night air is sweet, but not pleasantly so. It's
more like a syrup gone bad, the stench insinuating
through my nasal cavity into my skull. Here I am, in
the place I long-dreamed of living, but how shallow
such dreaming was. The sheer naiveté of it! Did I ever
consider how this place treated our enslaved sisters
and brothers? How they were plagued by insects that
bite and burrow, heat that dehydrates and sucks you
dry, and predators, including the most dangerous of

all, fellow *homo sapiens*?

Crickets and katydids scream, go silent, then resume their demonic wailing. The song of tree frogs, which I used to find soothing, grows sinister. Just below the chirr of cicadas, I hear the pattering, foraging, and wing-swoosh of nocturnal creatures. Coon, possum, Barred owl. Each sound sparks an image of Wink, scared and vulnerable, facing night predators. Can they smell my dog's fear pheromone as he stumbles through the swampland or rests on a bed of rotting leaves? The hawks, the copperheads, the alligators — can they smell my boy?

Images of Wink wandering in this hostile environment chill me in the warm, muggy night. They rotate in my brain like meat on a spit. A grisly metaphor, true, but such are my thoughts. An owl hoots and I see it swoop in a deadly arc to pluck Wink in its talons. He's too heavy to be carried off for a baby-owlet breakfast, but what if he's injured? I see his fur, creamy-white and silky-smooth, torn apart by the hooked beak of a Great Horned owl. I see his wiry body with its well-defined muscles ripped and crushed.

When back pain grips me, I move from the rocking chair and lay prostrate on the porch. I think about calling Ben. He adored Wink and would surely offer solace. Or would he? There's a four-month gap between us now, and, unlike me, Ben is expert at compartmentalizing. I have no doubt he missed Wink at first, but me? He used to gaze into my eyes and see my love, but, in the end, he said my eyes had become a mirror of his own soul. Is that a bad thing, I asked? He replied as if I'd uttered the most treacherous question imaginable, "Depends on what I see."

I remember holding my breath, terrified of asking the only question that *could* be asked in that moment. But how does one walk away from that? What *do* you see, I asked, to which he responded, A desperate man on the verge of massive failure. A week later, he asked me to leave.

So goes the first interminable night without Wink. I create vignettes of where he might be, what he might be experiencing and feeling and thinking. None of it is good. When I try to imagine a reassuring tableau — Wink asleep in front of a fire in his rescuer's cottage, the rescuer who will call the animal shelter first thing in the morning — I can't sustain it for more than a few seconds. It seems the only way to divert myself from all the horrific possibilities in the present is to unbury good times from the past.

Our first date. Ben and I walk around a lake, flat and glistening like a silver platter. Bikers and runners pass in both directions. Ben talks about the books he likes to read, depending on the season. I say I'd never considered such a thing, that my selection of books is motivated primarily by whichever book raises its hand when I close the last page of another. I don't do long-range planning well, I tell him. It simply isn't my nature. He's intrigued.

We drive to a Moroccan restaurant a couple of towns over and eat with our fingers. Ben says he likes my disquietude, my analytic bent, my imagination. Before we return to the lake, we swing by my apartment and grab Wink. The three of us walk around the lake and Ben drapes his jacket over my shoulders.

Slack Tide

When it grows too chilly, we go back to my place and he makes us hot toddies. Later, in bed, our kisses are deep and our skin slides over each other's like heavy silk. I look in his eyes and know I have never felt more vulnerable with a man.

A man with a consequential moustache, for heaven's sake. A gentle, smart man. A man who loved me wildly . . . until, one day, he didn't.

Between the dramatic beginning and the dramatic end, there was little melodrama. I told Ben everything, which, at the time, didn't feel like a mistake. I assumed that his attentiveness signaled his willingness to be similarly vulnerable with me. It didn't. What it did was make him mysterious and, for a woman like me who's easily intrigued, it was not a big leap to fall hopelessly in love.

Did we ever fight? I don't think so. Even our disagreements were careful and civilized. It was easy not to push deeper because we clicked on so many levels. We talked books and politics and, often, about how much we genuinely liked each other. We shared an abhorrence of pop culture and an appreciation of opera and road trips. We asked each other all kinds of questions, but, until it was over, I didn't realize I'd been asking the wrong ones.

"How are you?" I'd say, walking in the door after work or when he returned from a long walk with Wink. Even when I awoke in the morning and found him looking at me, I'd ask, "How are you?" But what I really meant was, 'Are you happy?'

I wonder now why I simply didn't ask that? In the beginning, when Ben and I were over-the-moon in love, I think it would have seemed redundant. Our happiness, his happiness, was apparent. Then, as the years passed, I persisted in using the code, 'How are you?' because 'Are you happy' smacked of neediness. Lord, that sounds strange now. Who *doesn't* need to know if their beloved is happy?

That said, the primary reason I asked 'How are you?' was to offer him infinite responses, including the ubiquitous and banal, 'Fine.' On the other hand, 'Are you happy?' — well, that's complicated, and subconsciously, at least, I was fearful of an honest answer.

But even that doesn't quite get at the heart of it. In the months-long meltdown that preceded the end of our relationship, when a discussion of happiness would have been particularly relevant, it was Ben's emotional fragility that kept me from asking. I wanted to protect him because the one woman who should have, didn't.

Ben was only two years old when his mother abandoned him. I spent years mining the mysterious seam of this— the story *beneath* the story — but all I really know for sure is that she dropped him at an orphanage in the hinterlands of Wyoming and never returned.

I don't claim to understand the nuances of abandonment syndrome, but I grew intimate with its symptoms. There were times when Ben plunged headlong into deep crevasses of self-doubt. When he expressed feelings of unworthiness, I pressed, but he always insisted he couldn't care less about his mother. So, yes, I witnessed the effects and had the words to discuss the 'what,' but that's the easy part. 'Why' is where the real story lies.

A few times in our years together, I experienced
a powerful, nearly euphoric sense that Ben was
on the verge of cracking open. Out would pour his
vulnerability and humanity and I, star empath that I
am, would be there to catch it. I wasn't so naïve that
I believed I could make his pain disappear. But, until
those last weeks, when I assiduously averted my eyes
from the writing on the wall, I was sure that our
relationship could be salvaged. That sheer need, on
both our parts, would prevail. I was wrong.

I hear a rustling near the porch and am pulled
back to the present. Wink? I stumble down the steps
and through the side-yard, but it's only a couple of
squirrels chasing each other up the rough bark of a
palmetto tree. When I return to the porch, I curl up on
the floor and doze. I dream a dream that seems to last
for many minutes, although scientists say our dreams
are mere seconds-long, more like technical-difficulty
flashes on an old newsreel than a full-length film.

In the dream, Wink and I are in our house in
New Jersey. I know this because I'm sitting on the
flowered couch that Ben and I bought. Wink is at my
feet and he turns to snap at something on his back,
an itch just out of reach. I bend down and rake my
nails down his long spine. When I hit the right spot,
he whimpers in gratitude and looks up at me as if I've
slayed a dragon.

I wake disoriented and it takes a moment to
stitch myself back to reality. I sense a life-force near
me, but it's only a moth, small and brown, thrusting
itself repeatedly against the porch light. I watch it,

the whisper-thud mesmerizing in its repetitiveness. The moth's single-mindedness in killing itself shocks me. What must its poor wings and body feel? I am overcome with tenderheartedness for the poor creature, so alone and desperate in its mission. But my compassion quickly turns to anger: "Live, goddamn it! *Live*, you fucking fool . . . do you think life is so inconsequential that you must kamikaze yourself like that?"

Do I say this aloud? I don't know. Finally, in a fit of exhaustion and tears — suspecting that my anger is directed at Ben and not at the helpless moth — I switch off the porch light, sit in the dark, and listen to the breathing of the night.

six

In the hour before dawn, I'm overcome by an urgency to find and set up my computer. I must pull photos of Wink off my hard-drive and create a missing-dog poster. I turn on all the lights in my still-curtainless house. What a sight I must be for passersby, as I frantically scoot towers of boxes around. But a passerby is unlikely at this hour on a side street in a little burg like Beaufort. I try to tip boxes at the top of stacks gently, hoping nothing fragile lies within. But, in truth, I don't care what might break, as long as it's not my computer.

I'm momentarily calmed by my friend Becca's fat, black lettering on the tops and sides of the moving boxes. The day after Ben announced he was leaving or, rather, wanted me to leave, Becca swooped in from Asheville like an avenging angel. She simply appeared at our front door, brandishing a Magic Marker like a switchblade.

"When I get my *hands* on him—" she snarled, then opened her arms wide and I fell into them.

For all I know, Ben walked out the back door the moment he heard Becca's voice at the front. I have no idea where he went, but for two days, Becca and I worked nearly round-the-clock. When our possessions were not intermingled, the packing went quickly. Our books, for instance, were on different shelves. When I moved in, Ben informed me that Barbara Tuchman would be mortified to live next-door to John Banville, and, throughout our relationship, we honored each other's book spaces. So, books and clothing, of course, were easy but artwork was tough. Although we brought our respective treasures into the relationship, Ben and I also purchased some nice pieces together. In the end, I simply walked away from more than I could have.

Why Becca and I saved the kitchen for last, I don't know, but there we were after midnight on Day Two, running on fumes. I was teetering on the edge of another meltdown when Becca held up a cheap potato peeler that had seen better days.

"His or hers?" she asked, and we collapsed in fits of exhausted laughter.

I vow to call my savior-girlfriend as soon as I distribute Wink's posters around the neighborhood. She'll probably drop everything and drive the five hours from Asheville to Beaufort to help in the search. That's the way it's been with us from the moment we met in 7th grade. I picture us as kids, jumping high to pluck dandelion seeds blowing in the wind. I'm actually not sure if that ever happened, but that's been the *feel* of our relationship since the beginning. Seeing wonder wherever we looked. Experiencing delight, even in the bad times. Especially in the bad times. Becca and I have always seen the core strength in each other and, if one of us needed reminding of it, the other reminded.

I paw through every box in the living room, but don't find my computer. I'd given the movers scant directions about where to put boxes because I'd been anxious to get back to Zeke's. I don't find the computer in the guest bedroom either and, as I search other rooms, I feel myself getting smaller and smaller, like Alice after drinking the potion. Finally, I find the box in my bedroom. I hurry to set it up, only to remember that I'm not connected to the Internet yet.

I turn off all the lights and sit in the dark. Eventually, I use my phone to do a Google search: "Missing dog Beaufort SC." Within what Google boasts is .2 seconds, ten websites pop up. I click on the first and read:

"Dog Thefts Are Massively on the Increase"

What?! How could this be? *Why* would this be? I'm not so naïve as to think dogs are never snatched, but isn't this extremely rare? An isolated case of mental illness, a neighborhood grudge or a teenage prank? The glow from my cell screen casts flickering shadows on the walls, as I continue to read:

Do not leave your dog unattended at any time:
- **Thieves are looking for the opportunity to steal dogs left outside shops and in cars.**
- **Never leave your dog outside alone, even on your own property.**
- **Do not let young children walk your dog.**
- **If you know an elderly person who has a dog, help them walk it.**
- **Make sure your dog is microchipped and the details are up-to-date.**

EVERY DOG HAS A VALUE, WHETHER FOR RESALE, RANSOM, BREEDING OR BAITING

God help me. Theft. Something else to add to the fetid stew of possibilities simmering in my brain. I can't continue to read, let alone scroll through other websites. Scrolling is simply too passive and I fear I'll go crazy if I don't *do* something.

By the time the sky begins to pink, I've created the template for a flyer with my cell number, Wink's attributes, both physical and behavioral, and a big space for a photo. I pull two head-shots and a full-body shot of Wink off my hard-drive, and am surprised by the wee spasm of pleasure I take in photo-shopping Ben out of one of the photos. I'd taken it six months ago on the Jersey boardwalk: Ben and Wink, both in perfect profile, had stopped to watch some gulls bickering on the sand. Just as I clicked the photo, Wink turned and looked right at me.

I find a box marked "supplies/paper" in the

kitchen and am startled to find a staple gun, which I've never owned. It must be Ben's. Beneath that box is my printer. I hook it up and begin with 30 copies. Wink's brown and white face slides into the printer tray, over and over. It's almost too much. I feel like a victim of some acute stress disorder, suffering recurrent, re-traumatizing events. And maybe I am. Each time Wink's face drops into the printer tray I feel a stab to my heart. Yet I'm unable to look away.

I'm on the street as the sun begins to fill the clouds from the bottom up. My plan is to tack Wink's poster on telephone poles in the neighborhood. How much sense this makes, I don't know, but at least I'll be doing something until I return to Zeke's.

So, there I am, mechanically moving from pole to pole, balancing a sheaf of posters and the staple gun, fixated on my mission as the firing of the staple gun punctures the dawn stillness. I'm not expecting to run into anyone.

"Z'hat your dog?"

I whip around. It's an older woman and the first thing I notice are her pearls, which seem to contradict her raw and raspy cigarette-voice. Her matching earrings distend her old lobes to the unnatural ovals you see in some African tribes. She strikes a combative pose in the tawny light, wrinkled hands planted on narrow hips, apparently waiting for me to explain myself.

For a moment, I'm confused, thinking she's referring to Wink trotting by my side on our morning constitutional. Then I feel the freakish weight of the staple gun, still raised to shoulder-height. I lower it and look again at the poster.

"Yes. That — *this* — is my dog. He's missing—"

"Well, you can't put him up there like that."

I turn back to her.

"But I, I—"

"There're rules, you know. About this kind of thing."

This kind of *thing*? Waves of anxiety course through me and my mind becomes more befuddled than it already is. Her words make no sense. *This* kind of thing? This *kind* of thing? Perhaps I missed some obvious reference, a way to put her words in context? How had I reached the age of 60 and not known that a missing dog falls into a category? A thing or a kind of thing.

"Pardon, ma'am?"

I look into her rheumy, white-blue eyes. Her face is as lined as parchment paper and she gives off a sweet scent. Lavender, maybe.

"There are rules, I mean. Oh, this neighborhood! It's become so lackadaisical! I said to Earl when I saw you out here hammering, I said, 'Earl, we simply must start *somewhere*!' So out I came and here I am" — at this, she pats her pearls — "to inform you that you simply cannot attach things willy-nilly to *utility* poles. Or *any* pole, for that matter."

What can I do? Perhaps I should stand my ground and muster a kind but firm reply. Perhaps I should declare that barring law-enforcement intervention, I fully intend to staple my missing-dog poster to this pole. Maybe I should take out my cell and fake-call the police, then fake-assure her that I am completely within my rights. All the blood rushes to my head and I wobble a bit. Am I having a panic attack? I'm operating on auto-pilot and have no stamina for a confrontation, which begs the question: If I can't figure out what to say to a little old lady, what the hell do I intend to say to Zeke?

I look at her again. Notice her widow's hump, hear her noisy breathing. I look at the pile of posters at my feet and think one pole, *this* pole, is not likely to make a difference. I bend and scoop up the posters. As I step off the curb, she speaks again.

"About your dog . . . ?"

I turn.

"Yes?" I say, breathlessly, hoping she's seen Wink or possesses some vital information.

"Well, I'm sorry, dear. But, as I say, there are *rules.*"

seven

Yes, rules. As the old crone walks away, I want to scream, 'Hell *yes*, lady! You *assume* there are rules. You hope and *pray* there are rules. Rules that govern doggie day-care establishments, for instance. Rules that keep animals *safe*!'

But I say none of this. I return home, collapse on the couch and weep. Eventually, I muster the resolve to start posting on lost-and-found animal websites. Again, I log onto my computer only to remember that the Internet isn't scheduled to be hooked up until tomorrow. I take my phone to the front porch and begin the mechanical exercise of posting: Wink's name, breed, markings, age, weight, special needs or personality quirks, place last seen or circumstances of disappearance. Doing it on my cell is a mind-numbing and arduous process. Find the URL, click on 'new posting,' fill in the data fields, add a photo.

I decide to use the most recent photo, taken just yesterday. We'd crossed the North Carolina/South Carolina border, blasted past the kitschy "South of the Border" amusement park, and pulled off at the next exit. I filled up the tank, then let Wink out to do his business. He trotted over to a scrawny tree and peed on the trunk, then walked to an old Standard Oil sign that was propped against the side of the building. There he plunked himself, in front of that fossilized sign with its Corinthian pedestal spouting a plastic flame, and I snapped the photo. The powdery, golden light hit him just right, accentuating his half-brown, half-white face, the dividing line as straight as a ruler all the way to the tip of his nose.

I'm in my bedroom dressing when I hear a soft tapping. At first, I think it's a branch against the window, but it comes again in perfect four-tap meter. I freeze, foot raised, sock mid-pull. It's still before 7 a.m., a time when strangers with good intentions generally do not come knocking on a person's door. And at this point, there are only strangers in town. In the next instant, I think of Wink and dash down the hall. But I pull up short before opening the door. *Be smart, CiCi*, says the little bird in my head. I side-step to the window to look outside, but there's no one there.

Another knock, louder this time. Or perhaps it's louder because I'm standing mere inches from whoever is on the other side. I tiptoe closer, press my ear to the door.

"Wink?"

I whisper his name. It's silly, really. I'm not so

far gone as to think my dog would knock. Yet, for an instant, I'm sure that whoever is on the other side of the door has something to do with Wink. But as quickly as the thought comes, I dispel it. I hadn't included my address on the posters. Also, Wink is microchipped. But, in all the hubbub of the move, all the address changes and utility shut-off's and switch-on's, I have neglected to update our address in the nationwide chip database. At this point, however, the only way someone would know that I am Wink's and he is mine is via my phone number and no one has called my cell.

I crack the door. A tall man gazes down at me.

"Yes? May I help you?"

He backs up a step. He's neatly dressed, dapper, actually, with eggshell-colored pants that look to be linen and a brocade vest with swirls of magenta and blue. The fabric is shiny in places like it's shot-through with gold thread. Who wears vests anymore? I've had no sleep and am not thinking straight. Who even *thinks* of the fashion-currency of vests when their dog is missing?

"Good morning, madame," he says, bowing at the waist. "I believe we met yesterday on the Bluff. My neighbor, well our neighbor, our *mutual* neighbor, Mrs. Eloise LaFitte, told me of your predicament."

Through my muddlement, I indeed recognize him as the man who commented yesterday about Wink's sexual preference, although the transformation in his appearance is remarkable. Where yesterday there was chin stubble, today his face is a smooth, healthy pink. He's not hunched at all, which had been my initial impression, but in fact, he stands ramrod-straight. I open the door further and see a bag at his feet.

"Oh, my goodness, dear," he continues, extending a hand. "Where are my manners? Professor Julian Phineas Ruopp. But please call me J.P."

I shake his hand and am about to tell him my name, but he catches me mid-breath and forges ahead.

"Oh, dear — another *fax paux*, I fear. Predicament is *entirely* the wrong word. *Je me regrette.* Tragedy, ca*tas*trophe" — he dramatically emphasizes the second syllable — "is more fitting. I fear your canine companion, the four-legged love-of-your-life, is still missing?"

At this, he cranes his neck, looking for all the world like a turtle as he ogles left and right over my head. His movements are stiff and formal, or perhaps I simply project an aristocratic bearing because of his waistcoat and elegant mane of silver hair.

"I'm Cecilia Gilbert," I say, opening the door and gesturing him inside. "Please call me CiCi."

"I shall do no such thing, Ms. Gilbert!" he sputters, then bends to retrieve the bag, which is monogramed *JPR* in flat gold thread.

"Horrors!" he exclaims.

Or I believe that's what he exclaims. It's the only word I catch in a kaleidoscope of utterances as he strains to lift the bag and I simultaneously lean in to help. We bump heads, beg each other's pardons, and each end up holding one of the bag's straps. It's a *pas de deux* reminiscent of our meeting on the Bluff. A modest tug of war ensues amid a flurry of protestations before he releases the bag. He smooths his vest over his stomach and tugs at the points that fan out at his waist. When he reaches again for the bag, I tuck it against my body out of his reach, and we do an odd little shuffle down the hall to the kitchen.

"I've brought you some shrimp and grits, Ms. Gilbert. Unfortunately, it's frozen, so of no help at the moment. I wish I could say it's homecooked dog food, but I'm a sensitive man and won't even *think* of preparing such until—"

"Wink," I say.

"Yes, your Wink has returned to his right and proper domicile."

I might have burst into tears, but I will them back.

"Oh, *do* put that down, dear," he cries. "We cannot be worrying about food now, can we, with Wink in such dire straits!"

I open the fridge, put the bag on the bottom shelf, and take a good look at Professor J.P. Ruopp. He's as quirky as a Dickensian character, a little off in the head, perhaps, but his spirit seems bountiful. Immobilized as I am by Wink's disappearance, nearly catatonic with grief, all I want to do is rest my head against this man's chest and be close to his big, generous heart.

I usher the Professor back to the living room. He sits on the couch and I sit next to him.

"Do you know anything about my dog, Professor?"

"No, I don't, my dear. Eloise, that's Mrs. Eloise LaFitte, the idiosyncratic granddame who lives next door to you, saw your poster and, of course, I immediately investigated. She feels terrible about this, poor Eloise. Dismayed, utterly. Now, please, tell me, what we *know* . . . both as a matter of fact and conjecture?"

He reaches over, takes my hand. I scooch closer so he doesn't have to lean. He's very tall and, perched as he is, precariously close to the edge of the couch, I worry he might topple into the coffee table, which is piled high with all manner of paraphernalia capable of damaging a gentleman's head.

"Well, I searched the neighborhood where Wink disappeared—"

"Zeke's."

"— yes, Zeke's, until well past dark. Stayed there until a few hours ago. I've posted on missing-dog websites and left two messages at the animal shelter. I haven't contacted the police yet, but I intend to. And, as you know from Mrs.—?"

"LaFitte."

"LaFitte. I put posters up around the neighborhood."

He pats my hand like a spinster-aunt consoling a protégé.

"Today is a new day, dear."

For some reason, those platitudinous words plunge me into sadness. I find nothing hopeful in them, although I don't doubt J.P. intends them to be. All I hear is pity, the artificial cheer of bucking up and mustering-on. Which immediately makes me feel monumentally ungenerous, of course.

"Wink is chipped, you know. That's a very good

thing."

"Chipped?"

He is trying very hard to keep up, to offer solace.

"Wink has a little microchip implanted in his body. If he's found, even if it's hundreds of miles away, even in another state, they can find me through a database."

He shifts his body slightly and looks intrigued. Again, he tugs at his vest tails, awaiting further explanation.

"There's a number stamped on Wink's chip, you see — and, when he's found, they scan between his shoulder blades where it's implanted. They use a little wand to scan the number."

I make like I'm waving a wand, back-and-forth. J.P.'s eyes, or rather his entire head, track the imaginary wand.

"My, my," he says. "Precisely, how does it work?"

"Well, I don't know precisely, but the scanner puts out radio waves that activate the chip-thingie."

"I *see*," he marvels. "A modern-day miracle, *n'est-ce pas*?"

"It *is*," I respond, allowing a sliver of hope to pierce my heart.

Professor Ruopp stands and smooths his vest. Apparently, this is a ritual or nervous habit. The gaze he casts upon me is immeasurably earnest and, in that moment, I almost believe Wink will be found.

"We must devise a plan," he pronounces with great solemnity. "Something strategic, yet tactical, is required, as your Wink may not remember where he now lives."

And this is true. My heart sinks.

"If you would allow me," J.P. says.

I'm lost in thought, and wonder if I've missed something.

"Excuse me?"

"If you would allow me, Ms. Gilbert, I shall put together a posse and we will report at fourteen hundred hours. In the meantime, might you acquaint me with your plan?"

I feel a hard kernel of aggravation in my belly. I need every ounce of energy to look for my dog. To scour the miles between here and Zeke's. Or no, to actually fan out in all directions from Zeke's trailer. Except I have no idea how to canvas this marsh-choked countryside. Even a half-mile outside Beaufort city limits, it is quite rural. I can't coordinate a "posse" when I have to be on the phone, calling county, city, and other shelters in the area, following leads, disseminating posters, asking commercial establishments to display them in their windows. I have to spend time on my computer, checking lost-and-found sites and, of course, Facebook. But I don't really do Facebook and I'm not quite sure how to start or what value it would have in this situation. I need . . . oh my, I need a local posse.

J.P. sits again, awaiting my response. He looks spry enough, but could he tramp through fields and the back-country around Zeke's? I have no idea if he can use a computer and he's so soft-spoken I can't imagine him calling for Wink without falling into paroxysms of coughing. No, Professor J.P. Ruopp may not be able to bring the computer-savvy or the legs or even the lungs to the search. But he could bring the heart.

I lean over and kiss his forehead. The move surprises me, but doesn't seem to surprise him in the least.

"I'm going to the county animal-control offices when they open," I say. "I don't want to just file a report by phone. I want them to see my face . . . to understand my terror" — my voice catches.

"You want them to care," he says.

Oh, my. That's *exactly* what I want, but without J.P. there to name it, I fear that wanting such a thing would be naïve. Overly optimistic. Or just plain stupid. I'm not sure Professor Ruopp can help, or if I'll end up taking care of him, thus compromising my focus. Still. The man is so very earnest and the only soul I know in town. But what a soul.

"But before that, I'm going to go to Zeke's—"

"Where I'll accompany you."

I gaze at him for a long moment. Over his shoulder, I see the leaves on the old oak in my front yard quivering in the breeze. I hear the air-splintering beeps of a truck backing up, signaling the relentless continuation of life's routines. Routines now lost to me. The Professor tugs the points of his vest, poised to carry out my every wish.

"I'm going back to Zeke's, to search for Wink in the daylight," I say.

"*And*," he adds, "to confront the son of a bitch."

eight

J.P. and I agree that he will follow me to Zeke's, then I'll go to Animal Control on my own. I finish dressing while J.P. goes home to get his car, and I'm locking the front door when he pulls up in a late-model BMW. My stomach starts to cramp. I haven't eaten in nearly 24 hours, but it's not hunger. It's fear. I'm terrified of seeing Zeke's Paws Spa again in the daylight. The forest, the marsh, the sheer isolation of where Wink vanished will horrify me. I'm already feeling ashamed of myself, but now I'm mortified that Professor Ruopp will see how naïve, how unforgivably stupid, I was to leave Wink there.

Although it's only ten miles outside of town, it's so rural it might have been 100. Most of the homes out here are trailers, some well-kept, some not so much. The land looks deranged to me this morning, as if it can't decide whether it wants to be forest or marsh. I keep my eye on J.P. in the rearview mirror. Perhaps it's silly, but I have visions of his car, which he calls his "conveyance," disappearing into a bog, swallowed whole.

There's no sign of life at Zeke's. I drive slowly past the trailer to where the dirt road straggles to an end. J.P. parks behind me.

"Are you okay, my girl?" he says, joining me at the edge of the marsh.

We look out over the tidelands and I tell him about my recurring image of his car sinking into the earth. He's not surprised.

"You've had no sleep, my girl, and it *does* seem as if our Wink has been swallowed up whole."

He rests his hand on my shoulder. It is remarkable the benevolence I feel in that gesture and his reference to 'our Wink.'

J.P. says he's glad we've driven past the front of Zeke's trailer, as this vantage point allows us to better surveil the premises. I see the partially downed fence that I skirted last night. It parallels the marsh, separated by low dunes. Lots of wrack has washed up, and I think how this stew of eel grass and kelp, crustacean shells, feathers and all manner of litter left on a beach by high tide would be an olfactory bacchanal for Wink. But if he's hurt, would he even notice it?

At one end of Zeke's property, a magnolia forest nearly abuts the fence. I walk ahead of J.P. and venture into the trees but can find no sign of a path or trail. J.P. warns me to be mindful of snakes, and we pick our way to the fence until the back of the shed where Zeke put the dogs comes into view. The morning is warming. The birds have stilled and even the cicadas have gone quiet. I wonder if, in this eerie silence, Wink is watching me? Is he out here somewhere, playing a ghostly game? But no, of course not. My boy would never — ever — willingly keep himself from me. I'm on the verge of a sobbing collapse, but J.P. bolsters me with a gentle nudge.

"Are you ready to confront the scoundrel?"

A few minutes later, we stand at Zeke's door. I raise my hand to knock, but J.P. is quicker. He pounds the door like a battering ram and it sets off frenzied barking from within. Against all hope, I close my eyes and listen for Wink's voice among the others. The door opens a few inches and I see the outline of a man's head. J.P. moves a step closer.

"Sir," he says, officious as a tax collector. "We are here about Wink. More information is required, you see."

The door eases open a bit and I see Zeke.

"What business is it of yours?" he sneers.

J.P. leans to the side, allowing Zeke a glimpse of me, then places himself squarely back between us.

"I told this woman last night, I ain't seen her since she went in the kennel."

J.P. shoots me a look. There's not a speck of fear in his eyes. I hear his breathing, deep and even.

"*Him*," J.P. says, enunciating slowly. "Please be so kind, sir, as to put your dogs somewhere so we can talk. Your explanation to-date is woefully insufficient."

Zeke looks mystified. In the next instant, the

door closes and I wonder if he might be retrieving a shotgun, but then we hear the dogs yowling in the backyard. The door opens again and Zeke squeezes onto the stoop. His next words are chilling, despite, or perhaps because of, the obsequious grin that accompanies them.

"Not a step further," he says. "We can talk out here."

He tugs at his pants and, as he tucks in his shirt, I suspect he is intentionally all elbows and knees. It's a tight fit, the three of us on the stoop, and it's apparent he wants us to stand down. We don't. He shuffles another step towards us, again with the smirk, but J.P. gives no quarter. He bombards Zeke with questions: When did he put the dogs in the shed? Was he sure Wink was among them? Could anybody else have entered the backyard? Appearing sorely aggrieved, Zeke spits out his responses. Around dark. Yes. No.

Then, J.P. gets personal. He steps closer and assumes a slight crouch, compressing his body like a cat preparing to spring.

"Have you, sir, ever received an animal-abuse violation?"

"Hey, man, I—"

"Are you acquainted with any local dog-fighting rings?"

"Ac*quaint*ed?"

My stomach lurches. Dog-fighting? Before seeing the notice online last night, I never considered such a possibility and the shocking reference to "baiting" made me sick to my stomach. Wink is not a fighter, but he is a scrappy little dude. I shake off the image of my pup being used as training bait.

The Professor's body tenses when Zeke repeats his question.

"Did you just ask if I'm *acquainted* with dog-fighting?"

Does he not understand the word or is he mocking J.P.? Regardless, no one could misunderstand the Professor's next hissing words.

"Do. Not. Fuck with me, sir. I will bring a Shakespearean tempest down on your head if you fail to tell this fine woman everything you know. *Now.*"

Zeke cowers a bit but sticks to his story. He put all the dogs, including Wink, in the shed about an hour after I left. No one else was around. He heard nothing. He has no idea what could have happened. He refers to me as "that woman," jerking his head in my direction, but refusing to look me in the eye.

J.P. says we want to investigate the shed. Zeke grudgingly grants permission but does not accompany us. He instructs us to go around the side, then retreats back inside and closes the door in our faces.

Daylight confirms the sorry state of the shed. I get down on my knees and crawl over the nasty wall-to-wall mattress. Lifting each corner, I check for holes in the walls or flooring. There are none. J.P. and I then walk the perimeter of the yard, stopping at sections where the fence is bent. It looks like it's been hit by a mortar bomb, or a number of them. We lean in closer, looking for blood, prints, fur. Any sign of Wink's escape.

When I look up, Zeke is standing at the back door. His hostility is unmistakable and, for the life of me, I cannot understand why, if he has nothing to fear, he is treating me like the enemy. But there I am, already giving him more grace today than I did last night. Why do I think, '*If* he has nothing to fear?' if I truly believe that his behavior — putting Wink in a cramped, dark space and failing to keep an eye on him — constitutes negligence? I must resist the temptation to assimilate things that feel totally wrong, to accept more and more as time goes by.

      The Professor and I have seen enough. Zeke is on his back stoop, watching us. As we turn to leave, the Professor doffs an imaginary hat. The gesture is so flamboyant it screams of barely suppressed rage. Before we disappear around the side of the trailer, Zeke and I lock eyes. He slowly draws his finger from left to right across his neck. And grins.

nine

I don't mention Zeke's gesture to the Professor. It's obvious that he has not seen it and, frankly, I'm not sure I even saw what I think I saw. I want to ask the Professor if he finds Zeke's attitude as disturbing as I. Why, if indeed he knows nothing about Wink, if he is truly mystified, would he not be more sympathetic? More willing to offer advice or assistance — or something? But before the Professor and I can talk, I must go to the animal shelter and file a report on Wink's disappearance.

As we say our goodbyes, J.P. assures me that, together, we will "meet whatever challenges necessary to find Wink." The way he speaks, his very demeanor, offers some hope.

I inch down Shug Lane, grab my cell and punch in the number for my New Jersey veterinarian. Wink's microchip records are buried in one of the moving boxes and I'll need the information for the county shelter people. Although it's still shy of 9 a.m., I know someone at Family Vet Clinic will pick up. The vets and the technicians and even the front-desk folks at Family Vet are a devoted bunch. One time, I drove by the building at two a.m. and saw Dr. Yates, my favorite vet, locking up. She and I had become friendly and, when I brought Wink in the following morning for his annual check-up, I asked if she made a habit of keeping such strange office hours.

"Ha!" she barked, tossing her head in the general direction of a sign with the office hours. "Those are purely aspirational."

Sharon, a vet tech I know well, answers the phone. I tell her about Wink and her response is so empathetic that I know she'd hop a plane and join the search if she could. That's not hyperbole. Sharon's daughter and son-in-law were killed in a crash on the Jersey Turnpike two years ago and she has been raising their granddaughter ever since. She is the epitome of compassion and resilience.

Sharon pulls up Wink's registered chip number. Just as we're hanging up, I hear a faint moan.

"Sharon?"

"You know I'd come if I could."

She can barely choke out the words.

"I know, Sharon, I know."

We say goodbye and my heart swells. I don't know if I'll find people like Dr. Yates and Sharon down here to take care of Wink, but their very existence is evidence that I might. Mercy is all around us and I'd do well to remember that.

Slack Tide

A few minutes later, I'm passing the one-room schoolhouse-cum-fruit-and-vegetable stand on Highway 21. A hand-lettered sign announces 'Ochre & Corn' and 'Beans & Ochre.' In another mile or so, I see a sign for Beaufort County Animal Shelter & Control. I take the left turn and am immediately engulfed in dense, subtropical vegetation. Without warning, the road turns from asphalt to dirt, and, for the next mile, I bounce over rutted road. Just when I'm sure I've missed a turn, a low, concrete-block building emerges from the jungle. An old sign for the facility is propped against a tree trunk. It, and the old oak itself, look like they've weathered a hurricane or two. One of the tree's massive limbs veers right where an old injury was suffered, perhaps a lightning strike. It's eerily quiet, but when I shut my car door, barking and yipping starts up as suddenly as a switched-on radio.

I open the door and enter a sparsely furnished lobby. Against one wall is a single molded-plastic chair. Next to it, a hat-rack, which strikes me as odd. Beyond the high counter, bare except for a clipboard and an old-fashioned bell, are two metal desks. Atop each is an old IBM personal computer, yellowed with age. A vintage metal-spike spindle perches menacingly on one of the desks. There is no one in sight.

I walk to the wall where some official-looking documents are hung. They're bunched close together as if someone planned to decorate the rest of the wall but never got around to it. A certificate for a building permit, a State of South Carolina business license, and the high-school diploma of one Robert M. Schwartzman, June, 1968.

I stand in the empty office, as the barking dies back to an occasional yip. Off the reception area, two closed doors appear to lead to private offices, but I see no lights therein. I think about ringing the bell, but it's likely to set off more barking and, truth be told, I'm terrified of being close to so many canines talking to me. Deep-throated, confident voices saying, I'm here, I'm here! Tentative, anxiety-ridden voices saying, Who's there, do I know you, please don't hurt me. Voices swollen with boredom, hunger, excess energy turned to angst. I wait.

And wait.

Five interminable minutes pass. I realize Wink might already be here. Dead or alive, Wink might be 40 feet away at this very moment. I ring the bell once and the feeble ding mocks my wretchedness. I punch the bell again, three sharp stabs. Then, just as I'm ready to walk behind the counter and back to the kennels, one of the doors flies open. Out comes a middle-aged woman, rubbing her eyes. Her hair is the color of plums and it's spiky-glued into impressive little spears. A lit cigarette dangles from her lips and her eyes squint against the smoke. She hasn't seen me yet, so I reverse a trespassing step or two.

"Jesus *Christ*, lady!" she yelps. "What the hell are you *doing*?"

In that instant, my timidity vanishes and I become righteously indignant. I'm a taxpaying citizen, after all, who's been waiting many minutes during business hours at a public facility, an agency whose mission demands the greatest responsiveness to its citizens. I'm ready to launch into my accountability rant with this public servant when a lone dog begins to howl. It's not Wink, but he or she reminds me that I'd be well-advised to befriend, not alienate, this woman.

She approaches and removes the cigarette from her lips. I extend my hand.

"Brenda Lee," I say, reading her badge. "My name is Cecilia Gilbert, and my dog has gone missing."

Brenda Lee offers a weak handshake, then bends over, giving me a nice long look at an inch of grey-white roots. She pulls something from under the counter and plunks it down, emphatically, in front of me. It's a blank nameplate. I stare at it. Then, with an exaggerated harrumph, she turns it around.

"Mrs. Brenda Lee Hoenecker," it announces in block letters. I look from the nameplate to her face. I attempt a smile, but I suspect it's more of a grimace. Her expression of monumental annoyance doesn't change. Mrs. Brenda Lee Hoenecker seems bound and determined to piss me off. Oh Wink, give me strength.

"Did you say something?" she says.

Did I? I'm sure my little Wink mantra had been silent.

"I—"

"No matter," she responds, shaking her head like a parent whose child has disappointed yet again. "You may call me *Ms.* Hoenecker. Do *not* call me *Mrs.* Hoenecker. Buck, that lyin' sack of shit, left two months ago."

"Oh."

The word escapes my mouth, but I'm not sure Ms. Hoenecker hears it, as she is once again bent over, busy under the counter. Another birds-eye view of the dome of her head. Large patches of scalp are visible through her thin, heavily processed hair.

"I'm sorry to hear—"

"Oh, for Christ's sake, don't be *sorry*! Didn't you just hear me say Buck is a miserable son of a bitch?"

Seriously. I am on the verge of tears. This woman — this Brenda Lee Hoenecker recently left by the SOB Buck — telegraphs so much negative energy that it nearly swamps me. I want to get away from her immediately, but of course I can't. If the way to Wink is through Brenda-freaking-Lee, so be it. My professional careers as a paralegal and a reporter taught me how to steamroll over the toughest of cookies.

"*Miss* Hoenecker," I pronounce emphatically. "I am here because my dog has disappeared. I am here to fill out paperwork — or whatever you folks require. I did not sleep last night. I'm exhausted and terrified and I am barely, *barely,* able to hold body-and-soul together."

For an instant, it seems she might throw me a crumb of mercy. But no.

"Well, excuuuuse me," she breathes, pushing a piece of paper in my general direction. "Fill this out. Ring the bell when you're done. I got more to do than stand here."

She turns and walks through the door from which she entered.

The form asks for Wink's weight and physical description and last-seen location. But nowhere is there a place for his microchip number.

"Miss Hoenecker?" I call, tentatively. Nothing. But what do I expect? She instructed me to ring the bell. I call more loudly, then ring the bell twice. The same door opens and here she comes, marching or stomping, I'm not quite sure how to describe it. Another cigarette, this one unlit, hangs from her lower lip like a magic trick.

"Done?"

"Well, yes, but I have a question."

She sighs, shifts her weight to the other leg, lights the cigarette. Never have I seen a person silently communicate exasperation more convincingly. If this were a movie scene, she'd be guilty of over-acting. I wait for her to ask what my question is, but after a moment, it's clear this hellcat has no such intention.

"About Wink's microchip," I venture.

"Wink? Microchip?"

"My dog, Wink. His implanted ID number, you know. His *microchip*. There's no place for it on the form and I was wondering—"

"You mean, your dog wasn't wearing a collar with identification?"

"Yes, but—"

"Now, you're going to tell me she wasn't wearing a county-license tag, right?"

"He. And no, I wasn't going to say that. I'm actually talking about an implanted ID that you can scan. In case you, you know, find Wink?"

I'm becoming flustered again. My cordiality has a shockingly short shelf-life today. But then, so does Brenda Lee Hoenecker's. She continues to stare at me. Impassive. Silent. Smoking.

I relent.

"No, ma'am," I say. "He does not have a county

license. We just moved here. Yesterday. Just yesterday. I
haven't had time—"

She sucks smoke deep into her lungs,
summoning her Jobian patience, and stubs out the
half-smoked cigarette.

"Miss—?"

"Gilbert."

"Gilbert. Yes, in fact, I *do* know what a microchip
is. This may be South Carolina — I hear the Yankee in
your voice — but we have a passing familiarity with
modern technology down here. In fact, our scanners
put out the same radio waves as y'all's up north."

She fake-grimaces.

"What we do *not* have," she continues, "are funds
to print an up-to-date form."

I have no idea what she is talking about.

"*With*, I mean to say, a specific line-item for
one's microchip number."

Concluding her disquisition, she turns the
form 180 degrees and slashes a heavy black line at the
bottom. Then ceremoniously slides the form back to
me.

"Microchip number, please?"

Were it not so preposterous, so blatantly passive-
aggressive, it would have been funny. But it isn't, and
I'm beginning to take it personally. Is it me? Am I
pissing her off? I print Wink's ID digits. Brenda Lee
looks at me, her face as impassive as an executioner's.
I can almost see the strain in her eyes as she struggles
to seem aloof. I want to say more, but what? I turn
and walk to the door, silently pleading that Brenda
Lee will not send me back into the cruel, cruel world

without a word of hope. A statistic, perhaps . . . 80% of missing dogs are found within the first 48 hours. Some encouraging words. I'm so demoralized I would have regarded a simple "Good luck!" as a blessing. A sign of human connection. That, however, is me: I tend to be brimming with an implacable faith in my fellow man and woman. But it is clear where that got me with Wink.

I open the front door, then turn. Brenda Lee Hoenecker is studying something, head down. When she raises her eyes, she looks surprised to see me standing there.

"I'm sorry?" she says.

I want her to see me. Really see me.

"You'll want to know that Wink is not here, of course," she says. "We've got no dog here under 50 pounds. Dead or alive."

I'm stunned by the harshness of the statement, but of course that's the way someone in Brenda Lee's position might see it. Still, I can't seem to speak.

"When Wink is found, Ms. Gilbert, you'll be the first to know — I'll call you myself."

I'm encouraged. I believe Brenda Lee Hoenecker. The woman has zero bedside manner, but she clearly is a force of nature. And that's what I need on my side.

ten

I am too lonely to be in my cottage and I have no energy to start unpacking. Although I really should go to the grocery store, my brain is not functioning properly and I would only wander aimlessly up and down the aisles. I decide to walk downtown, get a quick bite to eat, and call Becca. When I shut the front door behind me, I don't lock it. In my exhausted reasoning, leaving the door unlocked is somehow connected to Wink being brought home while I'm out. It is completely illogical, but the very concept of logic has lost all meaning for me.

I walk to the river and turn left on Bay Street. Across the street on the Bluff, a runner plants his foot against the trunk of an old oak and leans into a stretch. His calves are thick with bulging, achingly defined muscles and his tendons flex as he rocks back and forth. I pass the pizza place downtown and catch a whiff of burning hickory. At the end of a wide alley, I glimpse sparkling water the color of sapphires, so I follow it down to the riverfront park. Kids play frisbee. A big thrumming sidewalk-sweeper creeps down the sidewalk towards the marina. I spy an empty swinging bench and head toward it. A woman dressed in pink, beret included, passes me with her beagle and invites me to marvel at her glorious specimen.

"Oh, Ladyhawke *likes* you," she says.

But I can't pet the dog. Lord knows I want to, but I just can't. Even fleeting contact with Ladyhawke's glorious fur might do me in. I sit on a bench and look out over the heartbreakingly lovely vista. This, I think, this glorious riverwalk is where Wink would put on quite a show. The wide tabby sidewalk to strut down, lined with bushes to pee on, and every twenty feet or so, a ready-made audience swinging on benches in Zen-like contentment. It's a perfect pooch trifecta, and I think how my boy will soak it up. But is that correct? *Will* soak it up? Or *would* have? Or *should* have? I feel pathetic, tormenting myself over verb tense. Yet isn't verb tense everything? A ragged wire of pain shoots through my left hand, the one usually connected to Wink's leash, and I wonder if simply *imagining* my dog in this scene could prompt phantom pain?

I watch yellow-vested workers empty the park's garbage receptacles. Two young men, tattooed and white-aproned, huddle at the back door of a restaurant, smoking, crouching, trying to be invisible. Near the city dock, a gaggle of pre-teens is roughhousing, poking at each other, pretending they're about to topple into the river. A man in a sleeveless undershirt walks past and tells the kids to pipe down. I pull out my cell and dial Becca. On my first two tries, her line is busy with no opportunity to leave a voice message. The third time, she answers.

"Cecilia?"

"Wink's gone, Becca. I can't find him. He's disappeared."

The line crackles. I hear muffled noises, like she's moving around or switching the phone to her other ear.

"I can't hear you, Cees. Did you say Wink is *gone*?"

A sob catches in my throat.

"He disappeared, Bec. Yesterday."

I tell her everything, or as much as I know, which, upon the telling, is pretty paltry.

"Wait, Cecilia. Stop. Let me understand. You took him to a kennel and a few hours later, he was gone? And the owner knows *nothing*?!

"Yes."

"I'll come, CiCi. Just hang on. I'll catch a flight tomorrow. I'll get Rommie and we'll drive down. What do you think happened? I mean, where *is* this place? Could he get away? Is he *lost*-lost? I mean, outside? Okay, that's what I'll do. I'll fly home and Rommie and I will come. If anyone can find Wink, she can."

My head is swimming. Becca is not making sense, she who has always made more sense to me than anyone. Catch a flight? Fly home? Where is she?

"Becca," I say. "What do you mean, fly home? Where *are* you?"

"Oh, CiCi. I'm in Paris, remember? But I'll

reschedule. It'll piss off my publisher, but, seriously, this is *Wink*!"

Of course. Yes. Her debut novel has been translated into French and she's on her book tour. My beloved friend's offer is genuine — Becca *would* drop everything and fly back across the Atlantic — but I cannot ask this of her. Plus, I'm convinced Wink will soon be found. Aren't I?

I ask her how the tour is going, but she doesn't want to talk about it. And, really, neither do I. Focusing on anything other than Wink feels like a betrayal, and I know Becca feels the same. I wish her luck, she tells me she loves me, and we hang up.

As I gaze out over the river, I flash on one of our favorite topics of-late: how to grow old — should we be so lucky — gracefully. Becca posited that graceful aging has something to do with keeping one's sense of humor, and we were off to the races. I segued into forgiveness and whether graceful aging might involve forgiving past wrongs. As both the grantor and the recipient of forgiveness. Invariably, the discussion, *any* discussion, would lead to Ben, and how his abandonment colored his ability to commit . . . or even to believe in love.

Shortly before Ben ended our relationship, Becca came for a visit. We walked on a wide Jersey beach about twenty miles south of town, as the sea crawled up the sand, then released it with a sigh. A squadron of brown pelicans skimmed the ocean's surface, gliding in the troughs between waves. Rommie, her dog, dashed in and out of the waves, barking at them like a maniac. Wink trotted by my side, occasionally casting a sympathetic look at Rommie as if she might be crazy . . . but, if so, that was just fine. My all-accepting Wink. Once again, Becca and I found ourselves on the topic of graceful aging, which morphed into a discussion about grace.

What do you think grace *is*, I asked, not knowing where the question would lead, in the way all good inquiry will, if you keep an open mind.

"Hmmmm," Becca pondered. She is a great ponderer.

"Perhaps it has something to do with someone loving you and thinking you're absolutely wonderful," she said. The wind picked up and I had to lean in to hear her over Rommie's barking. "If you can accept it, that's grace. Maybe grace is learning how to be loved?"

Two weeks later, I called Becca to report that Ben didn't love me anymore. Blubbering and inconsolable, stream-of-conscious blather poured from my mouth.

"I'm 60 years old!" I sobbed, as if she didn't know, as if our birthdays weren't three days apart.

"Oh, CiCi."

"I'll never — ever — love again," I cried, wiping a strand of mucous from my upper lip.

"Stop," she sighed. "You're the biggest lover I know."

And that, I thought, was true enough. I do love quite easily.

I head down the sidewalk towards the coffee shop, but a man is blocking my path. He is standing at an easel. In his left hand, he holds a painter's palette; in his right, a paintbrush with its end poised between his pursed lips. I veer to give him wide berth, but he turns and speaks.

"Sometimes you just get buck fever, you know?"

I have no idea what he's talking about, but I respond, "I can only imagine," and keep on walking. But he stops me with a sharp, "Ha!" I turn.

"You haven't the slightest idea what buck fever is, do you?"

"Nope."

He sweeps his brush in an arc over the sun-glinted river and the gold and green grasses beyond.

"It's when you simply must paint outside! Buck fever. It's a compulsion. To smell, to feel, to taste your subject. En plein air, n'est-ce pas? Some call it paintbrush fever. I, however, call it buck fever."

N'est-ce pas? Does everyone in this Southern village pepper their English with French? At that, he turns back to his canvas. To smell, taste and feel, indeed. But if one wants to speak of the 'all' of it, one must acknowledge the abominable as well as the fantastic, n'est-ce pas? As the Buddhists say, nothing left out. True, the marsh scene before us is glorious, but ten miles away at this very moment on this very body of water, Wink could be gagging on the hypoxic, rotten-egg fumes of marsh bacteria. He could be hungry enough to eat poisonous weeds. He could be fending off liana vines that clutch at his throat, sentient as a snake. There's always the sinister beneath the lovely and the thought of that, the damn totality of it all, crushes me. I walk on, past scenes of life, bucolic and ordinary, and am stunned how the world keeps on spinning while I flounder in a private hell.

When I dash into a coffee shop, I avert my eyes.

Nancy Ritter

The cashier tries to engage me in conversation, but
I offer one-word responses and keep my head down,
pretending to be inordinately interested in the napkin
dispenser. She hands me a bag with my bagel and
fruit cup and I jog home, swiveling my head like a gun
turret atop a tank, darting my eyes to the undersides
of bushes and down narrow alleyways. Looking for a
little white dog.

eleven

Some folks think Wink is a Jack, or Parson, Russell terrier, but I suspect this is not strictly true. Although he has the face of a Jack, his body is more dachshund. And his mellow disposition is all Great Dane. I adopted Wink, the year before I met Ben, from a rescue agency, so, like most rescues, his provenance is unknown.

Wink was found running along the side of a highway in East Texas. After testing positive for heartworm, he was brought to New Jersey for treatment. I later learned that many places in the rural South simply don't have the funds for heartworm treatment and, particularly with a case as severe as Wink's, the animal is usually euthanized. But the Dachshund Rescue of North America got ahold of my boy and he was transported, one caring middle-aged woman at a time, in 300-mile stints, to Jersey for treatment.

Having had dogs most of my life, I knew about heartworm, but I never understood its insidiousness. Heartworm is transmitted through the bite of a mosquito and the parasitic roundworms work their way into an animal's heart, lungs, and blood vessels. It's hard to fathom, but a single heartworm can grow up to a foot long, and a dog can be infected with hundreds.

During his treatment, Wink was given three melarsomine injections deep in his lumbar muscles. The shots can cause such severe pain that the animal can experience difficulty standing. Some experience nausea and lethargy. Before, during and after treatment, the dog's exercise must be severely restricted because exertion increases the rate at which the worms damage the heart and lungs.

Along with the injections, the animal receives other drugs to help combat the notoriously awful side effects, which include a bad reaction to the death of the worms. It is nothing short of a miracle that my boy tolerated all this and still became the best dog I've ever known.

Once he was heartworm-negative, Wink was put up for adoption. I knew from the website photos that meeting him would be risky — risky, I mean, in the best possible way. He is so damn cute that even a friend who thoroughly dislikes dogs saw Wink's online photo and said, "If you don't rescue him, I will." Suffice it to say, I was predisposed to regard him as perfect based solely on his cuteness and the hardships he endured to survive. But a Jack Russell? Frenetic, yippy, high maintenance? Still, I made an appointment with his foster-mother, Michelle, to meet him.

For the first thirty minutes, Wink sat with his long body glued to Michelle's thigh. I couldn't take my eyes off his creamy-white coat and extraordinary puzzle-like markings, which range from russet brown to a lovely taupe with hints of dusky rose. But it's his face that stops people in their tracks: from the back of his skull to the tip of his nose, it's perfectly divided into half white and half brown. As Michelle and I talked, I held his gaze. I detected no nervousness or fear. Sometimes, he looked back and forth, up at Michelle when she spoke, across at me when I did. I'd never seen a dog do that. Then, without warning, invitation or coaxing, he jumped off the couch, walked to the armchair where I was sitting, and sprang onto my lap. No big display or neediness. Just a simple declarative statement: I choose you.

After that, the adoption fell quickly into place. I'd already completed the paperwork and the rescue agency had conducted phone interviews with three personal references. That afternoon, after an agency representative made a home visit to confirm the suitability of both my house and me, Wink became mine and I became his.

I called Michelle and arranged to pick him up the following morning. A couple of hours later, however, she called back in tears. Through the snuffles and the silences and a generally unsuccessful effort to compose herself, Michelle asked if I could possibly pick him up at 6 a.m., when her children would still be sleeping. During his grueling nine-month heartworm treatment, Wink had been with this family, and I couldn't imagine their sadness. Here, I had been celebrating my good fortune and, twenty miles away, a family was grieving.

And so shortly before 6 the next day, with the sun spilling pink and orange at the horizon, I pulled into Michelle's driveway. I didn't shut the car door for fear of waking her kids. Moments later, she walked out the front door with Wink at the end of a leash and tears shining on her cheeks.

"I snuck into my little one's bedroom and stole him from under the covers."

She appeared stricken, as if she'd just committed a mortal sin. Which, in a way, she had.

"You can come visit," I choked out, strapping Wink into his new car seat.

"I couldn't," she said. "I just couldn't."

She walked back to the house and turned. I was still standing next to Wink's open window, stroking his back. He was watching her, too.

"My husband was right," she said. "This is hard. Last night, I told him I'd never foster another dog again. But, seeing you now, I know I will."

And with a pitiable shake of her lovely head, she went inside.

On our first day together, Wink and I walked in the woods and later romped on the beach. We took a short nap. When I woke, Wink's chin was resting on my foot. He was long and lean, and in this posture, I could see the wiener dog in him. Trying not to disturb him, I pulled my laptop over and logged into my email. I wanted to send Michelle and her family a note, reassuring them that Wink was okay. I wanted to tell the kids that I would never forget every ounce of tenderness they bestowed on him.

In my Inbox were two emails from names I didn't recognize. The first, from a Rachel MacKain, said she volunteered with the Dachshund Rescue of North America and was making her routine rounds, looking to save dachshunds destined to end up in high-kill facilities in rural Texas. When she saw Wink, her message said, she knew he may not have much dachshund in him, but she rescued him anyway.

The second email said "Wink" in the subject line. I'd already decided to change his name to Puccini . . . until I opened the email, that is.

> *I beleeve you adopted the dog I found running in a ditch next to the hiway when I was driving from the mortuarie where my mother died and I want to ask if your going to keep his name. You don't have to, when I rescued him I thought he might have receeved my mothers soul. Not that he is an angel, I don't beleeve in them, but I think her energie went into the universe and it was fate I found you dog that day. My mother was called Wink so thats what I name him.*

Oh, my. All these years later, my heart still swells when I think of that email. It was signed, "Yours truely, Victoria" and I didn't think twice about my reply.

I told Victoria how sorry I was about her mother's passing. I said that if her mom raised the kind of daughter who, in her deepest sorrow, would pull over and rescue a lost dog, she was a good person and I'd be honored to have Wink bear her name forever.

And now my Wink is lost again. It seems cruel that one dog should be forced to endure so much, but, of course, so many do.

I look at all the moving boxes arrayed around my living room like errant chess pieces, and, for a minute, I forget if I'm moving in or out. I should go to my car, dig my Swiss Army knife out of the glove compartment, open more boxes, and begin the process of settling in. What are you *waiting* for, I think? But, of course, I know what I'm waiting for.

And so I sit, listening to the suffocating silence as reels of images unspool in my mind. Wink mired in mud or caught in a dense tangle of undergrowth. Wink in a ditch, broken and bleeding, as flies bedevil him and fire ants boil and move in a silent, barbaric line towards him. I find the quiet completely unnerving, which is ironic because it's one of the reasons I left the cacophonous hodgepodge of New Jersey. I longed to escape the rumble of subways, the screech of trolleys, the sudden sparking of tram wires. I yearned to leave behind the crush of people, speaking many languages, often pushy and always opinionated. Will I begin to pine for noise as an antidote to all the ugly images that thrive in this breeding ground of silence?

I've always had such romantic ideas about silence. I was intrigued with a medieval order of monks who, as a means of redemption, structured their lives around silence. Was I seeking some kind of redemption in moving to the Lowcountry? No sooner does this thought arise than panic grips my non-Christian gut: Would my new community hold my nonbelieving against me? I know the South has more than its share of Baptist acolytes and some are quite rabid about their faith. Yet, isn't that, too, why I moved here? I want to be more open-minded about issues like faith and politics. Living in Jersey was like living in an echo chamber, and I found myself hungering for greater diversity of opinion and sensibility. Something that would help me shuck my sense of entitlement and reclaim a more generous spirit. Or so I reasoned.

My romantic self also sought greater intimacy, which comes, I believed, with a smaller locale. Although New Jersey is modest in size, no one thinks of it that way. In fact, the state is larger than life: big freeways, big beaches, big hair, big egos that nip like a rat terrier at the heels of Manhattan. Years of East Coast brashness — the pace, the noise, the intense commerce — changed me, and one morning, a few months before Ben's pronouncement, I realized I had become hard. It happened gradually, organically, and no doubt some of it was due to Ben's waning commitment. But the lusty, spirited life of my fellow Jerseyites, so stimulating in the beginning, had grown exhausting.

And then there's this: Once heard, the siren call of the South is not easily unheard. I imagined life in Beaufort would be gentler, more serene. I know how stereotypical that sounds: Small-town simplicity, Southern gentility, etcetera. I do understand the risk of judging a book by its cover — the charming manner of a Rhett Butler masking the soul of a slave-owner —

but I was desperate to leave behind a particular East Coast ethos: Having to be right all the time *and* being loud about it. After Ben and I had been together a few years, I began to regard Jerseyites as unnecessarily argumentative. Their brash, in-your-face manner, while not intended to be malicious, often left me feeling a bit knocked about. Whether Ben noticed this, I don't know. During that last year, he was focused on opening the antique store, which was perfectly situated in an up-scale market to ensure success. Except that it wasn't. It limped along, under-capitalized and overextended. Ben was doing 90 percent of the work: buying, valuation research, photography, ad design and sales. The enterprise demanded all his attention and energy . . . until there was simply none left for me.

At the end, he couldn't even talk to me and took to passing missives under his office door. I think he felt so badly about himself — about me, about us — that he just couldn't look me in the eye. For all his talents and kindness, despite his brainpower and good nature, Ben was a deeply unhappy man. Early in our relationship, he informed me of his plan to commit suicide at the age of 70. We were lying in bed, listening to the rain, and that's what he said.

"Stop it!" I cried. "How could you even *think* of killing yourself?"

"Oh, CiCi," he said. "Don't you know I've been working toward killing myself for years?"

It still chills me to remember that conversation. But now I simply must stop all this remembering. There's too much to do! I put that dog-napping notice I saw last night behind me. I post on more lost-dog websites, pushing through all the stories, all the photos of darling, pitiable faces, all the anguished pleas of their humans. I remind myself that dogs are found and rescued all the time and I need look no further than my own history for proof of that. All my pooches — before Wink, there was Molly and Guido and Snooter and, my first, Brandy-the-Weiner-Woman — came to me through rescue groups. Which proves, doesn't it, that happy endings are possible?

twelve

ometime in mid-afternoon when the
sun is high and I'm treading old ground
on lost-and-found animal websites, the
Professor calls. He invites me over for a debriefing on
my animal-shelter visit and "to plan our next line of
attack." It's apparent he had not seen Zeke's threat. The
more I think about it, the more convinced I become
that Zeke's throat-cutting pantomime was intended
for the Professor, who had just doffed his hat in a way
that clearly communicated, I am *watching* you, sir. I,
who can doff and bow and speak the King's English,
am *more* than capable of bringing a scoundrel like you
down.

Still, in my exhausted state, I continue to
second-guess whether I truly saw what I think I saw.
On one hand, the throat-slashing pantomime seems
childish. Something a frustrated sibling might perform

behind his mother's back. But, in conjunction with Zeke's malevolent smile, it certainly seemed more sinister than childish.

Although J.P.'s house is just a few blocks away, I decide to drive. I want maximum flexibility if I have to pick Wink up at the county kennel or even at Zeke's. In my rearview mirror, I see Wink's car seat, more than a little ratty after seven years of trips to the vet, parks near-and-far, friends' houses for dinner, fall hikes in the mountains and long vacations at the Shore. I'm drowning in despair and begin to weep. Wink may be scared and hungry, but through the tears, I will myself to stay strong. He's been gone only 24 hours, so, yes, he's scared and hungry, but he's still okay. I start the engine and turn up the air conditioning. I'm hyper-aware of these pedestrian acts and assure myself that the mere fact I'm capable of performing them is a good sign. I swipe my shirt sleeve across my eyes and steel my spine.

That resolve lasts for only a minute because thoughts of dog-fighting invade my brain. Ever since I was a kid and learned that people are capable of perpetrating heinous acts upon animals, I've been unable to "look." If I come upon a scene of animal cruelty in a novel, I skip ahead, sometimes just a paragraph or two, and sometimes, an entire chapter. I've even been known to set a book aside because I do not trust the author to not spring a depraved scene on me. Perhaps that's a form of denial? If so, I say, bask me in denial.

I pull into the Professor's narrow driveway, flanked by dense stands of Crepe myrtle. He greets me, I follow him inside, and before he closes the door behind us, I catch a glimpse of tall bookcases along an entire wall. Although open, the Professor's draperies are a dark, heavy damask like one might see in a Renaissance drawing room. As my eyes adjust from the bright sunshine to this mottled twilight, I take in a remarkable mishmash of antiques. Cabinets abut writing desks, which, in turn, bump up against highboys. On every drawer and cupboard, brass pulls fastened to intricately designed brass brackets have been polished to such brilliance that I'm reminded of gold jewelry sold on the Ponte Vecchio.

"Have I mentioned my antique obsession?"

His tone is solemn, almost confessional. I feel his quiet energy and how different it is from the energy that abounded in the courtrooms and newsrooms of my professional life. The Professor is careful and deliberate in his movements. Obviously, he has a big, active brain, but it operates like a stealth jet. I detect no ego clamoring for attention. Rather, Professor J.P. Ruopp seems guided by the type of focused, curious energy I hunger for. Especially now in my wretchedness.

The Professor's antique-engorged home doesn't surprise me, as I had sensed in him a reverence for beauty and for the past. I follow him past graceful Queen Annes with cabriole legs; mahogany Chippendales with intricate chair backs; and three of the Georgians: Adam, Hepplewhite, and Sheraton.

Everywhere I look, there are books! Old mahogany bookcases rise, floor to ceiling, along two of the parlor's walls. I scan the spines at eye-level and see some of my favorites. *The Sea* by Banville, *Mrs. Dalloway* by Wolff. Near the top rung of a library ladder, I spy a red leather-bound book that is not flush with the others. Although I can't read the title, I think an entire story might be written about this one book. Is it pulled halfway out or pushed halfway in? Has the reader finished it or is he anticipating the sacred act of opening it to the first page? And what, oh what, interrupted the task? All around us, books form little pyramids on tabletops and are propped like dominos against the legs of chairs. I sigh for the sheer promise of them. But only after Wink is found.

J.P. watches me from the archway to the kitchen.

"You're deep in thought," he says. "May I ask what about?"

"It's silly, really."

I pause.

"I was thinking about a conversation Ben and I had years ago. Ben, the man who recently left me."

He nods.

"We're both avid readers and once I commented that reading nurtures one's humanity. You know what his response was?"

J.P. walks to a wing-back chair, sits, folds his hands between his knees.

"He said," I continue, "he actually *said*, 'Poppycock!'"

The Professor furrows his brow and clears his throat.

"What do you suppose he meant by that?"

"Books are intellectual matters to Ben," I say. "To me, they're matters of the heart."

He smiles.

"You're saying" — his eyes sweep the room — "that I could seduce you with books?"

Is it a question or a statement?

"You could seduce me *without* books," I say, and we lock eyes, hesitating on the precipice. Then, he speaks.

"I fear, however, that you are the wrong—"

"Gender?" I say.

"You knew?"

"Yes," I respond, "Wink told me."

We both laugh. His, a gentle glissando sliding up the scale.

Then, he seems to recognize the incongruity of the moment. He becomes sober and says with such certitude that it sounds like an edict: "We will find him, Cecilia. He. Will. Be. Found."

He asks if I want a bite to eat, but I decline. I must go to the police department, I say, but he convinces me to stay for tea. While he prepares it, I take in the living room more fully. The floor of the circa 1640 house — so validated by the Beaufort Historical Foundation on a bronze plaque by the front door — appears to be original heart-of-pine. The wide, rough-hewn planks are polished bright and clean and every surface of furniture is claimed by antique clocks, curio boxes, and silver settings. And, of course, the aforementioned books.

From the kitchen comes the same drone-like humming I heard when J.P. and I met on the Bluff. Even as he hands me a mug of tea, the humming continues. I look into his steel-gray eyes, which are shot-through with gold. I've never seen anything like it.

"This room feels precious to me, J.P.," I say. But as soon as the words are out of my mouth, they sound off. A precious room? Is that right? I scramble around my brain for a better, more precise word, but J.P. understands perfectly.

"Yes," he says so softly that I must strain to hear. "Everything here is dear to me" — he looks around, as if seeing his artifacts and artwork for the first time — "which makes the room, indeed, precious."

We exchange wistful smiles that speak of loss. My loss, of course, is more apparent: Wink's disappearance. But there is the loss of Ben, too, which I don't want to talk about. I want to keep my pain about Wink pure. Undiluted. As if that pain alone will rouse the karmic energy necessary to find him. As if the gods and goddesses of fortune will bow to my sole focus. Also, I'm not ready to talk about Ben because I don't know where to begin. You move to a new place, form a new community, make new friends. How much of your old life do you bring along? How many of your old heartbreaks do you share?

J.P. speaks.

"How did you pick Beaufort, Cecilia?"

"Oh." I take a deep breath. "I first saw Beaufort, hmmm, I guess 15 years ago, on a day trip from Savannah with my best friend. We were vacationing there, Savannah, I mean, and we drove up here for lunch. I thought it was one of the most bewitching places I'd ever seen. You, J.P.?"

"Well, Thomas, my husband — we lost him two years ago — well, when we retired, we wanted to leave the City. We were professors, both. Me at Columbia, English Lit. Thomas, bless his misguided soul, was devoted to Fordham. Mid-Eastern Poetry. *I* wanted to retire to a place where people are connected to the land, which is not so much the case in the City, you know? I was willing to roll the dice: The Great Plains? Maybe Kansas or Nebraska? Maybe "My Ántonia" stomping grounds, you know, where folks drive combines and tractors. Thomas, on the other hand, was partial to the Far West — the desert of Utah or New Mexico, where your neighbors can identify one hundred bird species and know their way, blindfolded, to ancient cave dwellings. Or so he believed."

J.P. walks over to the fireplace. The humming returns. I think he's about to trip over a massive volume of T.E. Lawrence's biography, propped against the hearth pilaster, and I nearly call out. But, at the last minute, he side-steps it. The scene becomes instantly imaginable to me: Late at night, he rests the book against the pilaster before taking the poker to scatter the ashes and burning coals.

Time begins to feel elastic. I sit on the couch, fidgeting, then proclaim that I must go to the police. But I can't seem to leave. Perhaps because I know that when I walk out the door, I'll encounter reality . . . or, rather, an *unreal* reality. Like stepping through a mirror.

I have no idea what to expect with law enforcement in a small, Southern town. And I also don't know what I can truthfully report about Zeke. Oh, how I long to stay in this book-brimming room with its seductive, diaphanous light. But I can't. My basic instinct is stronger and I believe that my very survival may depend on finding Wink.

Just as I stand to leave, the silhouette of a child appears in the kitchen archway. Backlit by sunlight, the face is undiscernible, but the body bobs up on its toes and rolls back on its heels. The motion is disorienting, like being adrift in a rowboat as the horizon tilts vertiginously. Behind me, J.P. hums. The person, a girl, I think, comes toward us. Then she is upon me once again. Eloise LaFitte! Was it only yesterday she flounced, uninvited, in my back door, wagging an odd letter in my face? Only yesterday when Wink was still here?

Eloise assumes a soldierly stance directly in front of me. She salutes.

"I understand I am to be deputized in the valiant search for your dog. I stand ready to be sworn in."

I look at the Professor. He's inscrutable, and, for a moment, I think it's part of some sick charade. I mean, Eloise LaFitte effectively recommended Zeke's, didn't she? I'd had little thought of boarding Wink before Carol mentioned it and Eloise seconded her opinion. But was I so befuddled by two days on the road, a sleepless night, the movers' delay, etcetera, etcetera, that an addled old woman could tip the balance in my rash decision to take — and leave — Wink at Zeke's Paws Spa?

"My dear Miss LaFitte," the Professor says, his tone gentle but firm. "I believe we can dispense with the oath. That is, if Miss Gilbert agrees."

I agree, but in what manner I do not know. Perhaps I offer a weak smile? A nod?

Eloise sits on the couch and pats a cushion, inviting me to sit. She takes my hand and her eyes bore into mine.

"Okay," she says, "I know this is going to be hard, but let's mine the minusculitude, shall we?"

For a moment, I go blank. I forget to breathe. But I must, I *must* ask why she recommended Zeke's. And, apparently, I must do it while she's holding my hand.

"Eloise," I say.

"Yes, dear?"

I look at J.P., who appears to be on high alert. Does he sense that I'm about to ask his friend something that may upset her? I know he has great affection for Eloise and is obviously protective of her. It's clear to me then that he has no idea Eloise recommended Zeke's. *If* she did, if I haven't misread the whole thing. What a potential landmine. I don't know these two souls and I have no basis for assuming what they should, or should not, know. And I have no idea how they'll react to my questions.

"I need to clear something up, Eloise, and I'm not sure how to say it."

"Well, my dear, it's always best to just out with it."

"Yes, well."

I squeeze her hand, then withdraw my own. The action is chillier than I intend, and the Professor notices. I try to reassure Eloise with a smile, although I suspect this confuses her even more.

"Well, it's this. You recommended I take my dog to Zeke's Paws Spa, which is where he disappeared from. And I'm wondering why you recommended him?"

"Oh!" she bleats.

"Eloise?" the Professor says. He looks confused.

Alarmed, Eloise looks at him, then at me.

Oh, my," she says, her voice choked with emotion. "Have I done something wrong? I ran into Zeke Johnson last week at the church bizarre. No, that's not right. Oh, dear, what—?"

She looks down at her hands, muttering.

"The church, the church . . . ?"

"Bazaar?" I whisper.

"Bazaar! Yes. Now back to Zeke, dear. Don't interrupt. I've known him since he was in short britches. Such a nice young man. Didn't get into any trouble, mind you. He's run that kennel of his for years, and when you mentioned boarding your dog — what with running into him and all — well, of course, I thought of him. But what are you saying, my dear? Zeke would never harm your dog."

I am flustered. Acutely embarrassed. What possesses me, I don't know, but I spring from the couch and run out J.P.'s front door. At the street, I turn right instead of left toward home, and a block later, I remember I drove. Oh, god, if I'm this disoriented a couple of blocks from my own house, how am I ever going to find Wink? A wave of hopelessness washes over me and I stop, paralyzed. The heat of the day is building, inexorably, and I have the feeling of moving underwater. In the distance, a gull cries. I look up. The sky is a shameless blue. I rub the heels of my hands in my eye sockets so hard that stars appear on the back of my lids. The next thing I know, Professor Ruopp is by my side, his hand on my shoulder.

"Eloise can be trying," he says. "Her monologues corkscrew and somersault. But I can assure you, Cecilia, she never would have said you should board Wink at Zeke's if she'd had even an inkling of anything untoward."

Eloise is inconsolable, he says, and will I come back, just for a moment, to comfort her? My initial reaction is to refuse, to keep the waters muddy so I don't have to face my own culpability. Regardless who put the idea of boarding Wink in my head, it is I who left him there against my better judgment. Now, J.P. is here, guiding me gently back to what is before me at this very moment: A fellow human, a befuddled, old woman who is only trying to help, needs a kind word. How could I possibly turn my back on that?

We find Eloise puttering in the kitchen, as if nothing has happened. J.P. puts his hand on the small of my back, leans close and whispers.

"I always say Miss LaFitte's perfume renders her more off-putting than she actually is."

There's a twinkle in his eye.

"You *do*?" I whisper back. "I *definitely* have not heard you say that."

He grins, tickled, I think, that a spark of humor still lives in me.

"Well, perhaps not, but I *think* it. And now that I've said it, it verily trips off the tongue, wouldn't you say?"

"Verily."

When she sees me, Eloise hangs her head.

"I—"

I rush to her, wrap my arms around her slender frame, and hold tight for a good long while. She accepts it, easily. When I break away, she reaches up and cups her hand to my cheek.

"I could not be more sorry," she says.

"I know," I say. "I know."

I begin to make my pardons, saying I really must go to the police. J.P. offers to accompany me, but I decline. He's not deterred.

"Then, I shall dress and decamp to your porch." His tone tells me he'll brook no dissent. "I will be waiting there in case Wink returns."

He opens the door and kisses Eloise, then me, on the cheek.

"Do you really believe that?" I ask. "That I will see him again?"

I swallow a sob and force a smile.

"I do, my girl, I do."

I flash on a painting I once saw. A woman stands in an old Victorian widow's walk, the turret where the wife of a seagoing man — a fisherman, perhaps, or a merchant sailor plying the seas — waits. She looks out over the ocean and waits.

And waits.

thirteen

The Beaufort Police Department is housed in an austere brick building, circa 1960. The signage is simple and devoid of any adornment. On a wall in the entryway, a hand-lettered sign reads, NO FIREARMS PERMITTED. However, the older woman at the front desk appears wholly incapable of enforcing such a policy. When she looks up, her eyes smile and she calls me "dear." Jersey, it's not.

"I'd like to report suspicious circumstances surrounding the disappearance of my dog," I say.

"Then, it's Sergeant Allen you'll want to see, dear." When she stands, I see the sidearm strapped to her hip. "Follow me, dear."

We wind through a maze of empty cubicles. I'm riveted by the way a pair of handcuffs sways from her belt. Eventually we arrive at a cubicle in which a uniformed officer sits, talking on the phone. He nods once and gestures that I should sit. Before she turns and leaves, the woman squeezes my shoulder.

It feels strange eavesdropping on an official conversation, but, so far, Sergeant Allen isn't revealing anything confidential or proprietary. Mostly, 'Yes, sir' and 'I can certainly understand that, sir'. He scribbles on a notepad, but even upside down, I can see that most of the page is covered with doodles.

I take in Sergeant Allen's classic crew cut and barrel chest. His eyes are the shade of blue you see in Husky dogs. He mugs a look of exaggerated boredom, I assume to convey how uninspiring he finds the phone conversation and to bring me into his confidence by sharing said assessment. I sit quietly and review the points I want to make, but as I tick through them, I begin to lose confidence in my story.

Yes, Zeke's place is ramshackle, but what do I expect? Although Beaufort is a gem of Antebellum history and architecture, it's surrounded by rural South Carolina and, in many parts of the country, rural and ramshackle go hand-in-hand — an indication of poverty, not nefariousness. I admonish myself to be careful how I voice my suspicions. How, for example, should I describe Zeke's face in the moment we realized Wink was gone? Had there been a hint of something in his expression? Some clue of what had happened? And then today? I've already revisited the throat-cutting gesture so many times it's etched on my brain, and, thanks to my years as a trial paralegal and investigative reporter, I know how memory works, particularly the impact of fear on the stunningly flawed phenomenon of human recall.

Sergeant Allen concludes his call, stands and introduces himself. We shake hands. Then he sits and squares off in front of his computer, poised to enter pertinent information. Should any be forthcoming.

I explain that my dog disappeared yesterday, only two hours after I left him at a boarding facility. The proprietor claims no knowledge of what happened, I say, but I don't believe him.

"Let's stop right there, Ms. Gilbert. First, his name? Then, your initial impressions, please."

"Zeke Johnson."

As he types, the Sergeant shrugs his shoulders, which I take to indicate he is not familiar with the name.

"First impressions?"

It's an interesting question, and not one I anticipate. But Sergeant Allen looks like a man who knows what he's doing, so I go with it.

"Well, I'd forgotten this until you just mentioned first impressions, but, when I met him — when I dropped off Wink—"

"Your dog."

"Yes, my dog. Wink. Anyway, Mr. Johnson looked like he'd been in a fight."

The sergeant perks up. His eyebrows tick up and down.

"Cuts on his face?"

"No, I don't remember any actual cuts."

"Bruising, perhaps? A black eye?"

"I'm sorry, Sergeant, I honestly can't bring to mind any bruises." Then I add, unhelpfully, "It was more of a general perception, really.”

He withdraws his fingers from the keyboard and issues a prodigious sigh. He's frustrated with my answers, and I can't blame him. In normal circumstances, I pay ferocious attention to detail. During my career I saw cases won or lost because of a single detail. Plus, my decades-long study of Buddhism has honed my observation skills and taught me that nothing is so precious as a simple detail. But now, all that seems to have vanished . . . my memory, my ability to express thoughts, my confidence in myself. I stare at my hands and am overcome with shame. How did I possibly think it was okay to leave Wink?

“A general perception, you say, Ms. Gilbert . . . as in, say, swollenness?”

I look up.

“What?”

“You mentioned Mr. Johnson may have been in a fight and I'm wondering if your general perception includes swollenness.”

I'm confused. For a moment, I think he's being sarcastic. But he looks so hopeful, and I'm desperate to offer a pertinent fact or relevant thread that might be unraveled to a fruitful conclusion.

“There was a smell of old bacon grease,” I say, fighting tears. “It was trapped in the soft furnishings.”

“Ms. Gilbert, I'm afraid—”

“And today he threatened me. His story changed and he threatened me.”

Sergeant Harold Allen turns in his swivel chair. His eyes are deadly serious. Intense. Alert.

“Oh, my dear,” he says, sympathetically. “I'm

very sorry. Impressions are not the place to start.
My partner Jeff — he's out sick today — told me
he's had luck encouraging folks to think about first
impressions. You know, before they try to recall
actual facts, which have a way of solidifying in a
witness's mind by the time they come to us. He, Jeff, I
mean, finds surprising memories can surface, which
otherwise might be buried forever through what we
call the misinformation effect."

I am surprised by his forthrightness and, like
most people as close to the edge as I am now, I'm
moved by his unexpected kindness.

"So!" he says emphatically, trying, I'm sure, to
steer me away from tears and keep me on track. "First,
I'd like to hear what, precisely, Mr. Johnson said when
he realized your dog was gone. Then, please tell me
about the threats."

"Well . . . I honestly don't remember his exact
words. When I returned to pick up Wink, he seemed
surprised he wasn't with the other dogs. But I might
not have been reading him correctly. He just didn't
act overly concerned. Said something like, 'I have no
idea what happened to your dog.' I was unsatisfied
with his response. It seemed like he regarded Wink's
disappearance as a riddle, not a responsibility."

I stop talking. The sergeant stops typing.
I suspect how dramatic this sounds. I've made
no allowance for differences in Zeke's and my
perspectives. Of course, it would seem like a riddle to
him and a tragedy to me. I am losing my composure.
I, an ace reporter who could spot barely perceptible
holes in a witness's statement and the mere tips of

threads begging to be tugged. How could I segue from being "unsatisfied" with Zeke's explanation to feeling threatened without losing credibility in this officer's mind?

"Don't overthink it, Ms. Gilbert. It's my job to figure out the whys and wherefores. Tell me about the threats, please."

I tell Sergeant Allen about the throat-cutting scene.

"Were you on his property, Ms. Gilbert?"

"Well, yes. In the backyard. But he had given us permission."

He doesn't miss a beat.

"Us?"

Oh, dear. Have I not mentioned that Professor Ruopp was with me? What else have I left out? If I'm unable to be a reliable witness, what hope is there for Wink?

"Ms. Gilbert. I think we should back up. You went out to Mr. Johnson's place again today? With someone?"

I explain everything, including the confrontation on the stoop where J.P. said, 'Don't fuck with me' and asked about dog-fighting.

"Dog-fighting? And what did Mr. Johnson say in response?"

I think hard for a minute, trying to recall his precise words.

"I don't think he really responded. In fact, I'm sure he didn't *say* anything. But it was after that, when we were out back looking at the shed, that he drew his finger across his throat."

Sergeant Allen plants his palms on the desk. The pity in his eyes is palpable.

"Ms. Gilbert."

He's stalling, searching for something positive to say.

"We don't have much to go on. We'll check for any prior complaints against the establishment, see if there's something on Mr. Johnson that might shed some light. I'll send one of my boys out there. Snoop around, ask some questions. Hell, I might even go 'round myself, see-n y'all just moved to town, and this is not the sort of welcome we Beaufortonians pride ourselves in."

"But," he continues, "I can't guarantee we'll find any signs of your dog. Dogs go missing all the time in this part of the world. I wish I could be more hopeful, but that's the truth of it."

I force a smile. Why do we do that, I wonder? We women, I mean. Sergeant Allen isn't smiling. In fact, he looks close to bawling. Women, though, we're nurturers. Through all my pain, as this man confirms my worst suspicions are probably true, I *smile*. I smile to let him know I trust him and believe he'll do everything he can. I smile to thank him. Perhaps even to bless him. I smile to assure him I will live.

He walks me to the lobby and we shake hands.

As I'm about to step on the automatic-door pad, I turn. The Sergeant is leaning down, speaking in low tones with the woman at the front desk.

"Sergeant Allen?"

They both look up.

"Yes?"

Slack Tide

"Is there dog-fighting around here?"

"Yes, occasionally. We try to keep a lid on it. We get tips, we raid 'em. Things quiet down for six months, a year. Then, well. There are still some good 'ole boys 'round here. Haven't all died off yet."

I'm rooted to the spot. Is he going to say more? I look at the woman, the matriarch with the .45 strapped to her hip. There's a fleeting look in her eyes. Compassion? Pity? It's there, then it's gone.

"I'll call you, Ms. Gilbert," the Sergeant says. "And in the meantime, I'd advise you to stay away from Zeke's place. Please."

fourteen

When I return from the police station, the Professor is dozing on my porch. It's a touching tableau: his head lolling to one side and an upside-down book in his lap, threatening to slide off. I hear the susurration of strings. Vivaldi. Then, I see my front door ajar, and I realize that the Professor has hooked up my speakers. Oh, the unexpected mercies of people.

I stand at the bottom step, not wanting to disturb a molecule of air that holds this peaceful scene in place. I yearn to stay rooted in this moment forever. A moment of pure tranquility.

When my mother died, when I couldn't stop weeping after Ben ended us, when I lost my job, it was the mere possibility of moments like this that kept me going. I hung on to a vision of sitting on my own front porch in Beaufort, South Carolina, the essence of tea olive on an early-evening breeze and Wink curled like a comma at my feet.

The Professor stretches, but his eyes remain closed, and I wonder if he's holding on to the kite-tail of a dream. I clear my throat and his eyes fly open, then relief washes over his face. Like a dad waiting up for a tardy teen who instantly forgets all the bad things that could have happened to his child when they walk in the door. Simply grateful that they are home safe.

"Tell me about it over a glass of wine?" the Professor says.

"Oh, J.P., I don't have any wine yet."

"I took the liberty of scrounging, my girl, and I can confidently report that you don't have *anything* yet. May I correctly assume that your kitchen is a virgin?"

I smile.

"My taking of liberties is endless, Cecilia. I have raided my own pantry and — with your permission, of course — I shall prepare dinner. Here. To consecrate your kitchen."

"You probably mean, *consummate*, J.P., as you are correct about my kitchen's virginity."

"Perfect!" he cries. "Let the deflowering begin."

He instructs me to stay on the porch while he cooks, and do I want a glass of wine? I do.

Over salad Niçoise, I tell J.P. about my trip to the animal shelter and my conversation with Sergeant Allen. I hear defeat in my own voice, a wavering of resolve, and appreciate that the Professor doesn't offer platitudes. He simply listens. Later, when we're doing the dishes, he turns off the faucet and faces me.

"Have you thought of calling Ben, Cecilia? To tell him about Wink's disappearance?"

"Oh," I say, flinging myself into a kitchen chair. "I did think of calling him that first night, but I don't think I will. It would only break his heart."

My breathing comes in shallow little gasps, like a toddler hiccoughing on the verge of tears.

"He's not part of my life anymore, J.P. I mean, *really*?"

My tone is harsher than I intend. But, after six years of all-out loving, then sudden termination, any middle ground with Ben strikes me as impossible. He had not said, "Let's stay in touch once or twice a year." He'd not said, "Drop me an occasional note." In the past three months, my shock and pain has turned to anger. Why hadn't he *told* me he was unhappy? I don't feel I owe Ben a phone call . . . even if 'owe' is not precisely the concept I'm looking for.

"CiCi?"

"Yes?"

"About Ben, not about Wink. What are you *really* feeling now?"

The Professor is right, of course. My heart is broken, and what I truly feel about Ben is not anger, but fear, which I learned long ago generally lurks beneath anger.

"I don't want to tell Ben about Wink," I say, "because I'm afraid my heart would break even more in the face of his sadness or compassion . . . or, yes, even his indifference."

"Yes, dear girl, I think I understand."

"The thing is, J.P.," I say. Now that I'm talking,

I can't seem to stop. "The thing is, I barely have the strength to hold two contradictory ideas at the same time — that Wink will be found and that he will never be found. I don't think my heart could hold *Ben's* feelings, too, you know?"

We finish the dishes and I walk J.P. home. I'm exhausted and my emotions are as ready to spark as a tangle of exposed wires. I have a nagging feeling that there's a big gaping hole in my plan. Except that I don't really *have* a plan. Maybe that's what the nagging feeling is about? I have no plan beyond checking found-animal websites, and that is impossibly passive.

When Eloise opens the door at J.P.'s, my impulse is to turn around and go home. What is she doing here? Does this woman simply come-and-go in other people's houses? It's not that I'm mad at her. Or not precisely. But she is so needy, and I think her fragile mind wants something from me, some kind of energy, that I simply don't have to give. Still, protocol requires that I step inside and exchange niceties, if only briefly.

That said, I should have trusted my gut. I should have simply turned around, said goodbye, and parted, because we are all walking on eggshells. At one point, the three of us — the Professor, Eloise, and I — are standing in an odd little triangle, discussing the weather forecast. It's supposed to rain overnight, Eloise says, and I experience a panic attack of sorts as I envision Wink's little body pummeled by rain and seized by trembling paralysis if there's thunder. When I exclaim that a torrential downpour will sweep into sewer and swampland every scent that Wink needs to find his way home, Eloise tries to comfort me.

"That's not how it works, dear," she says, stroking my arm. Which is what prompts my outburst.

"Works?" I bawl. "*Works*?! Tell me, Miss LaFitte, how *do* such things *work*?"

It is not my best moment. The two of them lead me to the couch and sit on either side of me. J.P. pats my back. They're clearly at their wits' end, as I sit rigidly, zombie-like, not wanting to accept their sympathy. Why do I become nearly insensate after my outburst? I truly don't know. Perhaps I fear that accepting their kindness will somehow validate my terror that Wink will never be found?

I watch shadows bruise J.P.'s damask curtains and believe that I might be slightly hallucinatory. God help me, but in that moment, I hope that Wink will be found dead . . . because I could not bear never knowing what happened to him. That thought, utterly hopeless at its core, may have been what brings me around, though, because I feel my body relax. With that, I realize I have few choices. I must accept all the help I can get, damn it. And help comes in all kinds of packages. Not just a search party or small army to comb the countryside. I also need moral support. Kindness, encouragement. If I intend to build a community in this town, I must begin somewhere. And Professor J.P. Ruopp and the slightly teched Eloise LaFitte are a good place to start. I steel my spine and summon my resolve. Frankly, they're *more* than a good place to start. They're here.

fifteen

I'm not sure I can survive another night alone and, as I say goodbye to J.P. and Eloise, I experience a tsunami of anxiety. Each step is an exercise in blind faith, because I worry the ground is not solid and will not support me. I'm walking like a marionette, lifting my foot too high, hovering it before I have the courage to step on it. It's an out-of-body sensation. Can J.P. see my slow, tentative gait or is it happening only inside my head? At the sidewalk, J.P. turns, hugs me, and strokes the back of my head. It feels like a benison.

I walk home, I try to breathe into my anxiety, my loneliness. I hear the call of an Eastern screech owl, her scale-descending trill like the whinny of a horse. I crane my neck to search for her. She calls again and I get a better bead on her position. I turn in a slow circle, tracking the span of the big oak's branches, but I can't find her.

"I saw that faggot coming out of your house, you know."

The high-pitched voice startles me. I whip around and there is a boy of nine or ten. He's hugging a skateboard to his chest, but I can make out some of the words on his tee shirt: 'I'm no longer accepting the things.' Below them, I recognize the silhouette of Angela Davis's Afro. The kid is glaring at me.

"What did you say, young man?"

My tone is brusque, which he may not anticipate because he cowers. Well, not precisely cowers. He actually takes a step forward, but I can smell his fear.

"I saw you ta-talking to the fa-faggot," he says again.

Despite the challenge in his narrowed eyes, he appears confused. Nothing about the boy looks like a bully. He's as skinny as a kid can be. His shoulder blades jut sharply from his back as fragile as bird wings. I detect a quivering in his hands. The child is struggling to broadcast an air of superiority, but I suspect his bluster, like diluted milk, will never offer the nourishment that his impoverished ego craves. It makes me terribly sad.

"What's your name?" I ask.

"Who wa-wants to know?"

He squints hard again, issuing a challenge. His teeth are perfect miniature white tiles against his dark skin. There's a cut on the underside of his arm where blood has recently congealed.

I take a deep breath. This kid's false bravado is familiar to me. I saw a lot of it when I was tutoring in

New Jersey. Bullies, even wanna-be-bullies like this quite lovely child before me, are mostly just scared. Afraid of being hurt, terrified of not being liked. Kids who resort to this kind of hostility — calling someone a faggot, seriously, in this day-and-age? — simply don't believe they'll ever be respected. Which is why empowering them is the place to start.

But first, I have to disarm the little wise-ass. Throw him off-guard with something unexpected and because I know he anticipates censure, I go for kindness.

"I beg your *pardon*! I've yet to introduce myself. My name" — I extend a hand — "is Cecilia Gilbert."

The kid gapes. His hand, when it touches mine, is limp and sweaty.

"Uh, Darius."

What happens next surprises us both. I start to cry.

"Darius," I choke out, "Darius, you break my heart."

Oh, my. My heart is already broken, of course, over Wink, but this kid's shaky swagger is the fatal arrow to my heart. His vulnerability is nearly palpable. Again, I resist hugging him, which I fully recognize as a blurring of this scared humanoid and my dog, who would be similarly scared, assuming he's still alive.

We stand for a few moments, Darius and I, sizing each other up, like boxers in their corners waiting for the bell.

"My dog has gone missing," I say, as matter-of-factly as my tears will allow. "I was going to put up a few more signs before it gets too dark. Do you have time to help?"

He eyes me suspiciously, then allows as he has a few minutes. I run inside, grab some posters and the staple gun. Darius tucks his skateboard under his arm and follows me. At the first utility pole, I hand him the sheaf of posters and instruct him to hold one against the pole at eye level. Dutifully, he holds it three feet off the ground.

"Eye level," I say, gently.

"*Whose* eye level?" he teases, and I'm reminded that everything in life is a matter of perspective.

We move from pole to pole, Darius holding the posters, me stapling. He flinches at each firing of the staple gun, as if it hurts him to see a sharp, metal object slam into Wink's image. At one point, after I've moved on to another pole, I look back to see him staring at the poster.

"Darius?"

"What color are *my* eyes, Miss Cecilia?"

I take him by the shoulders and turn him to me.

"The color of mahogany," I say.

"What's mahogany?"

"I'll show you back at my house. Why do you ask?"

"This k-k-kid at school," he says.

I give him an encouraging look. I want him to feel he's safe with me, that he can say anything and it'll be okay.

"This kid at school said my eyes are the color of a stink bug and I don't know if that's good or bad."

"Hmmmm," I say. "Well, let me ask you this: How do they *work*? I mean, can you *see* okay?"

"Yes, ma'am."

"Then, in my opinion, stink-bug brown is quite good, indeed."

It takes us 20 minutes to put up the rest of the posters. I want it to last longer. In the distance, a roll of thunder sounds and, nearer, a whistle, followed by a rasp and a scolding. I look up.

"They always fool me," I say. "It's a mockingbird."

"My mother is always mad at me," Darius says, flatly.

His candor, the complete incongruity of this statement, takes my breath away.

"Oh, Darius."

He becomes stoic again. I could have reacted directly to his stark confession, and perhaps I should have, but I want to empower, not coddle, him.

"Hey, Darius," I say. "What I said earlier about your breaking my heart, you know I meant when you called Professor Ruopp that bad name, right?"

He nods.

"Well, it's just that I wanted you to be a nice person. I mean, you're a kid and I *expect* kids to be nice, although I know that's not always true. I just so hoped *you* would be nice, you know?"

He picks up his skateboard and nods, solemnly. I feel the moment slipping away. As he walks down the sidewalk, I stare at the back of his head. The symmetry of his cornrows is a work of art.

sixteen

When I walk in the door, the absence of Wink's life-energy is a punch to the gut. I go to his half-empty water bowl in the kitchen, run the tap until the water is cold, and fill it. It's illogical, but the habit is deeply ingrained. To dump out the water and let the bowl sit empty, or worse, to know it's growing stale, accumulating dust and sprouting bacteria and all manner of microscopic pathogens is unimaginable.

I should sleep, but I'm afraid to dream. In the pre-dawn hours last night, just on the verge of unconsciousness, I bolted upright, panic-stricken. Intellectually, I understand why this is happening: my subconscious regards surrender to sleep as a betrayal of Wink. Because when I'm unconscious, I'm not trying to find him.

I sit on my couch and click through online

postings, which has got to be one of the loneliest, most demoralizing activities ever. Every missing dog, every missing cat, every precious face accompanied by a story of how much they're loved. I can't wrap my head around how many dogs are missing in an area the size of Beaufort County. True, it's a sprawling, mostly rural, county with dirt roads winding through scrubby pine forests, which, in turn, are surrounded by swampy marshland. Easy places to get lost.

But still.

I cannot stop scrolling through older found-dog listings as well. Of course, if you're a found dog, you're still most likely missing your person, so it's all a part of the same story. I'm guessing that the majority of found dogs were abandoned. But some, I assume, have chewed through leashes or scrabbled out of collars, game for a couple-hour adventure, but clueless about what actually lays ahead. I look at every one of those faces behind bars in animal shelters, the kennels bare and always too small. Why the people belonging to these animals have not yet reclaimed them requires a whole other level of comprehension. Moral weakness at best, outright depravity, at worst.

It's too late to call the shelters again, but that doesn't deter me. I call anyway and leave a message at every facility within an 80-mile radius of Zeke's Paws Spa. A phone message, I reason, may garner more attention than an online posting. Plus, underfunded, understaffed kennels may not be able to regularly update their websites on captures or turn-ins . . . or, if the animal is dead and chipped, contact its person.

Oh, that I could hold back the night! But

relentlessly it comes, this funereal gloom, this dark blindness that is so dangerous for Wink. I don't even want to know what night predators thrive in the Carolina backcountry. I turn on the porch lights, front and back. I retrieve his favorite blanket from the car. When I bought it, it was as pristine as a christening gown. Seven years later, it's a dirty beige and worn in places to near-opacity. I hold it to my face and inhale.

I spend a lot of time rearranging blankets on both the front and back porches in case Wink returns but is unable to rouse me. I put out fresh water, then tuck a few of his favorite treats into the nests of blankets. They may be devoured by raccoons, the blankets shit upon by river rats, but I don't care. One day, and one night, at a time.

I wake to gauzy strips of dawn across my bedsheets. In the next instant, I realize Wink is not in bed with me and it all comes flooding back. Although I don't want to lay drowning in sorrow, I seem unable to get up and confront another day. The thought that today will be no different than yesterday immobilizes me. Yesterday was agonizing with its endless online searching, the confrontation with Zeke, the report to police. What more can I do? Breathe, I tell myself, breathe.

I focus on a spot on the ceiling and do just that. I breathe. When a thought comes into my mind, I greet it, then let it pass through me. After years of practice, I'm a pretty good meditator. I can recognize areas of tension in my body. I can name sensations and release them. Often, the process brings tears of joy and gratitude. But today my tears originate in a deep well of pain.

Memories catapult in my mind: The smell of Wink's wet fur, the way he tracks my every move when I'm sick, the time we got lost hiking in the Blue Ridge foothills and I let him choose which fork to get us back to the car.

I must have fallen asleep again because when I look out the window, I'm surprised to see it's rained. For a moment, the world is rinsed clean. But then the abyss, the yawning emptiness, returns. Wink is gone.

I run to the front porch, then the back. The blankets are undisturbed. I call softly for Wink and listen acutely for something. A whimper? A bark? A cry?

Nothing.

I picture him slogging through swampland on his five-inch legs. Panic grips me when I realize that the rain will have ruined the posters I put up yesterday. I'll have to call the copy place as soon as it opens and order laminated posters, then do the rounds all over again . . . and does a staple-gun even work on lamination?

I move Wink's blankets so they don't get wet. The rain is mesmerizing and, at one point, I look down and see I'm still clutching Wink's travel blanket to my chest. Which is when the idea comes to me. I'll use Wink's blanket to spread his scent around the neighborhood. I'll canvas the streets like a burglar and rub his blanket against objects he's likely to sniff in his search for me: On shrubs and mailbox posts, stone carriage-steps in front of the Antebellum homes and, yes, on fire hydrants.

Nancy Ritter

Perhaps my plan sounds crazy, the desperate act of a mad woman, a grasp at futility. But in my wretchedness, it makes perfect sense.

seventeen

I realize that my plan would work better, if it works at all, after the rain stops. But my compulsion in that moment is urgent. It grabs and hangs on, undeterred by a little moisture. I pull my rain slicker out of the trunk, where I had tossed it after the downpour during our overnight in Richmond. I tuck Wink's blanket inside the slicker and, hugging it against my breast like a baby being smuggled across a border, I slip into the dripping world of green and gray.

Overhead, fingers of the sun reach through the branches of my oak. At the sidewalk, I stop cold at a Southern Wood fern next to my mailbox. I picture the scene as if it's happening now: Wink lifts his leg to anoint this particular fern. Perhaps, I think, the rain hasn't washed his scent away. Perhaps, instead, there's some alchemy at play, some magic by which the rain catalyzes dried pee and returns it to its full pungency. Years ago, I would have scoffed at such a hare-brained thought. But then I discovered the canine olfactory system.

In one of my first jobs as a reporter, I was assigned to cover the search for a missing child and somehow my editor got me embedded in the K9 unit of a local police department. After my first day with Tug and his officer-handler Captain Eggert, I came home jumpy with excitement. Ben was cooking a cassoulet. I stood in the kitchen doorway, flipping through my reporter's pad and regaling him with olfactory marvels while he peeled the pearl onions.

"Get this, Ben," I said, and he grinned the way he often did in the face of my childlike enthusiasm. "Humans have approximately six million olfactory receptors in their noses. Guess how many a *dog* has?"

He stopped chopping and considered the question with mock solemnity. Perhaps because he was so busy protecting himself as a child, Ben was a serious man who rarely allowed himself to be amazed. But he delighted in that proclivity in me.

"Twelve point three million?"

"Wrong!" I exclaimed. "Dogs possess up to *300 million* olfactory receptors in their noses. *And*" — I pause for maximum effect — "the percentage of the brain devoted to analyzing smells is 40 *times* greater than ours. *Forty*, Ben!"

"Lord-a-Mighty," he declared, dumping the onions into his special cassoulet pot. He was poking fun at me, but I loved it because he loved doing it, and I loved him.

Slack Tide

"I *know*. *Right*?!" I flipped through pages in my notepad. "According to one dude, a Mr. James Walker of the Sensory Research Institute at Florida State University, a dog's olfactory acuity is 10,000 to 100,000 times greater than ours."

He wagged his eyebrows at me.

"You scoff," I said, "but let's suppose it's only 10,000 times greater. The esteemed Monsieur Walker — in a rigorously designed study, I might add — found that if you apply this analogy to vision, what you and I could see at a *third of a mile* away, a dog could see 3,000 miles away . . . and see as well."

"Whoa!" he said, and Wink came running, thinking Ben was calling him.

Now, how many years later — five? six? — I stand in the rain next to my mailbox and stare at the Wood fern that Wink may or may not have peed upon, trying to summon the awe I felt for canine noses on that long-ago day. But, as soon as I pull Wink's blanket from its raincoat papoose, I realize my plan is flawed. I will need to use separate scents for what I have in mind: fur and skin cells from his blanket *and* the unique enzymes, hormones and acids in his urine, deposited on this Wood fern. I reach down and grab a frond near its base, but it resists sacrifice. With my other hand, I apply torsion, twisting the stem back and forth, then, at its weakest point, use my thumbnail to cut into the turgid tissue until it breaks free.

The rain is coming harder now, pelting my skin like a million tiny hypodermic needles. I hover over my precious fern frond to protect it and I rub it against the trunk of a magnolia tree. In this way, I continue, a block, then two, then three around my cottage, rubbing both frond and stem on plants and poles.

At the corner of Wilmington and Bay, I stop in front of a low brick wall. Along the entire length of the wall, Resurrection fern grows on the top. In dry conditions, the plant's delicate green fronds shrivel up and turn grey-brown, then magically revive in the rain. I look at the old bricks, discolored by a century of rain and the slow accretion of decayed plant material, and suddenly, the best use for Wink's travel blanket comes to me! Surely these brick walls are highly sniffable, and they're everywhere, surrounding many of the town's historic homes and cottages. I remove Wink's blanket from my jacket, bend to the wall and stroke the blanket against the bricks. As I move along the length of the wall, I see a lichened-stained cherub standing atop a fountain in the garden beyond. He holds his wee penis and spouts water into a large basin. A sob catches in my throat as I see a bird's-eye view of myself: A middle-aged woman, water pooling at the rim of her hood before dripping onto her face, trying to guide her lost dog home by frantically rubbing a ratty, old blanket against a rain-tattooed wall. Is it an act of sheer desperation or monumental hope? Is there a difference?

In my deepest marrow, I know Wink will try to overcome every obstacle to find me. And so, as pitiable it may be for a grown woman to be stroking a hunk of old flannel on an 18th century lichen-encrusted wall, I believe it matters.

Shortly before 9 a.m., I head home. At 9:01 a.m., I call Budget Print and order laminated copies of Wink's poster. Initially, I'm told they'll be ready late tomorrow afternoon, but, in a tone somewhere between coaxing and wheedling, I plead my case. Eventually, the clerk relents and agrees to have the posters ready in an hour. When I arrive 10 minutes early, I discover the acne-scarred teenager who ran the copy machine failed to notice the checkmark next to "laminate" on the order form. It's all I can do to not collapse in a puddle at the customer-service desk.

Since they have to do another print run, I decide to add a reward. Two days ago, a reward had been only a passing thought, but with Wink now gone 36 hours, I'm willing to pay anything. I don't want to encourage kooks or opportunists, but where would that fine line be? I stand at the counter, dithering, while the young man paces. Finally, I ask what *he* thinks the right amount would be.

"Two hunnert?"

He says it like a question. Tentative, simply a guess. But as good a guess as any. I realize how unfair it is to put this young man, a boy, really, on the spot. But he's upset with himself for messing up the job, so I take advantage of his desire for contrition.

"I think you're *right*!" I say, too fervently. "Let's make it $200!"

We edit the pdf and 30 minutes later, I'm back home, retrieving the laminated posters from my trunk where I barely remember putting them ten minutes earlier. I cart them to the porch, hear a mockingbird, look up, and notice I've left the trunk open.

The next hours pass in a blur. I staple laminated posters to utility poles and rub Wink's blanket on the poles near the ground. A heavy mist hangs over the river and I wonder how Wink will find his way home with his sightline diminished by this miasma. I pray that his extraordinary olfactory skill will compensate for not being able to see more than a couple of feet in any direction.

I'm nearly back home when my cell rings. The area code is local.

"This is Cecilia."

"Mr. Braxton here. I'm calling about your missing dog."

A beat, then two, before I can utter even a syllable.

"Yes?"

"I believe you said he disappeared from Zeke's place?"

In fact, none of my Internet postings, nor the posters, mentions Zeke's Paws Spa. The truth is, I'm afraid to, skittish about courting some kind of retribution from Zeke and still not convinced he's blameless. I simply used road names on the posters and postings: Last seen in the vicinity of Shug Lane and Highway 21.

The man — Brandon? Braxton? — chuckles. It's an odd, grating sound that feels manipulative and designed to put me off-balance. I sense we've been on the phone for a long time, although I know how strangely time behaves when one is in a state of hypervigilance. I've been in neurological readiness for days, believing that the first call, *the* call, would be good news, but also distrusting myself because I know the news could be bad. I hear the man breathing. He has yet to say why he's calling.

"Are you there?" I ask.

"I believe I can help you, ma'am. I'm prepared to offer the services of my drone. My going rate is $80 per hour, which I think you'll find quite reasonable."

I'm struck dumb. Drone? I know as much about drones as the average person, which is essentially nothing. Of course, I've seen video clips of their use at the U.S.–Mexico border, and a few years back, a friend's son used one to videotape the landscape around Cape Cod, which he edited into a creative marriage proposal. But the idea of using a drone to find Wink? It seems wrong-headed.

"How would it work, precisely?" I ask.

"*Precisely*? Well, drones — unmanned aerial vehicles, they're called, or remotely piloted aerial systems — give you a bird's eye view of what's below. There is *precisely* nothing mysterious about it. Say yer huntin' something on foot, tracking deer or some-such. You can miss things, owing to the large area. A drone can cover that same area lickety-split. *Precisely*."

I flinch. His tone is dripping with sarcasm, the way he repeats my word 'precisely.' As if he's sneering at me, finding me both pompous and clueless, a privileged princess who should trust him because I clearly know nothing. And while it's true that I know little about drones, I sure as hell could imagine what it would be like to be the target of one. I picture a birds-eye view of a drone moving in its eerie, herky-jerky fashion to flush out deer or coyote in Montana or elephants in Zimbabwe.

"You *know*," he sighs. "They're just used for

scouting . . . not actual *hunting*."

I don't believe him for a second.

"Mr. Branson—"

"Braxton—"

"*Braxton*. I'm sure your drone can capture stunning panoramas that you'd never see on foot. But the area where Wink disappeared? It's wooded. Heavily canopied, thick underbrush. What is it that we might actually *see*? I can't imagine my dog would leave a discernable trail—"

"Well, that we do not *know*, now do we, Miss?"

I feel chastised. He goes silent, as if expecting me — oh, ye of little faith! — to actually answer this question. True, I don't know what we might see, but doesn't common sense suggest that a drone flying over Zeke's property and the surrounding forest and marshland would show only vegetation? Could a drone drop below heavy canopy? Could Mr. Braxton actually command it to do so in dense, wild terrain? I have no desire to argue, though, because I suspect this person could out-argue me and might even derive pleasure in doing so. I go for what, to my layperson's broken heart, is the most compelling issue.

"Even if my dog is still in the area, Mr. Braxton, wouldn't the sound of a drone scare him? Isn't it more likely he'd run away, terrified, rather than sit still and wait for us to come get him?"

"My equipment has the best image quality," he persists. "The FPV camera has a CCD sensor with a much better image quality that your average CCD."

It's not that I think he's messing with me, but I'm feeling extraordinarily overwhelmed.

"I'm giving you a great deal—"

"I'm sorry, I'm not interested, I'm hanging up now."

As I disconnect, I hear, ". . . with 2.4 gigahertz."

Climbing my front steps takes every ounce of energy I possess. What was the man thinking? A drone is too loud, its mechanical hum more insistent and noisome than a swarming cloud of mosquitos. And malevolent, too, as if out for blood. The sound would frighten Wink. The erratic buzzing, the sharp turns of a mechanical monster overhead, would drive him further into hiding. I tell myself I've made the right decision with absolutely no evidence, except my gut, that this is true.

I collapse on the couch and turn the TV on with the sound muted, so I can hear if Wink comes scratching at the door. But I can't concentrate, so I move to the porch. In the distance, a siren wails. At one point, I swear I hear Wink breathing. I listen hard, but it's only the wind. I have never felt so bereft. I think I could accept Wink's death if there is proof, but in the absence of evidence? It would be unforgiveable.

Later that night, I walk again to the Bluff. The rain has ended and the night is balmy and clean. I think of myself standing here just two days ago: a blindfolded virgin on the lip of a volcano with no notion of what lay ahead. Especially that I would come to regard this beautiful, haunting landscape as malevolent. I smell the acrid stink of the mud and the damp of the earth. This is the natural world that Wink inhabits, and I want to be in it with him, not cloistered in a warm, dry house with filtered air. I scan the long

line of oaks for the one Wink peed on and recognize
it instantly. Four monstrous branches spread over the
grassy bluff like a benediction. I press my hand against
a huge knot on the trunk and feel for the message
deep within. I know it's in there, something important,
something I should know, but being a mere *homo
sapien*, I am incapable of understanding it.

Streetlights form islands in a sea of black, as
I wander aimlessly, spreading Wink's scent on walls,
bushes and tree trunks. A jet, first one, then another,
shrieks overhead. Night training at the Marine Corps
Air Station. Is Wink hearing this? Does he imagine
a massive unzipping of the sky, his own body in the
crosshairs? I look up and find myself in an unfamiliar
neighborhood. The houses are as grand as those closer
to the river, although not as meticulously maintained. I
stop in front of one grand old dame with peeling paint,
missing shingles and splintered porch rails. After a
moment, I sense a presence. Perhaps a shadow in my
peripheral vision? A slight disturbance in the air or the
sound of muffled breathing?

"Good evening."

The bourbon-tinged words emanate from the
porch. But, with no light from inside the house, the
porch, under its deep roof, is even blacker than the
night. Then, it lightens — maybe a cloud clears the
moon? — and I discern a ghostly shadow, rocking in a
chair.

"Good evening," I say and walk on. But the
shadow speaks again.

"I was going to play some piano," it says. "Would
you care to join me?"

Slack Tide

I balk. Wasn't this the same too trusting temperament that allowed me to leave Wink in a dangerous situation? But music! Music might be the only thing that could touch me tonight, the only thing that might keep at bay the growing capitulation to my anxieties, the shock of Wink's sudden absence and my shameful complicity. I must actively resist such capitulation, and if anything could do that — in this place, in this moment — it is music. No, I would not turn away from its power to release neurochemicals that my brain desperately needs: dopamine for pleasure, serotonin to boost immunity, oxytocin to lower anxiety.

The man stands, opens the screen door, and reaches a hand inside. Instantly, we are flooded in light: recessed lighting overhead, floor and table lamps arranged around the wide, wrap-around porch, and, blazing in the vestibule, the most elaborate chandelier I've ever seen.

He steps toward me and extends his hand.

"Hamilton," he says. "Hamilton Reeve the Third. This is my house. Or *was* my house, I should say. Mama died a few months ago and I can't afford to keep it up."

His smile is just a slight quirk at the corner of his mouth, but his eyes — an impossible blue — sparkle.

"Mama couldn't afford to keep it up either, but I let her live with the illusion that she could."

We shake hands.

"Cecilia Gilbert. CiCi."

Hamilton Reeve III is blonde and muscular and you could tell his craggy face was once very beautiful.

Actually, it is quite beautiful still, with its sun- and age-etched planes. He holds the door for me. The old floorboards are covered with thick Persian rugs, but apart from a grand piano, there is not a stick of furniture in the room. I glance back at Hamilton and he nods.

I walk to the instrument. The case is bleached of color in a few places and the ivories are yellowed, but when I tap Middle C, the action is quick. I play a chord. It's in-tune and its tone is rich and round.

"Do you play, Miss CiCi?"

"Not well. I left my piano behind . . . in the last place I lived."

He nods again. Mr. Hamilton Reeve III is a man of few words. I'm hesitant about playing, but there is something so vulnerable about him that I decide, if my middling performance might offer some solace, I am obliged to try.

I fumble the first bars of *Somewhere Over the Rainbow*, the only song I've ever memorized, but eventually catch the flow where bluebirds fly. When I finish, Hamilton silently applauds. I stand and curtsy, which is when I notice a framed photograph atop the piano. A man and woman in the 1940's, judging by their clothes. I don't have to ask if these are Hamilton's mama and daddy, the resemblance is that strong.

"Will you play?" I ask.

"I will."

His first offering is a luxurious rendition of Paul McCartney's ballad, "Maybe I'm Amazed." At the upper octaves, he adds scale-running flourishes and grace notes that tug at the heart.

I think about my piano, which really was Ben's, but in our six years together, he never touched it. Then, on an anniversary of our first date, he "gave" it to me. An anniversary gift, he said, which I suppose was a nice gesture, but, down deep, it hurt, because I'd always considered the piano "ours," not his alone to be bestowed. The following year, our last, was so full of silences, untruths and a hundred papercuts of disappointments that, when Ben ended the relationship, we both knew I would not take the piano. The "gift" was contingent on him loving me . . . and he didn't love me anymore.

When Hamilton finishes the song, I tell him he plays very well.

"Well, yes," he replies. "I do play well, but without the necessary spirit."

He rolls his head side-to-side, working out a kink, and shrugs.

"Joy," he adds, "has been absent from my life for some time."

I sit on the carpet, wrap my arms around my knees, and cock my head, encouraging him to say more.

"I guess when your heart does not respond to McCartney," he says, running scales in the background, "you know you're in serious trouble. Perhaps that's what they'll put on my tombstone: 'His heart just wasn't in it.'"

A minute passes, in which he coaxes complex chord progressions out of the beautiful, old instrument.

"Is that what they're called?" he asks.

"Tombstones?"

"Gravestones," I say and smile, because who am I to talk this man out of being sad?

And, thus, the night unfolds: I sit on Hamilton Reeve's Persian carpet in his empty house that used to belong to Mama, and he plays for me. Or for himself. Or, perhaps, for anyone who's ever sat alone in an empty house.

It's stuffy in the closed-up house. Beads of sweat pop out on my forehead and behind my knees. I spread my legs and stretch the tendons and muscles along my spine. Only once does Hamilton look up, but I don't believe he sees me. His gaze is directed inward or maybe backward in time as he improvises counter-melodies from melodies, moving seamlessly from Petty's "Free Fallin'" to the Police's "Drive." Every song aches with sadness and yearning. He sways, eyes closed, seeing the music in his head. Or whatever it is that the dear man sees.

Wink's absence is like an anvil on my chest. He should be here, snuggled against my thigh or sitting at Hamilton's feet as he presses the pedals. But he's not. He's somewhere out there. The music is otherworldly and I'm so very tired that, at one point, I begin to whimper, crying silent tears. In an odd zoomorphic twist, I go from thinking about Wink to *becoming* him.

I want Hamilton to play through the night, but of course he doesn't. When he stands, I scramble to my feet.

"Thank you," he says, offering a *namaste* bow.

I return the bow and whisper, "You're welcome."

It's enough, I think. To say more would be

superfluous and wholly inadequate to the gifts we've given and received. My gift to Hamilton: unequivocal acceptance of his haunted self. His gift to me: a few precious minutes of forgetting that Wink is gone.

eighteen

I'm unlocking my front door when, in my
peripheral vision, I glimpse something that
doesn't belong. My stomach lurches. I inch
closer. A bouquet of flowers lies on one of the rocking
chairs. They're roughly bundled and tied with twine,
which I'm fairly sure is not J.P.'s style. There's no
note. An odd feeling comes over me that they carry
a message from Wink. Or, rather, from someone who
knows something about Wink. But that's exhausted-
brain thinking. I'm too tired to explore boxes for a vase
or a glass, so I empty Wink's water dish, fill it with
fresh water, and prop the flowers up in that.

As soon as my head hits the pillow, I'm gone.
I dream of a man playing a xylophone in a field,
although the dream is mostly sensations, not details.
The man is shrouded in the same pearly light that
surrounds Ben when I dream about him, and my

dream-self knows that the light is nothing to be afraid of. It's only sadness. The scene then morphs into one of Wink waking up in the morning, struck anew by the sight of me and the sound of my voice, as if each day is a re-birth.

Sometime in the middle of the night, I wake to rain thrumming on the roof. The once-soothing sound is now monstrous to me, as I picture rain lashing Wink's exhausted little body. I turn on my bedside lamp, Google the current temperature in Beaufort, and am stunned to see it's only 52 degrees. I search 'dogs and hypothermia' but find no clear data on how long Wink will last, wet, cold, scared and unprotected in a 52-degree night that can only get colder.

As I listen to the ferocious wind and driving rain, I'm not sure if I'm awake . . . or dreaming I'm awake? In truth, I cannot say if what happens next is a dream or a hallucinatory half-dream. A trance, perhaps, some state of semi-consciousness yet to be explored by neuroscientists. But this is what happens: From just outside my bedroom window, I overhear a tête-à-tête between Land and Water, the elements that make up the Lowcountry's unique half-water and half-*terra firma* landscape. Every word of the conversation is clear in my head.

> **WATER:** Just give up, Land! You have few natural defenses, and my wind-whipped self can overwhelm your puny 'low'-country self in a nanosecond. You're pathetic, vulnerable as all get out, the way you expose your mud-caked underbelly twice a day.

LAND: I bow to the power of your tides, Water, but I can bend without breaking. And that mud you call 'puny?' It can absorb the measly moisture you throw at it in a Single. Sucking. Swallow. Even when your savagery forces me to retreat — surrendering 1,000 trees here or 500 hectares there — I possess the awesome power of . . . wait for it! . . . rejuvenation.

WATER: Bravo. Rejuvenation is way cool. But speaking of puny, have you seen that little white dog wandering about?

LAND: Yeah, baby. Little dude's our plaything tonight.

Wait. "*Our?!*" I swing my legs over the side of the bed, or in my dream, I see myself swinging my legs over the side of the bed. What do Water and Land mean by "our?" But then, in the next breath, I understand. Of *course*, it's "our." The natural world doesn't have to choose a single method to kill my dog. It's not just Water vs. Wink or Land vs. Wink. No, the natural world can join forces, conspire, work collaboratively. And woe to humans who take it personally. How self-centered can a species *be*? Thinking it's all about us. But Nature is not trying to spite us. It does what it does to live, to thrive, to perpetuate. Nature is completely amoral, neither diabolical nor divine. Do Land and Water "care" about sin or salvation? Hell, no.

> **WATER:** My, my. Look how that insipid canine — not even a real canine, just a pet — cowers in the face of my torrential majesty!

> **LAND:** Nice. And see how he tries to beetle under my pine straw? Boyfriend doesn't know my Southern Copperhead, that venomous little motherfucker, is nocturnal during the summer months. And, oh, let me check the calendar, it *is* June, isn't it, Water?

> **WATER:** Whoo-hoo! Hurricane Season!

> **LAND:** Aw, cut it out, Water. Now you're just showing off! As I was saying, my Copperhead camouflages so well in the pine straw that one false step by a little white dog—

> **WATER:** Ouch! Well played. But I should note that my river's rising, which makes it easy-peasy for a bull shark to travel inland from the coast. They've little taste for humans, but a tasty little morsel like we have with us tonight?

> **LAND:** Chomp. Chomp-chomp.

WATER: Yeah, but you don't think that pitiful dog — pet or no — is so dumb he's going to fall into my rising river, do you?

LAND: Doesn't have to.

WATER: Uh-oh. Whaddya got up your sleeve?

LAND: My ace in the hole.

"Gator!" I scream . . . or dream myself screaming. Why have I not thought about alligators before? They're the apex of the predator world in the Lowcountry, aside from man, that is. I run from my bed to the front porch. The rain is lashing sideways, at a 45-degree angle. I hope Wink can find enough air to breathe in the sheets of falling water.

I realize I'm muttering to myself. I simply cannot stay on the porch any longer. I stumble to my car. There's no traffic on Highway 21 and, with no streetlights, the road is as pitch-black as a tunnel to the center of the earth. But at least the rain has let up. After seven or eight miles, I slow to a crawl, put on my brights, and peer across the east-bound lanes, looking for Shug Lane. Even in the daylight, Zeke's road is just a break in the forest, but eventually I see the faintest softening of black. I turn onto Shug and lower the windows to increase the odds that Wink might smell me or that I might hear something. But in the dead-of-night stillness, all I hear is the susurration of my tires on the wet, sandy road.

At the end of Shug, I do a three-corner turn and

back up to the edge of the marsh. Zeke's trailer is about 100 feet away. I can see part of the chain-link fence in the backyard, but not the shed where he put the dogs. I get out of my car, but leave the door ajar, because I don't want to wake Zeke or the dogs.

The water, a gun-metal grey, is ebbing. I listen to the ticking of my engine as it cools, then become aware of a faint popping sound coming from the marsh. Cavitation, I think, stunned that I can dredge up that obscure word from my wretched brain. The pop of a small bubble that forms when snapping shrimp clutch their claws.

I scan the horizon and as far as I can see along the shore, but don't want to risk walking the fence line. Sergeant Allen's advice to stay off Zeke's property is sensible, of course, but I am driven to be as close as possible to the site of Wink's disappearance. My heart rate speeds up. I don't know if it's fear of something happening or of something *not* happening. What will my life be like if I never find out what happened to Wink? Do I want to know? Do I *need* to know?

The unknown is terrifying. What lies just beyond my vision at this very moment? What unseeable thing is there? A paw-print in the mud that was visible yesterday, but is now erased by the tide? In the unnerving silence, I hear Mother Nature whispering confidentially in my ear: 'Here's this dazzling water, this sumptuous land. But mind your hubris, mortal. Let it inspire your awe, but do not forget its power to destroy. Love it . . . but beware.'

When the eastern sky begins to lighten, I return to my car, lean back against the headrest and close my eyes. When I open them again, the light is a bleary-eyed pearl grey. The Spanish moss shushes in the breeze. Then from out of nowhere it comes! A bone-rattling crash on the roof of my car. I flinch and my knuckles slam into the bottom of the steering wheel. My eyes flash from the rearview mirror to the side and back again, and just when I'm convinced it must have been a falling tree limb, Zeke's face fills my window. He's so close I can smell the stale tobacco on his breath and see the tiny red capillaries in his eyes. My stomach does a flip and I pull back from the window, but there's nowhere to go.

"Thought I told you, sister. Don't know nuffin' bout your damn dog. Ain't gonna tolerate no harassment from y'all. Zat clear?"

I swallow hard. Each word carries a venomous sting. But words are one thing and slamming a fist on the roof of a car is a whole other matter. Once I'm able to speak, I sound like I've swallowed gravel.

"Mr. Johnson. I'm desperate. I can't imagine how Wink just up and disappeared."

His eyes narrow. Does he think I'm making fun of him with "up and disappeared"? It's not the way I normally speak and it sounds contrived, like I'm trying too hard to be a country gal. I muster a weak smile, take another tack.

"I'm so new to the area — and, well, I know my friend might have seemed a bit hostile yesterday, but he was only trying to help. And I, well, I definitely do not want to seem untoward or anything . . . but *do* you happen to know if there *is* dog-fighting in the area?"

Zeke takes a step back and flexes his left hand.

Makes a fist, releases it. His arm hangs benignly at his side, but if he does decide to hit me, there's no escape. His upper lip curls, exposing one of his gold-capped incisors.

"*Untoward*? Is *that* what you said?"

He's toying with me, a barn cat with a mouse.

"I mean, no offense . . . it's just—"

"Lady, everything *about* you is an offense to me."

Normally, I would cower at such a tone. His tone, his words, his empty eyes. And that flexing fist, which he now slowly, rhythmically, pounds against his thigh, as if he's warming up. But I'm committed now and will not back down.

"Sir, I would very much like to talk to your nephew. Perhaps he might recall something out of the ordinary?"

He's obviously startled at my mention of his nephew.

"Didn't mention nuffin' when he come in from bedding the dogs down," he says, narrowing his eyes as if I'm up to something.

I can barely hide my shock. Maybe if I could get out of the car and stand face-to-face with this horrible person — maybe then I'd be able to gather my wits about me. Be a little smarter about my response. But I'm just too exhausted . . . and way too pissed off.

"Wade?! What do you mean, when *Wade* bedded the dogs down? You told me *you* did that. I clearly remember you— "

His smirk goes from amused to condescending. He glances behind himself and, when he looks back, our eyes collide. I feel a power shift, a change in the energy between us.

"Lady, I don't know what-all I told you. Maybe I did and maybe I didn't. All's I know is how I 'member it now. Wade definitely bedded them dogs down."

I gulp hard. Is this the chink in his armor I've been looking for? I must change gears — and fast.

"Oh, Mr. Johnson, great apologies. I'm sure I'm mistaken. But, I wonder, is Wade here now? Could I talk to him . . . since I'm here and all."

What transpires next, I may never clearly remember. He begins to yell. I'm never to come on his property again. And I am never, *ever,* to talk to his nephew. He inches closer and I see the roadmap of spider veins on his nose. I think he's moving toward the door handle, so I scream.

"Stop!"

It startles him for the seconds it takes me to start the engine and peel away.

My heart pounds like a tympani drum. Stones ping the undercarriage of the car. I pass an elderly gentleman on a bicycle, hair and beard gone white, fishing pole balanced across the handlebars. He waves. I want to wave back but can't seem to loosen my grip on the steering wheel. I check my rearview mirror every five seconds for signs of Zeke until I reach the highway.

nineteen

My hands are jittery on the steering wheel and my legs tremble so badly that I have to concentrate to move my foot between the gas pedal and the brake. I try deep-breathing exercises, but am monumentally unsuccessful at quieting my mind. Although perhaps I don't *want* my mind quieted? Maybe it's this very disquietude that propels me onward now. The change in Zeke's story galvanizes me. So, too, do images of Wink mucking through the marshland. I picture him mud-caked to his chest, straining one leg at a time until the viscous mud releases each paw with a sickening pop, and each pop strengthens my resolve.

I open all the windows to feel the chill morning air in my face. It does little to dispel visions of Wink. I see him seeking shelter from the stabbing rain. I see him huddled under rain-slicked leaves of a buttonbush shrub, pressing his body against its twisted trunk. Or trying to squeeze into a hollow log. Or burrowing under a mite-infested mound of Spanish moss. I do not know what psychology is at play, but I fear that if I *am* able to quiet my mind, I'll lose the image of him wandering endlessly through the long night, side-stepping vines with strangling arms that might wrap around his body like a diamondback, refusing to relinquish its grip. And as long as any of that's possible, I refuse to banish such images.

At home, I fall into bed without undressing. I dream again, and in the dream, I wonder why I'm dreaming so much. My dream-self knows I'm not getting enough deep sleep, and that insomnia, anxiety and frequent awakenings offer the perfect dreaming fodder. When I awake, it's a brilliant morning, and I can't bring back any dream-details. Only a hollowed-out feeling of loss and abandonment. I'm not even really sure if I'd been dreaming about Wink — or Ben.

Then it rushes back in a torrent of memories: driving to Zeke's before dawn, his threat, the change in his story about who put the dogs in the shed. I must tell Sergeant Allen about this. But why haven't I heard from him? For 48 hours, I've been suppressing the fear that I'm being blown off. But now that fear is fully upon me, and I simply will not allow that to happen.

Thus coalesces my plan for the day: I will go to the police station and report Zeke's threat and inconsistencies. I will ask about the use of a drone, confirm that I've made the right decision, and I *will* get to the bottom of the dog-fighting issue.

When I arrive at the station shortly after 9 a.m.,

the same female officer is at the reception desk. She's
on the phone and doesn't look up, so I stand patiently.
Two uniformed officers enter and cross the small
lobby. One gesticulates wildly and the other mock-
staggers, holding up a hand as if to fend off further
hilarity. When they see me, they become sober,
nod and say "ma'am" in unison. Then the laughing
one punches numbers on a security pad and they
disappear behind a door.

The policewoman finishes her call and looks up.
"Ms. Gilbert!" she exclaims.

I'm surprised she remembers my name. I smile
feebly.

"You're here to see Sergeant Allen, I presume?"

She puts the phone to her ear and, before I
can respond, punches in a few numbers and says
something, *sotto voce*, that I can't make out.

"The Sergeant will be out momentarily, dear."

I'm too flustered to sit, especially when I'm
minutes away from admitting to being at Zeke's again,
potentially trespassing even, in the middle of the night.
I mindlessly scan the photographs on the lobby wall.
Beaufort City Chiefs of Police over the decades. All
white males. Once again, I'm baffled by the race and
gender homogeneity in so many American institutions.
In 2018, for heaven's sake.

A few minutes later, Sergeant Allen comes out
and back we go through the cubicle maze. Although
he greeted me warmly in the lobby, he begins to fidget
as soon as we sit. He pushes papers to one side, pulls
them back, arranges them in a pile. For a moment,
I think they, the papers, may have something to do

with Zeke or Wink or both. But finally, he pushes all of them to the side, tents his fingers, and looks at me intently.

"You'll want to hear about my visit to Mr. Johnson's."

"Oh."

I want to proclaim my surprise that he's been there and not called me, but I resist.

"I drove out yesterday afternoon," he says. "Pressed him pretty hard."

He pauses. I don't know if he wants me to respond, so I simply nod.

"He insists he knows nothing about how your dog got away, Ms. Gilbert, and he gave me no reason to not believe him."

"But—"

"—please let me finish and then I'll be happy to answer your questions."

I hear a sharp intake of breath and realize it came from me. Tears sting my eyes. Damn . . . I so do not want to cry. The Sergeant's statement feels like a rebuke, and my normal reaction would be tears, then defensiveness. But nothing feels normal about this tangle of emotions in which I'm caught. He opens a drawer, pulls out a box of tissues, scoots it toward me.

"Mr. Johnson assured me he's had no contact with his brother since he was released from prison. In fact—"

The words 'brother' and 'prison' hit me out of the blue. I fast-rewind the last few sentences of our conversation for context, and, finding none, experience the disconcerting sensation of being dropped into the scene from another planet.

"Sergeant, I'm sorry, but I'm completely lost. Brother? Prison?"

A shadow crosses his face and I wonder if he's second-guessing what he just told me. But he recovers quickly.

"Forgive me, Ms. Gilbert. I forget you're a recent arrival to Beaufort. Of course, you don't know."

What I don't know is this: Ten years ago, Zeke Johnson's brother was charged with running a dog-fighting "enterprise." A jury found Harold Smithson guilty and he received a prison sentence.

I'm reeling. This opens an entirely new layer of questions. If true, why would Eloise LaFitte recommend Zeke? Why, when Wink went missing, did she not mention Zeke's troubles, pertinent or not? And why-oh-why, has J.P. not told me about this?

The Sergeant swipes his hand over his face like a cloth. He rubs his chin. I suspect he's giving me time to collect myself.

"Which means," I finally stammer, "which *means* I left my dog in the care of a criminal, an *animal* abuser?

"The *brother* of a criminal," he responds in a slightly scolding tone. "There was never any evidence that Mr. Zeke Johnson had anything to do with it. Or had knowledge of it, even. I worked the case myself, Ms. Gilbert, and I must tell you, in all sincerity, that I believed him then, and I believe him now. I'm sorry I didn't connect Mr. Johnson with Mr. Smithson when you came in before. But I can tell you that Zeke Johnson is basically a good man, been raising his nephew since his brother went to prison. He seems genuinely mystified about what happened to your . . ."

"Wink," I whisper.

"Yes, your Wink," he says, reaching to straighten a pile of papers that does not need straightening.

"Well, he may be mystified, but he also has quite a temper."

I catch myself before I say something even snottier. Sergeant Allen is only doing his job, I remind myself, and doesn't have the whole story yet. He looks wounded that I would question his opinion. And maybe I am, because if Zeke truly knows nothing, the likelihood is that Wink has been wandering in perilous marshland for nearly three days. Which means he's dead . . . or will be soon.

"I'm sorry, Sergeant. That's not the way I should begin. You see, I went to Zeke's this morning."

"This morning? *Already*?"

"Well, the-middle-of-the-night morning. Around 3:30."

He frowns.

"I couldn't sleep, so I—"

"Start at the beginning, Ms. Gilbert, please."

He's clearly exasperated, but I can't tell if he is exasperated with me or with himself.

I tell him about Zeke slamming his fist on the roof of my car. I tell him that Zeke changed his story about who put the dogs in the shed. I tell him that he became enraged when I asked about dog-fighting.

"You asked about dog-fighting?"

"Yes."

"Well, that could explain his reaction. Not that

it's justified, of course. Just that it provides some context. I talked to him yesterday, so he must be spooked, which, let's think about this now, could happen to anyone who believes their livelihood is threatened. I'm not saying it's okay to scare you. Certainly not. But, seriously, Ms. Gilbert, going out there in the middle of the night? What were you thinking?!"

I wait a beat to see if he's being rhetorical. I'm glad he is because I have no idea how to respond if he expects an honest answer to that question.

"Tell me, Ms. Gilbert," he says. "And this is important: What did he say when you asked about dog-fighting?"

He faces his computer again as I try to recall Zeke's words. But the scene my mind recreates is surreal, dreamlike in its improbability. It's dawning on me how stupid it was to go out there at that hour. Although what *would* be the "best" hour to find Wink . . . or let him find me?

"I don't think he responded," I say. "In fact, I'm sure he didn't *say* anything. But he became quite agitated."

"How so? This is very important, Ms. Gilbert."

He rests his elbows on his desk, clasps his hands and bounces them as if to coax a kernel of useful information out of me. I draw a deep breath.

"Well, at first it was not the words so much, but he was flexing his fist like he was warming up."

"Did he raise his fist towards you?"

"No. But he looked at me in a very peculiar way. I can't explain it exactly, but he clearly wanted to scare me."

The Sergeant raises an eyebrow.

"Like he was playing with me. *Torturing* me."

I should have left that last part out. I sound crazy.

"The thing is, Sergeant, it was when I asked to speak to his nephew that things got creepy."

Creepy? Oh, come *on*, CiCi, I chastise myself. Get a grip. The Sergeant continues to rock his hands. He nods, signaling that I should continue.

"After I returned to pick up Wink — and he was gone — Wade was there. He helped Zeke and me look for Wink. I hadn't seen the man before. Well, I guess he's only a kid, right? Maybe 15 or 16?"

"Mr. Johnson's nephew? Yeah, that'd be about right."

"Yes, sir. Anyway, when I went out there this morning, that's when he, Mr. Johnson, I mean, changed his story. The night Wink disappeared, he said *he* put the dogs in the shed. But, this morning, when I asked to speak to Wade, he said his nephew had not mentioned anything unusual after he, *Wade*, bedded down the dogs."

We sit in silence for a moment, and I see the wheels turning in Sergeant Allen's mind.

"So, the first time, Mr. Johnson said *he* put Wink in the shed, and this morning he said Wade did. Have I got that right?"

"Yes, sir. And, this morning, when I asked to speak to Wade, that's when he became hostile. When I pointed out the inconsistency, he said he didn't remember *what* he told me that night. But today, he seemed very sure that *Wade* was the last person to see Wink. Or put him in the shed, I mean."

"So, you asked to speak to Wade?"

"Yes, and that's when he screamed to never come on his property again or try to contact Wade. He was yelling and his face was getting red and he was moving closer to the car. I was scared."

"So you—"

"Drove away . . . fast."

"I'm sorry, Ms. Gilbert. I truly am sorry that you're going through all this. I'll contact Wade and see if he can shed more light. But, please — *please* — don't go out to Zeke's again in the middle of the night. Or *any* time. Let me handle this, please."

I nod.

"You'll call me as soon as you talk to Mr. Johnson's nephew?"

"I will," he says solemnly, and I want to trust him. I want to believe that he is a man of honor. But I really don't know.

Sergeant Allen escorts me back to the lobby. We shake hands, I thank him, he thanks me, and I turn to leave. But before I walk out the door, I turn back.

"Ma'am?" he says. "Something else we should know?"

The woman behind the desk looks up, too. They are waiting for me to say whatever I need to say. They wear identical expressions of patience and sympathy. My dog is lost, which as long as our species remains woefully humancentric, is hardly a high crime or misdemeanor. And I'm sure that a missing dog is not the greatest challenge these officers will face today.

How can I ask for their help while also acknowledging the importance of their jobs, the dangers they face every day when they put on the uniform and strap a gun and taser to their belts?

"My dog," I say, haltingly. "I just want you to know, officers, that my dog is . . . singular."

twenty

Geologic time. Time that passes so slowly it's measured in millennia. But even a millennium is simply the slow accretion of minutes, hours, and days. Since Wink's disappearance, this is how time passes for me. Every moment both a nanosecond . . . and an eon.

Eventually, I'll have to talk with Eloise and J.P. about Zeke's brother, but my heart is too heavy to face them this morning. I need to *do* something. But what? An entire day lay ahead of me. Four days since Wink went missing and I would not, *could* not, waste it with something as pedestrian as unpacking tchotchkes. Plus, unpacking would suggest my willingness to stay in this town without Wink, and I'm not sure about that. Wouldn't this place always feel haunted to me?

I decide to return to the animal-control facility. Am I being a nudge? Undoubtedly. I know they'll call if Wink is found, but I also think there may be leads, clues of some sort, that I'll never notice if I don't open my mind to them. Although I have no idea what such clues might be. I'm not so unhinged that I think someone walking in the woods would report a Wink scat-sighting. As special as he is, Wink's poop looks like every other dog's of his size and, frankly, I'm not sure even I would be able to tell the difference between an old Wink feces and the feces of a big racoon or a coyote, which I've heard are on the outskirts of Beaufort, venturing into backyards at night. A tired, dazed Wink would be one tasty morsel. Yet even that I could accept, as long as his body is found. If he were half-devoured by a hungry coyote, I wouldn't blame the coyote. I would cremate the remains of my boy and spread his ashes over a marsh at high tide. Grieve, heal. Friends would write and call with condolences. But this limbo is an entirely different matter.

It's a cloud-weighted afternoon when I pull up to the animal facility. One of those grey nondescript days when the air is still and the temperature makes your skin feel permeable. I sit in my car with the windows down and listen to the stillness. From the corner of my eye, I see a flash through the trees and, initially, I think it's just a breeze stirring the leaves. But the movement changes direction. A minute later, the apparition flashes through the heavy, green undergrowth and a person on a bicycle comes into view. I stand a few feet from my car, watching as he — for now I can see it is a he — turns the handlebars and pedals in my direction. Sunlight glints off old-fashioned pant-cuffs strapped above his ankles.

When he sees me, the man begins to pedal furiously, legs pumping like pistons until he's nearly on top of me. Then he brakes and skids in a half-arc, coming to a halt a foot away.

"I've been thinking about you," he says.

I have no idea who he is. When I don't respond, he continues. But in the instant before another word leaves his mouth, I feel something swell in the air around me. Is it fear, this bloating premonition in my gut?

"Your dog is missing, right?"

My breath goes shallow, as if even my breathing might spook him . . . or, if this is all a dream, make him vanish.

"Right."

"I seen you. Here, I mean. I seen you when you came before. My job. I mean, it's what I do. Pick up dead animals."

"Oh."

I am rooted. Speechless. My brain slams against my skull as he stands in front of me, straddling his bike. He's nondescript, somewhere around 30, medium height and build, nut-brown hair that grows like a baby's with no discernable style. His skin is neither white nor black nor brown, which may sound odd, but it's simply the impression he gives. Bland. Flavorless. Uninteresting.

Except, of course, he's the only person in the world besides me looking for my dog.

"You must find *lost* dogs and cats, though, right?"

He continues to stare. Not that he appears

hostile or uncomfortable, but as if we speak different languages. I experience a throb of dread but try again.

"Lost, but still *alive?* I mean, you also look for dogs that got away from their . . . from their *person*, right?"

Good Lord. *Person?* I feel like an alien, as far-removed from a Carolina native as one can get. Years ago, I started using the expression "person" to avoid referring to an animal's "owners." I know it sounds like a precious euphemism, but I persist. The presumption that man and woman should have dominion over animals is, in my opinion, ethically lazy. Yes, I understand that ship has sailed, at least for now. But any person who has ever lived with an animal understands, or should understand, the parity in the partnership. Particularly in the canine-human relationship, we are no more — and no less — than two species living in a symbiotic relationship. That said, using the word 'person' now, in the soupy heat of a scraggy-limbed forest with mosquitos at my ears and gnats at my ankles, feels contrived.

I take a deep breath, which may unnerve the poor fellow a bit. What other inanity might blurt out of this strange woman's mouth? He turns his front wheel, crab-walks the bike around, and makes to get back on. But I can't let him go. I know I should go inside and see the more official and officious Brenda Lee Hoenecker, but I have a powerful feeling that I need something from this man.

"*Please?* Can we start over? I'm Cecilia Gilbert and my dog Wink has been missing for four days. He's microchipped and Ms. Hoenecker told me you wand dead animals. I mean, if he's alive, you'd call, of course. And, I guess, if he was dead, you'd call, too, because he'd still have his name tag. And also, the microchip. If something bad happened to him and he lost his tag, I mean."

It is an exceedingly disjointed monologue and I only half-hear myself speaking. The man takes it all in, intrigued, perhaps, by my ardor. But he still straddles his bike, poised to take off if the crazy lady veers clean off the road.

"I seen you here. Like I said. But I don't know nothin' bout no wanding. We had one a dem gizmos a few years back, but I don't know what happened to it. Machete Mike took it, I suspect. He was always lifting things. I told Miss Hoenecker as much."

No wanding? During these punishing days, I'd taken some solace that, dead or alive, Wink would be identified by his microchip. When grotesque scenarios grabbed hold in my mind and I descended into every 'what-if' imaginable, it was only the existence of the microchip scanner that calmed me.

I retrieve one of Wink's posters from my trunk and hold it up.

"Have you seen my dog, sir?"

He gazes at it for a good long while, and I have no way of knowing if he's trying to excavate a memory or scrambling for some way to tell me an abominable story.

"Sir?"

I waft the poster at him, encouraging him to look harder or snap out of whatever trance he appears to be in. I do I believe they will contact me if-and-when

Wink is found — don't I? — but with every passing day, I'm increasingly convinced he is gone. Dead-gone. Putrefaction-gone. Fading are any Pollyanna visions of him being found by a loving family with great kids under whose covers he sleeps at night.

I think how pitiable this is, how pitiable *I* am. I've cornered a man who scrapes roadkill off highways, and I've used my age, gender and Yankee entitlement as a cudgel. Wink's poster hangs at my side as I mutter an apology under my breath and turn away.

"I can't be sure," he whispers. I turn back and see the pain in his eyes. "I seen so many, you know? I can't really look at them anymore. Not really."

I want to thank him for his time and honesty . . . and for doing such a sad job, day-in-and-day-out. I want to scoop him up in my arms and tell him everything will be okay. But I am paralyzed. Whatever is holding me together is eroding and I'm desperate to hold onto it.

From the side of the building comes the thunk of a slamming car trunk, and I scurry to see Brenda Lee getting in a car.

"Miss Hoenecker?"

Her hand flies to her throat and, for a moment, I think she's going to scream.

"Ms. Gilbert."

I can't read the tone in her voice. It is something akin to relief or maybe compassion. Or pity. Probably pity. What a mess I am.

I walk closer, as I try to frame a coherent, non-abrasive question. But I'm losing that skill. Unable to fashion anything diplomatic, I blurt it out.

Slack Tide

"You don't have a microchip wand, do you? Isn't it possible that my dog's carcass has been found and you don't even know it?"

Brenda Lee looks like she's going to cry.

"No. I mean, yes. Oh, I don't know, I'm so sorry."

twenty one

For a long minute, we stand there, Brenda Lee Hoenecker and I, two middle-aged women under a hot canopy of live oaks, breathing in the world's sadness and breathing out our own. I can say nothing in response. No good ever comes from recrimination. Plus, what I really want to do is console her and, in doing so, console myself. Finally, she speaks.

"Would you have a drink with me?"

At first blush, the invitation might sound odd, maybe even gratuitous, but because I'm so vulnerable, I hear it with my heart and see it for what it is: The deep human urge to make a connection with someone we've wronged. The urge toward forgiveness.

I say yes.

I follow her to a place further out on 21. White cords of clouds ghost the western sky. It's lovely. But then a cloud covers the sun and its shadow scuddles menacingly over the landscape. Ten minutes later, I face Brenda Lee Hoenecker — county animal-control worker and proven liar — across a table at Bruff's Lowcountry Tavern, she with a Jack Daniels and Coke, me with a glass of the house red.

Brenda Lee is clearly distraught. Again, I notice her poorly dyed hair, more magenta than plum-colored. Her face is puffy and pouches apron her eyes. She's either been crying or hasn't slept. One of her hands trembles and I wonder if she is craving a cigarette. I remember her smoking during our initial interaction, which seems like eons ago, but is only four days. Four days since she introduced herself with a nameplate. Four days since she told me her husband had left her and she showed no sympathy for my plight, pushing paperwork at me like a robot. All this I remember in the greatest detail, yet, for the life of me, I can't remember what she said about the county using — or not using — a microchip scanner.

"I was very rude to you about your dog's microchip," she says. "I should have told you that we don't have a scanner."

I take a sip of the mediocre wine. Normally, I would let her off the hook. I'm not a vindictive person. But there is something so confessional about the moment that I don't want to steer the conversation away from whatever she needs to say.

"Yes," I respond.

"I don't know why I said that. We used to have one, but it started acting hinky and then Mike, well, a former employee — I had to let him go — took it home to fix it and, well, he never brought it back."

I nod.

"That was months ago, and it was only when you came in I remembered I never sent the paperwork to my supervisor. For a replacement, I mean. That was around the time my husband left me and I was dropping balls left and right."

"Yes," I whisper. I understand.

"Which is no excuse for lying to you. I'm sorry, Ms. Gilbert. I'm so sorry. I've lost sleep over it. About your dog, I mean, not about my husband . . . although him, too."

At this point, I might have said something consoling. Forgive her or at least find a conciliatory way to move on. But I can't seem to find my forgiving heart. Perhaps because I can't forgive myself? My mind replays how she slashed a line across the bottom of the missing-animal form and instructed me to write Wink's microchip number thereon. Obviously, that was an implicit representation, wasn't it, that the county could, and would, wand pets?

Brenda Lee looks as wounded a person as I've ever seen. I slide a hand across the table towards her but stop shy of touching her.

"What happens to dead dogs that the county picks up?"

She pulls her hand back as if she's been slapped, as if my touch would be incompatible with what she has to say.

"We cremate deceased animals. Deer, racoon, cats . . . dogs. After our wand disappeared, I told my staff to photograph every dead dog. You can't imagine how many there are. Anyway, that policy was followed for a while."

She takes a breath.

"Until it wasn't. I was supposed to put in for a new scanner. I even filled out the paperwork, but I keep forgetting to send it in. My troubles were snowballing around that time. I'm sorry. So very, very sorry."

Brenda Lee slides to the side of the booth, turns and leans back against the wall, pulls her legs up on the bench.

"Leonora?" she says, raising her glass as our waitress walks by.

"Sure thing, B.L.," Leonora replies.

We let a minute of silence pass. I like that Brenda Lee is not a chatterer. Most folks are uncomfortable with quiet. I have friends who can't fall asleep without a late-night radio talk show murmuring in their ear. I'm not one of those. One of my favorite things is to be in a car with a friend, no talking, no singing, no radio, just panoramas filling up the windshield, then slipping away as we move down the road. I once did a cross-country trip with a friend, and I remember an entire hour going by without a spoken word. No narration about buttes ghosting red in the distance, no exclamation over fields of windmills as far as the eye could see. Just silence. It felt safe. It was heaven.

Certainly, there's a risk in moving from silence to intimacy with Brenda Lee Hoenecker, but Fate has brought us together, so I decide to risk it.

"Tell me about your life," I say.

Leonora brings the bourbon bottle over and gives Brenda Lee a generous pour. The two smile at each other, the way friends do.

"Well, Buck left a couple of months ago," she says. "I believe I called him a lyin' sack when we first met?"

"A miserable son of a bitch," I say.

Leonora returns with two glasses of water.

"Talkin' about Buck, ladies?" she says.

I feel a triangulated force field among us. The recognition of a sisterhood, an unspoken homage to all the women in the world who have been left behind. Leonora, long and lovely with a sheet of sandy brown hair that reaches past her waist, walks back to the bar. She is a study of grace in motion, fluid, poised, intentional, as she pulls a towel from over her shoulder and begins polishing shot glasses.

"Buck wasn't all bad. The man has a refined sense of humor. You know he owns Buck's Tire & Retread, where the motto is 'We Take the Slick Out of Your Tire.'"

I offer a noncommittal chuckle. No need to offend, but it's a pretty lame motto.

She shoots me a rueful look.

"Go ahead," she says. "Laugh all you want. The man is an idiot. But he was good in bed."

I nod. Talk about solidarity.

"I suspected Buck was catting around when Corey was over. Corey Greene, Buck's buddy, he works at the shop, too. He and Buck were sitting on the couch, polishing off a 12-pack and watching the races, the way they do most Sundays."

"Anyhoo, I said to them, I said, 'Boys, y'all are gonna get dizzy watching those cars goin' round in a circle.' And Corey — who never says anything to me, really, the strong, silent, dumb type, doncha know? — Corey says, 'Oh, don't worry, Patty, that ain't gonna happen.'"

"*Patty*?" I venture.

Brenda Lee exhales dramatically.

"Yeah, Patty. Normally, I wouldn't have noticed. As a general proposition, I try to ignore those yahoos when they're together. But I happened to be walking right by, carrying a load of Buck's tidy-whities, as the Fates would have it, and I see Buck blanch, and Corey blurts out, 'Oh, *fuck*! I'm *sorry*, Buck!' and, right then and there, the jig was up."

"Patty," I say.

"Patty," she says.

"The bitch," I say.

Brenda Lee cracks a smile, but she's obviously deeply injured. At least, that's how she seems to me, but what did I know about this woman who I'd talked to for all of an hour? Who scorned me at our first meeting and now sits across from me, opening her heart?

"What did you do?" I ask.

"There was nothing *to* do, nothing there, nothing to salvage."

I understand completely. I want to tell Brenda Lee about Ben. It feels like lying *not* to. A lie of omission. But I'm not ready, plus she is already witness to the latest tragedy in my life. Wink.

We nurse the last of our drinks as more people arrive. Men mostly. I'd describe them as rugged, although I've never been precisely sure what that term means. They arrive in twos or threes, these men, carrying their denim-clad bodies gingerly, like it would hurt to raise an arm too high or bend to tie the lace on a work boot. They come from machine shops, I imagine, and the clanking and buzzing in their ears won't subside until bedtime. Some are undoubtedly fishermen, fresh off the shrimp boats, sweat and sea water staining their shirts.

I ask Brenda Lee about the photos of dead dogs after the scanning wand disappeared. She can't remember how long that had gone on. Only that her crew — really, two men, a regular shift and a relief-and-weekend guy — had stopped taking photographs about a week ago. Wink, I remind her, has been missing for four days. Is it possible photos were still being taken?

"Yes," she says. "It's possible, but I don't think so."

"Could I look?"

"You could, but I'd rather go through them first. It's my *job* and, damn it, Cecilia, I've fucked up *enough* already. Please let me look first? They can be pretty gruesome. I mean, you can see any that even remotely might be Wink."

We exit the bar into the deep purple twilight. The air is filled with evening birdsong. Among the warbles and whistles, I recognize the call of a nightingale, but not the grating double-bark from the canopy above us.

"Corncrake," she says.

We stand and listen. Brenda Lee cocks her head and closes her eyes. It comes again. A *crex-crex*, like a nail file pulled across the rough end of a matchbox.

"I love that corncrake," I say.

"I bet that corncrake loves you, too," she says.

We hug and Brenda Lee walks to her car. I have one foot in my car when I holler over the roof. Perhaps it's just the wine speaking, although I'd had only a single glass. More likely, though, it was our proximity to where Wink went missing.

"Would you want to drive over to Zeke's Paws Spa with me?"

"Oh. Talk to him, you mean?"

I've not told Brenda Lee about my confrontation in the wee hours of this very day, Zeke's threat, and my second trip to the police where I learned about Zeke's brother. But I could tell her everything on the 10-minute drive to Shug Lane.

"No, not talk to him. I guess to just look for Wink. Or not really look, cuz that might be on Zeke's property and—"

I'm rambling and can't seem to string events, or even words, together in logical order. I know this is a wrong-headed idea, going back to Zeke's, but the pull of "what if's" is fierce. What if today, tonight, now, this very moment, is when I find him?

Brenda Lee gets in the passenger seat. Ten minutes later, we turn onto Shug Lane and crawl ten miles an hour down the dirt road. Without me saying a word, she lowers her window, listens hard, and stares into the opaque forest. I actually feel a pitched energy in the air as she fine-tunes her senses. Or maybe I'm transferring my own sensibilities onto her? Either way, I feel an immense gratitude for this woman who sits by my side.

Two hundred yards before Zeke's trailer comes into view, I kill the headlights. There are no streetlights out here. The cloud cover that persisted all day now obscures much of the moonlight and the heavy canopy filters out the rest. I venture another 50 yards, then turn off the engine.

"Are we there?" Brenda Lee asks, her hand on the door handle.

"No, it's up ahead."

I tell her about my middle-of-the-night encounter with Zeke. She wants to walk the rest of the way to get closer to his trailer, but I'm hesitant. My brain is not functioning right and I'm hyper-aware that a bad decision could diminish what little chance remains of finding Wink.

I tell Brenda Lee how Zeke changed his story about who put the dogs in the shed. She looks at me sideways and, for the first time all night, she pulls a frown.

"Brenda Lee?"

She says nothing. Then I tell her what Sergeant Allen said this morning about Zeke's brother being convicted for running a dog-fighting ring. She fumbles to unhook her seatbelt and turns her entire body towards me.

"Oh, Sweet Jesus! That was *him*? I remember something about a dog-fighting case, but Buck and I were in Atlanta then. So, you're saying this kid Wade is that man's son? The man who went to prison?"

"Yes."

"And where is he now?"

"I don't know. I got the impression that he served his time, but I don't think he's back in the picture. The cop said he'd look into it but couldn't imagine Zeke having anything to do with Wink's disappearance."

"I guess there are weird coincidences in life," Brenda Lee says, to which I respond, "There are," then we just sit quietly, cogitating on coincidences and breathing in the night air.

Eventually, I get out of the car and stand at the side of the road. The nocturnal whirring and chirring of insects is hypnotizing. Memories of Wink threaten to overwhelm me. How he emerges from under the covers in the morning and shakes off the night's sleep. How he runs full-bore on the beach, his short legs propelling him as fast as a whippet, the muscles in his haunches moving like a racehorse, sleek and defined. And that signature way of his, eyeing a visitor, stealthily so as to give no warning what he's plotting, then springing from the left, always the left, onto the waiting lap.

Brenda Lee gets out of the car, but she doesn't shut the door and, for that, I'm grateful. It's getting late. I imagine Zeke turning off the TV, putting whatever dogs are there tonight in the shed. He, too, could be standing for a moment, head cocked, listening to the sounds of the night. I wonder if he's listening for Wink in the forest beyond, or if he knows Wink is not out there?

I listen and remember how I used to love hearing the sounds of the night, the crickets and katydids and tree frogs. But now I wonder what's out there that I don't hear. The slow crawl of a gator, the slithering of a cottonmouth? I smell the night and think how I'm breathing the same air Wink is breathing. The next thing I know, Brenda Lee is by my side. She takes my hand. It startles me, but just for a moment. She doesn't say anything. She simply holds my hand as we peer into the deep, forbidding forest.

twenty two

That night, I dream I'm poring over photographs of dead birds. Creased and faded black-and-whites of crows hanging from telephone wires by their feet. Pelicans entombed in fishing nets. Photo after photo of violent death. Mutilation, decomposition, turkey vultures pecking at their still-screaming young. When I wake the next morning, I know I cannot look at any photographs Brenda Lee might be able to retrieve. She has a photo of Wink. She could compare.

Was this, I wonder, the new normal? Just days ago, I'd have gone through any trial to find my dog; and now I'm unwilling to expose myself to photographic evidence of what he might have suffered prior to death? But, yes, it's true. With photos of dead animals putrefying in the recesses of my brain, I fear the specter of Wink's painful, lonely death would surely populate my waking thoughts and nightmares, and I might never find a way to forgive my sorry self.

I'm in the bathtub when my cell rings. I don't recognize the number, but it's a local, '843' area code.

"Hello, this is Cecilia."

"Cecilia with the missing dog?"

A deep baritone, bordering on a growl.

"Yes."

I sit up straighter and the bath water sloshes. I press the slippery phone hard against my ear.

"I found your dog."

I start to get out of the tub, then realize I'll need both arms. As I sink back, I command myself to stay calm. There's something about the man's voice, something decidedly off, that demands I keep my wits about me. For one thing, how odd that he sounds so gruff. Wouldn't a person who found someone's dog be elated to share the news? But I push that thought away because, really, I don't have a clue how people should sound in this situation.

"You there?"

"I . . . yes, sir, I'm here. Is he okay? Is he alive? Where'd you find him?"

"Yeah, he's alive, all right. Can't see it matters where I found him."

"Well, no, I only—"

Although I desperately want to believe him, I feel bullied by his words and his tone. Still, a person will tolerate all sorts of indignities when they're desperate.

"Meet me in front of the Parker's on Ribaut. Do you know it?"

"Yes."

"And bring the reward. Cash. Understood? Fifteen minutes."

"But I have to stop at a bank."

"Then, you better get going."

The line goes dead. I scramble out of the tub. I'm still sopping wet and can barely pull my pants on. When I hook my bra and try to slide it around my rib cage, it sticks like adhesive tape. It may seem odd that I wouldn't take two minutes to swipe a towel across my body, but who would stop to dry themselves if it delays, even by a minute, their reunion with a lost child or husband or best friend, or, yes, even a beloved pet?

The nearest bank is just 10 minutes away, but the drive-through ATM is out of service. I park in a no-parking zone next to the walk-up, aware that people are looking at me. My blouse adheres to my torso in Rorschach splotches, more frightening, I'm sure, than revealing. I keep making mistakes at the ATM, putting my card in upside down, twice punching in the wrong PIN. Finally, I withdraw $100, the maximum. I consider going inside to withdraw another $100, but I'm down to five minutes to get to the Parker's gas station. There'll likely be an ATM there, so I'll withdraw the rest when I get Wink back.

An elderly woman exits the bank, looks at me and stops. I see concern in her eyes and wave. Why, I don't know. Perhaps to reassure her, make a connection, signal hope. To camouflage what is actually happening, which is this: I am coming undone.

A mile down the road, I pull into Parker's and back up along the side of the building. All the cars in the lot are empty, except for a blue van with a caved-in front bumper, in which a young woman sits, staring straight ahead. I'd been given no further instructions, but if Wink is near, I'm not going to simply sit and wait. The unease I'd been suppressing, that this is a hoax, now gnaws at me in earnest, and I can almost smell the stench of fear in my sweat.

I get out of the car and circuit the lot. A man in a plaid jacket exits the store, carrying a small paper bag. It's too warm to be wearing the jacket and I track him with my eyes as he gets in a car and drives away, not even glancing at me. Eighteen minutes now since the call. Should I go inside? No, the man had been clear about being in front. Perhaps he's watching me from across the street? I study the trees and signs and buildings on the other side of Ribaut Road, like a coyote scouring the hills. A woman comes out of Parker's, trailing a fussy toddler. The child clambers into her car seat, every muscle in her face strained, mad at the entire world. A dog barks and, reflexively, I whip around, despite knowing immediately that it's not Wink.

Twenty-five minutes have passed since the call. Am I at the wrong Parker's? Is there another one on Ribaut? I'd not put my address on Wink's posters or online postings, so how would the caller know I'd come to *this* Parker's? I walk to the front, lean against the building, and tell Google to search 'Parker's Beaufort South Carolina.' The sun-baked asphalt smolders, rank in my nose, as I strain to read the search results through the glare.

"You're the lady with the dog?"

A young girl, barely out of her teens or not even,

stands five feet away. Her shoulders are hunched, her fists jammed into the kangaroo pocket of her sweatshirt. She's skittish, eyes darting, breathing in little gasps.

"Where's my dog?"

I don't intend to speak so loudly, but every synapse is on high alert, ready to fire.

"My uncle has the dog. He said to see the money and he'll bring her over. Or him. Whatever."

"Have you actually *seen* my dog?"

She begins hopping from foot to foot, ready to bolt. I simmer, recognize I'm being scammed, and am equally ready to spring into action, although what sort of action I don't know.

"Yeah, I seen him. *Course* I seen him. Whaddya *think*? You think I haven't *seen* him?!"

I drop my voice to a whisper. I want to disarm her and pull her eyes, which are skittering around the parking lot, back to me.

"What color is he?"

In my peripheral vision, I see a blue car creeping up on us. I hear the throbbing bass from an overamped radio. The sun slides behind a cloud, and I feel the tide turn.

"You don't have my dog, do you, dear?"

An undecipherable emotion flashes across her face and she nearly crumples to the sidewalk. I think I may actually have to catch her.

"No," she says, as her eyes fill with tears and she runs towards the blue sedan. It takes me a second, but I quick-step behind her. The driver, a fat, bald man, leans over, pushes the passenger door open, and the girl throws herself in. "Fuck!" the man yells, and the car lays rubber out of the lot, the passenger door flapping like the broken wing of a bird as they careen south on Ribaut.

I return to my car and slump in the driver's seat. I might just stay here forever, I think, encased in this steel cocoon, safe from an outside world that I no longer understand. I feel dirty. I take deep breaths to forestall the urge to wail. First Mr. Drone-Man and now this? What kind of people seek out others in pain and exploit their desperation? Was I to lose Wink and my faith in humanity, too?

I pull up Brenda Lee Hoenecker's number at Animal Control Services and dial. When she answers, I tell her everything.

"I should have told you things like this might happen, Cecilia. I'm so sorry."

Dear Brenda Lee. She seems to be perpetually apologizing to me. I know she's doing everything in her power to help, but I suspect, to her, it will never be enough. Oh, how wearying her job must be. Yet surely there are bright spots? Slivers of joy? Monumental moments of reuniting a lost animal with its person? Or rescuing an injured animal and seeing it through to adoption?

I consider inviting Brenda Lee over for dinner. I'd have to sacrifice search time to grocery-shop, but it might be worth it just to be in the presence of her empathy. And it could be good for her, too. In the end, though, I can't bring myself to ask. She knows too much about the horrors Wink might be going through — might have *gone* through — and I couldn't bear for that to seep out along with her sympathy. We stumble through our goodbyes and well-wishes, and just as we're about to end the call, she blurts, as if the words have been building inside and she can no longer contain them.

"I went through the photos of deceased dogs. None is Wink, Cecilia. I'm sure of that."

I can't speak. Of course, this is good news, but after a moment of relief, the hollowed-out feeling of hopelessness rushes back in. I begin to tremble, despite the fact that it's probably 90 degrees outside and even warmer in the car. Each day is bleeding, inexorably, into the next, and all I feel is the slow erosion of hope.

"You can still . . . I mean, if you want."

Can what? What were we talking about? Oh, of course . . . looking at pictures of dead dogs.

"No," I finally squeak out. "I trust you."

Again, the awkward goodbyes and we hang up.

I sit and watch the traffic on Ribaut Road. My heart is bitter, yet, down deep, I'm hoping the girl and her "uncle" will return with Wink. It's illogical, but we humans are prone to last gasps as hope dies. I pull up lost-and-found websites, ensure that Wink's postings are still there. I scroll through the found animals, but only glance at the pictures. Never the names. I can't bear to know the names. On every site, there are so many more dogs lost than found. The simple math of it crushes me.

twenty-three

The prospect of driving home to sit in an empty house is more than I can bear. I need to talk to J.P. and Eloise about Zeke's brother, but I simply can't face them on the heels of the attempted scam. So I drive downtown, park on Bay Street, and ask for an outside table at Plum's. With its back porch and river-facing patio, the restaurant is where Anne and I lunched on my first visit to Beaufort.

Although I'm not sure I can abide the chitchat of strangers, all happy and ignorant of the tragedy unfolding in my life, I know the distraction could be just what I need. I've been self-absorbed for days now. Not to suggest that there's anything wrong or inappropriate in that, but I'm trying to tell myself that life goes on. Even in the face of a terminal diagnosis or a school shooting or a tsunami that sweeps thousands to a violent, watery death . . . even in the face of the disappearance of one's beloved dog, life does go on. The issue, however, is how quickly it goes on. How soon does some level of normalcy return?

It's still early for the tourist crowd, and I'm relieved that the only other people on the patio are two middle-aged men in white shirts and ties. They speak in low tones and nod to me when they leave. I order a salmon BLT from a lovely, ponytailed teenager with skin as translucent as bone china. She's wearing short-shorts and a multicolored tattoo snakes up her thigh. When she brings my sweet tea, I ask her about it. She scoots sideways, perhaps to shield two women on the porch above us from any objectionable immodesty, then tugs up the hem of her shorts, exposing three inches of her bum.

"It's a map of New Jersey!" she says with glee, then checks my face to ensure that I'm not offended or mistake what I'm looking at.

"Ah," I say. "I just moved from Jersey."

"A very *natural* state," she responds, as she smooths her shorts over the swell where tanned thigh meets white ass. She's clever, this one.

"The biggest little state in the country," I say.

"With hidden treasures," she replies, and winks at me before turning back to the kitchen.

Ah, Jersey, I think. Jersey and Ben. There's so much I miss about him. An extraordinary conversationalist, he is. A dreamer and a risk-taker. A good listener with a big brain. There's precious little Ben couldn't get curious about. He could fashion the most mundane topic into a philosophical paradigm. But, oh, he was damaged and, when he wanted to shut down, it was beyond devastating to watch.

On the day he told me we were over, I tried to get to the bottom of his feelings, but he just wasn't having it. He had shut down, crawled into a cave, removed himself entirely from human interaction. When I began to weep, he said something that sent me into even greater emotional upheaval.

"You deserve to be happy, CiCi."

I stared at him as if he'd lost his mind. Did I verbally respond? I can't recall, but suppose I did because the concept of 'deserving' to be happy has long been a pet peeve of mine. More than a pet peeve, actually. Anathema. An abomination. I have a visceral reaction when people say someone deserves to be happy. What does that even *mean*?! How on god's green earth does one *earn* such entitlement? Deserve, indeed. If one is extraordinarily good, does he deserve happiness? What if she is fantastically bad — should she be denied happiness? If someone is brave, are they deserving? What if someone is a coward or a fool or downright cruel? Who decides what's deserving? It is extraordinarily arbitrary, so subjective as to be meaningless. I have no doubt I said all that, and more, to Ben that day.

I'm nibbling my last sweet-potato fry when the waitress places my bill on the table.

"There we are, dear," she purrs, and I chuckle. A young woman, just a child, really, calling me "dear." Is it because I am alone? Aged, in her tender eyes? Is it a sign of Southern gentility . . . or, perhaps simply a connection between two lost souls from Jersey?

I lay a twenty-dollar bill on the table and, when she takes it, I tell her to keep the change. She hesitates a few seconds, her nearly violet eyes locked on mine. She becomes shy and tentative, such a contrast to her bravado in revealing her tattoo. Upriver, the Woods bridge bell starts clanging, signaling descent of the traffic arms and imminent opening of the old swing bridge. We both turn and silently acknowledge this quintessential Beaufort moment. It's all I can do to hold back tears.

"I'm sorry you're sad," she whispers, and I put my hand on her arm. But I don't say anything disingenuous, like 'That's okay.' I don't even say, 'Thank you,' because the brief warmth of my skin on hers says it all.

When I leave the restaurant, I walk to the river and sit on one of the swinging benches. The river glistens like shards of glass. Mesmerizing, hypnotic. Another blast of the horn, and I watch the red-light-studded traffic arms descend. In both directions, cars stop. The locals say, all you can do when the bridge is open is enjoy the view. And what a spectacular view it is. On the far side, motorists are treated to a panorama of Antebellum waterfront homes and church steeples that rise from groves of oak and cypress. I spy a runner on the far side of the bridge and she, too, must stop and watch the seagulls swoop, over and under the bridge, and listen to their cries. Those stuck on the town side of the bridge have a picture-postcard view of tidal channels, lined with emerald and gold Spartina grass, snaking east to the sea islands. As the old bridge swivels open on its axis, I tear up. How, I wonder, can a place of such aching beauty become so cheerless and dangerous? For years, I regarded the

Lowcountry as a place to revere. I chose this place
because it nurtured my capacity for awe, but never did
I consider its potential to devastate. But that is my way,
too optimistic, too easily impressed, impulsive to a
vexatious degree.

Intellectually, of course, I know that beauty can
also be terrifying. But, before Wink vanished, that
was merely a poetic construct. Little did I know how
sinister the Lowcountry is at its core. A place that
cruelly flaunts its beauty to mock my shameful naïveté.

From my right comes the clatter of wheels on
the oyster-shell sidewalk. It's a kid on a skateboard. His
left leg sweeps back, pumping, propelling himself in
my direction. Then, his knobby knees bend and torque
to the side as he lifts the front wheels off the sidewalk
and executes a neat 180-degree turn on the board's
back wheels, coming to a smooth stop three feet from
me.

Darius. He reaches down, picks up his
skateboard, and holds it against his chest like a shield.
He says nothing, and, in that moment, I know who left
the flowers on my porch.

"Oh, Darius," I say with more enthusiasm than
necessary. "I'm so happy to run into you. I want to
thank you for the flowers . . . if, indeed, you are the
giver of said flowers?"

My little speech embarrasses me. Am I starting
to sound like the Professor? In his mouth, phrases
like "said flowers" are eloquent; in mine, fusty. Darius
doesn't seem put off in the least, however. He comes
over and sits on the other end of the bench.

"I picked them from Miz Lookabill's garden,"

he says to the river. Eye contact is difficult for him, but what pre-pubescent male doesn't have difficulty talking to an older woman? We all probably remind him of his mother . . . or grandmother.

"Oh!" he exclaims, suddenly horrified. "I mean, Miz Lookabill *likes* me to cut her flowers; she's on a fixed income, you know, and that's how she pays me for mowing her yard."

I nod. I want him to know that I take him seriously.

"That's very nice of you, Darius. You confirm my initial suspicions about you."

He turns to me, but I keep my eyes on the bridge as it rotates to rejoin the two spans of road.

"Uh, like *what* su-su-picions? About *me*?"

I debate going over old territory, but I've long-believed that we owe children our guidance, our encouragement and, when necessary, our correction. And by 'we,' I mean *all* adults. I take friendly jabs from friends who regard my "community policing" as inserting my nose into a parent's business. But I believe we're all parents, even those like me who never had kids. If we're not vocal about what we value, how can we nourish the kind of community we want? Shouldn't every adult be willing to speak truth to kids, all kids, in kindness and tutelage? As my father used to say, If not me, who? And there is simply no two ways about it: Calling someone a faggot is unacceptable.

"Yes, Darius, *you*. I suspected you were a really nice kid — a *great* kid, even — but when you referred to the Professor using a hateful word, it made me very sad. But I have returned to my original suspicion: You *are* a good person. Your help with Wink's posters and the flowers you left on my porch confirm that. Thank you very much."

He cracks a smile.

"A good person, but not *great*, right?"

I chuckle.

"Well, you're teetering on the precipice of greatness. How 'bout we get a couple of hot chocolates to-go and you help me with some unpacking? Do you have the time?"

Darius has the time. We stop at a coffee shop and, while we're waiting for our hot chocolates, I ask him what color my eyes are.

He moves an inch closer and stares hard.

"Green?"

"Hmmm," I say. "Can you be a tad more descriptive?"

He looks like I've asked him to jump off the Woods bridge.

"I mean, like your friend at school—"

He frowns.

"I mean, your *acquaintance*. Sorry. Anyway, he didn't just say your eyes are brown, he said the color of a stink bug. You know, descriptive. Plus more *fun*, right?"

He chews his lower lip for a few seconds, then his entire body spasms as if he can barely restrain himself from leaping in the air.

"Your eyes are the color of a field of clover after a summer rain."

"Oh, my!"

"I know. *Right?*" he says.

"What do you know about clover, Darius?"

"Duh, Miz Cecilia, like, Lucky *Charms*. On the box, you know. *Clover*."

We get our hot chocolates and he insists on carrying the precious cargo extended in front of himself like a Magi bearing gifts. Then I remembered I'd driven, not walked, downtown, so we back-track to my car. Darius sits in the back because, as he puts it, "It wouldn't be *great* to spill hot chocolate in the front." We have a theme of 'greatness' going. I like this kid.

In my living room, we take in the daunting towers of boxes. I feel overwhelmed, but Darius's face lights up as he pulls a small Swiss Army knife from his pocket and anoints himself Senior Box-Cutter. At that, we jump in, but, before long, he confesses to a phobia about newsprint.

"What about it?" I ask.

"Don't know," he replies. "It just ma-ma-makes me squeegee."

Eventually, we develop a tidy little operation whereby he slices a box open, I remove the newspaper, and, at my direction, he carries the item to the kitchen, bedroom or bath. It's not as seamless as it might sound, however, because the packing was hurried with Becca wadding the newspaper in a way that may, or may not, contain a fragile object. Her goal had been to get me out of the house as quickly as possible thereby "limiting further skullduggery by, and unnecessary contact with, the n'er-do-well."

As we work, Darius opens up. He likes school but is being bullied by boys who call themselves The

Enforcers.

"What do they enforce?" I ask.

"Hell if I know," he says, and I giggle.

"Sorry, ma'am. Shouldn't have said 'hell,' right?"

"Oh, I think 'hell' is quite appropriate in this case. In my opinion, a properly placed cuss word can move a sentence from good to great."

He giggles. We are co-conspirators.

"Do you know what my dad would have called The Enforcers?"

He looks intrigued, as if another swear word might be forthcoming.

"Nogoodniks," I say and laugh at the memory of my dear, gentle father using that word for everyone from the kid at the Red Owl, the slowest bag-boy on the face of the planet, to the Russians, who we kids were told wanted to nuclear-bomb us into oblivion.

Thus, the afternoon progresses as Darius and I work our way through boxes and pieces of our lives.

"Do you believe in haints, Miz CiCi?"

We're breaking down some of the boxes, stacking them flat on the back porch for recycling. I arch my spine backwards, stretching out a kink.

"I'm not sure," I say. "What's your opinion?"

He looks surprised that I've asked. All I know is that haints originated in the beliefs of the Gullah Geechee, descendants of enslaved people in the Lowcountry and barrier islands. But I have never understood if haints are good or evil.

"Well," he says, drawing out the word, as if he's about to share a great secret. "Mama believes, I think, but MawMaw . . . she *definitely* believes."

"Your grandmother?"

"Yes, ma'am. But me? Don't know that I've come to . . . an *opinion*."

I laugh. He's adorable, this kid.

"Well, let me ask you this, Darius, if a person *were* to believe" — I widen my eyes, dramatically — "would they be believing in a good spirit or an evil spirit?"

"Don't know. But I guess they'd scare the bejeebers out of you."

I pull a wad of newspaper from a box and out tumbles one of Wink's squeaky toys. Darius grabs it and quickly hides it behind his back. He thinks I haven't noticed.

"It's okay, Darius."

"I just don't want you to be sad," he says, handing the stuffed squirrel to me. One ear is detached, torn off, no doubt, in a bone-rattling tug-of-war. I press its wiry fur to my face and inhale the ghostly scent, both sour and sweet. One of Wink's favorite play routines is me pulling on the squirrel's tail as he clamps his powerful jaws around the head and shakes it like there's no tomorrow. All the while, he growls his low guttural warning, pretending to be big and vicious, while I pretend to be little and dazzled by his prowess. In another routine, Wink races around like he's just been released from a maximum-security prison, running in circles at full tilt and leaning into the turns like an Indy car driver. He stops on a dime and reverses course, then lets loose a single yip, as excitement in the room builds. Then, pretending like he suddenly spies the squirrel, he skids to a halt, drops into a hunting posture and belly-crawls towards the unsuspecting victim. He pounces! Then shakes the beat-up squirrel like it's a rat and shoots me sideways glances to make sure I'm watching. I usually am because how can a person avert their eyes from that kind of joy?

Oh, Wink.

I take the squirrel to the bedroom and prop it in a corner. It reminds me of the Velveteen rabbit with its snowy white chest and my body shudders as I experience a sear of regret. I was such a poor playmate in those first weeks after Ben ended our relationship. I'd grow distracted after a few minutes of play, anxious to wash the dog-slobber from my hands, and, of course, Wink always picked up on my disinterest. He'd tuck the squirrel under his chin and pout, and I knew what he was thinking: My three-minute effort was a poor showing indeed.

Time I will never get back.

When Darius and I return to the unpacking, our sense of adventure is gone. We've become sad, which is probably what prompts me to ask about his mother and why he thinks she's always mad at him.

He looks confused. I remind him what he said the first time we met.

"I think she's an alcoholic," he says and turns away. I don't press. I simply go to the couch, sit, and begin unwrapping what feels like a heavy rectangular box. Once I hear rattling inside and feel the way the contents shift slightly, I know it's an old silverware box, an inheritance from my mother. I call Darius over.

"You asked about mahogany?" I say, running my

fingers over the box. "This is mahogany."

"Pretty," he whispers, touching it lightly, as if it's ancient treasure.

"*My* mother," I say, as I place the box on the coffee table. "My mother was an alcoholic, too."

If he doesn't want to go down this path, I'll say no more. We've already talked about being bullied and how that can lead to someone becoming a bully, something Darius is interested in preventing in himself. We've had a good conversation about homosexuality. For it being 2018, the kid has the most arcane understanding of sexual orientation, harboring all the old tropes about the likelihood of a gay person being a sexual predator or "catching" homosexuality if he talks to the Professor. In our discussions, Darius has shown himself to be a curious, sensitive boy. But alcoholism, especially when it involves one's mother, is as close to the bone as one can get.

"Did she get mad at you when you were a kid?" he asks.

"If you mean when she'd been drinking, yes, she got mad because, when she drank, she lost her patience. And not just her patience with me — with everything, really. Mostly, I think, with herself. It's a bad disease, alcoholism. It steals the best parts of you and everyone who loves you."

"Hunh. Like, how does *that* work?"

He moves over to an armchair. My heart melts at the body-language of it all. Darius doesn't want to get too comfortable and who can blame him? I wonder if he's ever talked to another soul about his mother's drinking? I sit back and swing my legs up on the couch so I'm facing him directly. I try to appear casual while threading the needle in a conversation that could be no big deal or maybe the biggest deal ever.

"How old are you, Darius?"

"Eleven."

"Ah. Well, definitely old enough."

Is it my imagination or does his entire body relax?

"Well, one important thing to understand is that alcohol makes it harder for a person to accurately assess a threat. Do you know what 'assess' means?"

"Like, figure something out?"

"Precisely. Good. So, this can be any kind of threat. It can be physical, like when The Enforcers bully you—"

He's rapt. Hanging on every word.

"Or it can be emotional. Alcohol makes it especially hard for someone to assess an emotional threat. So, say, someone who's been drinking gets upset over something you say. They might feel they're being attacked, even if they're not."

"Yeah. I think that's what's happening with mom. I mean, my mother."

I nod. A few days ago, this child had been hostile, confronting me, using a slur about the Professor. And now. Now he is as vulnerable and open as a night-blooming cereus.

"My mom, too," I say. "After she'd been drinking for many years, she got paranoid. Defensive, like everyone was criticizing her, like she thought she wasn't good enough. Well, actually, like she just wasn't . . . *enough*. She knew she was disappointing us kids.

Not being a good enough mother. But she *was* a good mother, you know? Except when she was drunk."

"Did you ever talk to her? About, um, the drinking?"

"Yes, a few times."

I stop and think about that.

"*More* than just a few times, actually. It's funny, Darius, but I think I've forgotten all the times I talked to her or my dad. I mean, *did* I really talk to them all those times or was some of it just in my head? Because sometimes, you know, when I did talk to my parents about the drinking, I felt so *mean*. So *judgmental*, you know? Like I was making my mom feel terrible about herself . . . which I didn't want to do. I just wanted her to stop drinking. But she couldn't."

"Same as me."

"Sounds like it."

I want to wrap my arms around his skinny body and tell him he can always talk to me. But I don't because I can see he's shaken to the core. Probably not by *what* I've said. I'm sure he's heard or gleaned, or *experienced,* much of it all already. The lowering of inhibitions, the change in personality, the paranoia. But I wonder if he's ever talked to anyone about what is actually happening?

Especially that it is not his fault.

twenty four

Before Wink vanished, I thought grief was an internal thing. But now I know it's also external. A hulking, predatory creature that I cannot outrun. When I think of Sergeant Allen's revelation about Zeke's brother, I cannot banish images of Wink being used as training bait. The line between my waking images and my dreams has become so very thin and permeable. That night, I may have dreamed about dog-fighting, but I'm not sure. The lingering images are hazy and ghost-like, like when you look at the sun then look away and the after-image remains. What clings is a profound sense of chaos and terror. And the smell of blood. The sharp, iron smell of it. Warm, fresh blood. Spilled blood.

I toss and turn and finally turn on the bedside lamp. Thinking it may calm my fevered mind, I resolve to meditate on the tides. I stare at the ceiling and contemplate the slow inundation of the sea as it fills the creeks and bayous and estuaries. I breathe deeply for six counts, then think about the moon's gravitational pull of the sea back out to Mother Ocean. Four times a day, two high tides and two lows. For a few minutes, my mind quiets. But where I once found the tides seductive — an intoxicating seesaw of replenishment and release — now they seem nefarious, hiding then revealing infinite threats to Wink. Fields of viscous pluff mud to mire him, rank with decay. Will the stink of it confuse him? Drive him to distraction? And when the tide floods back, ferrying copperhead and cottonmouth, will it become a briny coffin for my dog?

And then I remember a third type of tide, one I'd not thought of in a long time: Slack tide. Between the ebb and the flow, the water ceases to move in either direction. A mere breath of a moment, but in that moment, before the tide reverses direction, the water is completely unstressed. Then — and only then, in this unstressed state — does the slack tide mark the tipping point in this amazing oscillation of Nature.

My next thought is altogether unexpected. Could yesterday have been *my* slack tide, the tipping point in my search for Wink? When Zeke changed his story about who put the dogs in the shed, I felt the tide turn. Now, I'm sure that Wink's disappearance is not merely an unfortunate, unforeseeable event. In my heart-of-hearts, I know that Zeke, and maybe Wade, is at the center of Wink's disappearance.

I throw off my blanket. I must talk this over with someone, but it's only 4:30 a.m. in Colorado. Too

early to call Anne. And just 5:30 in Minneapolis, so
also too early for Carol. Other friends would, no doubt,
listen and try to help, but if this is truly my slack-
tide moment, context is crucial, and the one person
who could provide context is J.P. I dress hurriedly and
swing by Starbucks to pick up a couple of scones. At
the cusp of dawn, I'm standing at the Professor's front
door.

He is wearing a green silk robe with elaborate
gold embroidery at the collar and cuffs. The tie-belt
hangs loose in the loops and, under the kimono, his
azure-blue pajamas also appear to be silk. It — he — is
breathtaking. Full-throated Beethoven pulsates from
his speakers.

"I prefer Tchaikovsky and Shostakovich," he says,
scurrying to turn down the volume. "But I never listen
to the drunk Russians unless I'm drunk."

The Professor seems unperturbed by the early
hour. In one hand, he carries a book, spread open with
two fingers, and in the other, a coffee cup.

"May I offer you one?" he asks, tilting the book
in my direction.

I look at the spine.

"Proust? Too early in the morning for me."

He grins.

"I'd adore a cup," I say and lift the bag of scones.

"*You* are the adorable one, CiCi," he says. "I don't
know when I last met anyone like you."

I follow him to the kitchen. His robe undulates,
as if caught by an invisible spring breeze, and, as he
moves, golden morning light plays on the billows and
troughs of silk. I sink into a chair, feeling the weight of

the world on me.

"Ben said something like that when he left."

"Yes?"

He turns.

"Well, sort of," I say. "Maybe not *precisely* the same."

I pull a mock grimace.

"Okay, not even close. He said I was a 'piece of work.'"

"Ah."

J.P. hands me a mug, sits across from me, takes long draws of coffee and studies me over the rim, as I tell him about the last few days. The ransom call and discovering that the animal shelter doesn't use a wand to scan dogs, dead or alive. I save for last my middle-of-the-night confrontation with Zeke, his anger when I asked about dog-fighting, how his story changed about who put the dogs in the shed. And my second trip to the police where I learned that Zeke's brother had served time for dog-fighting.

At this, J.P. jumps up, heads to the coffee pot, then turns back as if he cannot process all of it.

"Oh, Cecilia!" he cries. "This is too much."

After he gathers his wits, he pours more coffee for us, then drops back in his chair.

"This may be unfair, J.P., but what I can't understand is why Eloise would have suggested Zeke's in the first place? I mean, I'm assuming she didn't know about Zeke's brother?"

"Oh, my girl, I'm beyond heartbroken for you. And I know Eloise is, too. I can't *imagine* she knew anything about Zeke being associated, even

tangentially, with dog-fighting. And, if she did ever
know, she's obviously forgotten. You do know her mind
is slipping?"

I had seen signs, of course, thinking about the
blank letter she confronted me with after she walked
in my back door my first day here.

"But I'm thinking," he continues, "if you asked
Zeke about dog-fighting *after* the police talked to him,
might this explain his anger? Perhaps it has nothing at
all to do with Wink?"

This pulls me up short. An hour ago, I'd been
sure that Zeke or Wade knew the truth of what
happened. But now I gaze at J.P. because I don't want
to turn my gaze inward. Inward, where the truth lies.
Because, if neither Zeke nor Wade knows anything, I
am unlikely to discover what happened to Wink.

I am at a total loss what to do. I long for J.P. to
take the lead and remove the burden of "doing" from
my shoulders.

"Have you noticed my humming?" he asks.

The *non sequitur* is startling. He walks over to
the piano, lifts the fall board, and nods.

"Well, of *course*, you have. E-flat. Go ahead. Test
me."

I join him at the lovely old spinet and hit E-flat
in the center octave. It is, indeed, his humming note.

"Pitch perfect," he says and a smile flits across
his face. It's the first time I've seen anything akin to
vanity in the man.

"Impressive," I say.

"Well, it's not *all* perfect. I often wish for a
volume nob, so I might turn it up with someone I'd

rather not speak to and dial it down when I want
to encourage conversation. But, alas, my humming
is — oh, how shall I put it? — white noise. Since the
accident, I can't seem to turn it off. Perhaps, deep
down, I'm afraid that if it stops, if *I* stop, I will simply
disappear."

I don't know how to respond. He may not even be
expecting a response because he pivots quickly.

"So, CiCi," he says, "tell me something about
your life before Beaufort."

And suddenly there it is: The inevitable
conundrum everyone encounters when starting over in
a new community. How much of our story do we tell?
How much do we omit? Just the facts, ma'am, or the
whole kitchen sink? Should one's initial telling include
after-the-fact analysis, too? And be sugar-coated, just
in case?

J.P. regards me with curiosity and kindness.
It's a wide-open look and, already, I know I can trust
him. He gathers his robe demurely around his legs,
smoothing the fine silk over his knees, and I begin.

twenty five

"I've mentioned Ben," I say, surprising myself that this is where I'm apparently starting.

J.P. nods.

"Well, his mother left him when he was two years old. *Really* left him, I mean. Dropped him off at an orphanage and never returned."

I tell J.P. about Ben's abandonment, or as much of it as I know. By the end, the dear man is slumped further in his chair, as if the sheer sadness of the story is a nearly unbearable burden.

"Classic abandonment syndrome, then?" he says.

"Yes."

"The poor lost soul. Every day his mother didn't return, he was abandoned anew. And the father?"

"Raymond. A sweet man, but he didn't retrieve Ben from the orphanage for more than two years. Why,

I don't know."

"Perhaps *he* doesn't even know?"

"Perhaps. From what I can tell, Raymond had some sort of psychotic break after his wife took Ben to the orphanage and left. Apparently, he didn't feel he could take care of Ben—"

". . . and probably couldn't," J.P. interjects.

He shakes his head in sympathy. This is the part of the story that always rips my heart apart. For Ben, of course. But for *all* of them. Who can imagine the pain his mother must have been in, to abandon her child like that? And Raymond? Wandering in the wilderness for years, doing who knows what? I'm not sure even Ben knows that part of the story and, if he was ever told what those years were like for his father, I doubt he was told the truth. All I know is that, shortly after Ben's 5th birthday, Raymond returned, married to his mother's best friend, and they retrieved Ben.

Emotions shunt across the Professor's face.

"Ah, the acreage of the human heart," he says.

He looks down at the table, a fine-grained oak, and shuttles the salt and pepper shakers back and forth in front of him. He clears his throat, then stands, hoping, I suspect, to dispel the sadness that grips both of us.

"Tell me what you loved about him?"

"A lot," I respond. "I loved a lot about him."

"Like?"

"Oh, how much he loved words. Ben was a reader."

I sweep my arm dramatically around the room.

"Of course, a lot of men read," I continue. "But

words, now *there's* something Ben could truly love—"

"— without fear of being abandoned by them," J.P. interjects.

Oh, my.

"I also loved that he cared so much about Wink. Ben never had a pet and, at first, even the idea of that kind of attachment was foreign to him. But he grew to love Wink and even *admire* him. Which sounds like a funny thing to say."

"Why funny?"

"Sorry?"

I've lost my train of thought. Somewhere in the house, a clock chimes. The Beethoven that had accompanied my story ends and I hear the mechanical whir of the CD player changing over. Then, a bow is drawn slowly across a violin string. The single, sustained note continues longer than expected. So long and so very soft that it becomes haunting. Other strings join and the chord progressions ascend the scale — now I recognize Samuel Barber's "Adagio" — all the while maintaining the aching pianissimo. Oh, has there ever been a more heartbreaking note than that first uninterrupted B-flat? A solitary, subdued note that foreshadows what's coming at the end of the movement. But the finale is not some crescendoing, chest-numbing wall of sound that leaves the listener stunned. No, it is far more portentous than that. It is simply this: A pause. The famous Barber pause, the most poignant pause ever "written," the pause that captures everything worth loving and yearning for in life.

"You said it sounds funny that Ben admired

Wink."

"I did? Hmmm. I guess because Ben is more capable of admiration than love. He believes, actually, that admiration exists on a higher emotional plane."

"Than love?"

"I never quite understood it, but yes. When one admires, he says, one is still in possession of one's faculties. But with love—"

"One loses oneself and relinquishes all control," J.P. says, finishing my sentence, and I realize he's gleaned something about Ben that took me six years to recognize.

"You understand love, then," I say, but he doesn't respond. He stands, so I stand, and he takes my elbow and guides me to the living room. I sit on the couch, but he walks to the fireplace and stands with his back to me.

"I loved Thomas, of course, but in another way, a way I can barely speak of" — he pauses — "I also loved Maura."

I don't repeat 'Maura' as if he needs encouragement to say more. That would be utterly graceless. People do that, I think, because we're desperate to fill silence. I think again of the long pause at the end of Barber's "Adagio," and know the Professor will say more if he wants to. Or not.

"Maura," he says again, then turns. "The girl I killed."

He sits on an armchair across from me.

"It was twenty years ago. A lifetime. Yesterday. It was raining and I was taking the back roads from Burton, trying to avoid the afternoon traffic from the Air

Station. I saw a blur to my right—"

His voice cracks and he issues a single bleat.

"The blur . . . was a child. On a bike. She came from between two parked cars. Right into my path. I wasn't traveling more than 15 miles an hour, but it was enough."

"Oh, J.P."

"She died. Maura Annette died. I was holding her head in my lap. To this day, I don't know who called the ambulance. I don't even remember the ambulance itself."

He gulps back an animal sound.

"I remember the investigation later, of course. No charges were filed—"

"How old was Maura, J.P.?"

He looks up, surprised.

"Ten. She was only 10."

"She'd be 30 now," I say.

I can see how grateful he is that I ask about the child and not the prurient details of the accident. I want to honor her and hold both of them in my heart. Not because I presume to share J.P.'s burden or lighten it. We always *say* we want to do that for each other, but, really, we cannot. I simply want to feel his pain along with him, so he's not so alone.

"It was raining that day. Did I already say that? I held my body over hers, over Maura's body, so she wouldn't get wet. I rocked her and rocked her . . . and hummed a lullaby."

It all becomes clear then. The Professor's humming is not a quirk or a peccadillo. It's a tribute. An ode to a dead child.

twenty six

That afternoon, the fifth since Wink vanished, I finally go to the grocery store. After I unpack the bags and put the food away, I feel inordinately proud of myself, as if this demonstrates my ability to perform daily activities again. Thus energized, I unpack a few more boxes and look at found-animal websites. But the day is interminable.

When my phone rings, I see it's Eloise LaFitte and consider not answering. But I am so lonely, so very lonely. Within a couple of breaths of saying hello, Eloise proclaims her intention to take me to dinner.

"A welcome to Beaufort gift," she says, then goes silent. She must have remembered about Wink.

I have yet to ask Eloise if she knows anything about Zeke's brother running a dog-fighting ring and, if so, why she would have recommended Zeke. I consider not bringing it up, but I must. I accept her dinner invitation, but ask her to come over first, so we can avoid any potential scene in a restaurant. I'm as worried about myself in that regard as I am about Eloise.

A few minutes later, Eloise walks in the back door. Without knocking. As I guide her to the living room, I make every effort at nonchalance. There is no reason to distress her, but I also can't afford to let any nugget residing in my neighbor's befuddled brain go unexamined. We sit, I take her hand, which she likes, and ask if she's ever heard about dog-fighting in Beaufort. The term throws her.

"Dog-fighting? Whatever do you mean, Cecilia? Oh, my goodness, not that nasty creature down on North Street? Has he been at it again?"

I clarify as gently as possible.

"No, Eloise. What I'm wondering is about Zeke. You know, Zeke Johnson who you knew from school?"

She looks relieved.

"Yes, dear. What about him?"

I swallow hard. Get it over with, CiCi, be done with this line of questioning. But it's not easy to find the words.

"What I mean, Eloise, is do you remember anything about Zeke's brother? Harold? Smithson, I think. Do you remember anything about him being involved with the police? Any mention of him training dogs to fight so people can bet on them?"

I see this is going nowhere fast. Good Lord. My query has distressed an already-confused woman even more. She pulls her hand out of mine and gasps.

"Whatever do you mean, child? Someone *makes* dogs fight? Well, I declare, I have never *heard* such a thing! It's just not *right*!"

"No," I reply. "No, it's not."

"Well, at least we can agree on that!" she says, standing to smooth her dress over her narrow hips. "Shall we go?"

With Eloise giving directions, I drive east across the Beaufort River towards St. Helena Island. It's low tide and stilt-legged birds with long beaks comb the shallows for fish. It's as hauntingly lovely as a moonscape, but I'm unable to appreciate the stark beauty because all I can see is Wink trying to navigate it. This is wild, this place, and like any wild place, it beckons . . . love me, admire me, but remember to fear me.

"I'm sorry," Eloise says. "Did you say something?"

"Whaaa—"

"Oh, nothing. I thought you said something."

"The tides," I say after I collect myself. "I was thinking of the tides."

But I couldn't tell her precisely what I was thinking, which was the tide slinking back to the Atlantic twice a day, exposing a gooey muck teaming with oysters capable of simultaneously slicing and poisoning a puppy's tender paws.

As we continue east, the poverty becomes more apparent. Past the bleached bones of dead oaks littering the pluff mud, I catch glimpses of trailer homes and modest wood structures in need of shoring-up or paint or both. Then, quite dramatically,

Nancy Ritter

the landscape explodes again into lush vegetation —
towering cedars, wide, emerald-green magnolias, live
oaks in massive groves that shade football-field-sized
meadowlands. It is a perfect June twilight, and, in the
rearview mirror, I see the sun low on the horizon.

"The sea islands," Eloise says, reading my mind.

Occasionally, there are mailboxes along the two-
lane road, but rarely do I see houses, tucked back as
they must be down long dirt roads. Ten miles out of
town, Eloise instructs me to slow down, then points. I
see the small "enter" sign at the last minute and brake
hard. We park on an odd patch of asphalt that was
obviously poured to give wide berth to the root system
of a huge oak. A few minutes later, we're sitting at a
table on the back deck, overlooking a tidal creek. I peer
over the railing and see fiddler crabs scuttling over the
mud, dipping into holes and out again. The overhead
fans waft the humid air, and we drink sweet tea out of
Mason jars.

"You're probably going to pooh-pooh this," Eloise
says. "But hear me out."

"I'm hearing you out."

"A couple of years ago, Trudy Lyn — she's my
friend, you know, been close since second grade, boy-
howdy, can that girl *talk* — anyway, Trudy Lyn lost her
bracelet."

"Her bracelet."

"Yes, her bracelet! I know, *right*? Imagine! So, this
bracelet — little diamonds and black onyx, as I recall,
and I *do* recall since her mother gave it to her right
before she, Trudy Lyn's mother, I mean—"

She pauses to make sure I'm tracking, and I nod

215

to indicate I am.

"— died. Her mother died. Sudden-like. But whoever expects these things, you know?"

Again, she pauses. Apparently, her question is not rhetorical, so I dutifully reply.

"No one," I assure her. "No one expects these things."

"I mean, how *could* you?! Anyway, Trudy Lyn looks everywhere for that damn bracelet. For months and months, she looks. And then she gives up. Says, 'Eloise, I've given up on ever finding Mama's bracelet.' So, I take her to Charlie's for a martini. And shrimp. I think we both had the shrimp."

I glance at my watch. Six o'clock. I don't intend for her to see me looking, but she does.

"I'm sorry," she sighs. "My mind slips easily."

"That's okay."

As far as assurances go, it's weak. I vow to do better.

"Anyway," she breathes, indicating she would hurry to her point. "That's when Trudy Lyn told me about the psychic."

I nod again and her expression becomes grave.

"*Which* . . . is where Wink comes in."

I rearrange myself. Sit up straighter.

"I know, *right*?" she cries in a manner that suggests I'm bound to be amazed, if I can only keep up. "I was skeptical, too, Cecilia. But here's what happened."

Eloise plants her elbows on the table, and her bangle bracelets tinkle as they fall halfway down her arms. She leans in closer and her eyes say, Here comes the *coup de grace,* ignore at your peril.

"Trudy Lyn knows this gypsy. Well, actually, it's her friend Minnie who knows the gypsy, but I don't really *know* if she's a gypsy, I just call her that. Which I probably shouldn't, should I?"

She furrows her brow.

"She probably wouldn't mind," I say.

Oh, my god. There is nothing remotely consoling about being here. I'm beginning to feel claustrophobic, as Eloise's verbal wanderings tangle my brain.

"*Still,*" she says, as if my response had been unkind. For a moment, I fear she's lost her train of thought.

"Anyway" — she shakes her head — "*anyway,* she's all yakkety-yakkety. You know what I mean?"

I assure her I do, indeed. But, truly, at this point, I have no idea what she is talking about. I narrow my eyes and I suspect the inadvertent flicker of smile sneaks in, but the irony of her statement doesn't register with her. I let a couple of beats pass, then prompt her.

"About Wink?"

"*Please*, CiCi," she says, taking a long draw of tea. "I am *getting* there."

Eloise is becoming exasperated, more perhaps with herself than with me.

"So. Six months later, Trudy Lyn and Marvin—"

"Her husband?"

"*Ex,*" she corrects.

I admonish myself to be more patient. Ben was sometimes like this, telling tales not for the bottom line, but simply for the telling. Of course, with Ben, I could get lost in his eyes, while he got lost in the story.

"As I was saying, Trudy Lyn and Marvin go up to Dollywood, this was probably a year after the bracelet went missing, and she decides to go to a psychic — mostly for Marv, I think, not the bracelet, though the bracelet was worth more, if you catch my drift. But there she was, so she asks. And the psychic-gypsy says, 'Why, your bracelet's not lost, missus, it's at the bottom of your dirty clothes hamper.' Now, isn't *that* something, Cecilia?!"

She sits back, pleased as punch

"And it was?" I venture.

"Well, of *course*, it was! That's why I'm telling the story, isn't it?"

The waitress comes, we order shrimp and when it arrives, I encourage Eloise to not dawdle. I'm getting antsy. Not because I mind sitting here with her, which I am actually beginning to enjoy, but because I'm frittering time that should be spent looking for Wink.

When the waitress returns, I notice for the first time how lovely she is. Her Afro is clipped short and she's added a streak of platinum that sets off her impossibly high cheekbones. She sets another Mason jar in front of me, swapping it for my sad, now-iceless tea.

"Looks like you could use some freshening, sister," she says, her voice soft and kind. I wonder if she thinks I look befuddled because she adds, "On me."

I thank her then take a sip and gaze out over the darkening marshland. I'm grateful that Eloise lets me. Now that she's finished saying her piece about the psychic, she's handed the baton to me.

"Do you have a psychic in mind, Eloise?"

"The same one who found Trudy Lyn's bracelet."

"But I thought you said—"

"Oh, she's ancient now, of course. But I don't think finding things — lost things, I mean — goes away with age."

Eloise holds out her Mason jar and clinks the rim against mine.

"Hells-bells," she says. "For all we know, that kind of thing just gets *better* with age."

Someone calls Eloise's name. She turns and waves at four women clustered at the bar. Their voices are loud and they're talking over each other, so I catch only snippets — "awful prom dress," "light-years ago," "most definitely *not!*"

Eloise shoots me a look that suggests she's half-dreading, half-welcoming the impending encounter. She slides out of the booth and stands.

"I don't suppose you'd like—"

"Oh, please, Eloise, no. I haven't the energy."

"Who does, sweet pea?" she says, patting my hand as if I, not she, is the 80-year-old. "If I'm not back in 10 minutes, you come drag me out of that-there cabal, ya hear, darlin'?"

"Yes, ma'am."

I take my phone out and busy myself, trying to look unapproachable. I skim websites, most of which list ten or twelve dogs that have gone missing since Wink. This shocks me. Not that I have any idea the number of animals that lose their way — or are abandoned. Perhaps ten or twelve is even low compared to a typical week? I register the individual pain behind each dog whose posting now appears before Wink's. But at the core, my feelings are selfish because each new posting pushes Wink further down the page. I imagine the passing days and weeks, as Wink is bumped to page 3, then 7, then 20. A small cry escapes my throat, but no one seems to notice. Could there even *be* 20 or more pages of missing dogs in Beaufort County? In another week or another month, how many pages of lost dogs will someone have to scroll through to get to Wink? Would folks who spotted a dog on the way to the grocery store even be willing to *do* that? If they find a dog, yes, or a dog follows them home or appears on their porch, I assume most people would scroll through many pages to find information for that particular animal. But if they simply see a dog wandering along the side of a road, a quick glimpse, a tracking of the eyes as they do, or do not, slow down to get a better look? Probably not. The human attention span is such that, by the time a putative good Samaritan gets home, perhaps unloads her groceries, answers a phone call, remembers this is the afternoon she has to pick the kids up early . . . any memory of a wandering white dog would be gone.

A few minutes later, Eloise returns.

"Just so's you know," she says confidentially, "I don't listen to all the things I could hear."

She slugs back the dregs of her sweet tea.

"Ready?" she asks.

On the way out, I stop in the restroom. A single. As I wash my hands, I look hard at my face in the mirror. I don't look like me. The face in the mirror is puffy-lidded and limp-haired and much older than me.

Eyes glassy and rimmed in red. I lean in closer and see the blood vessels mapping the whites of my eyes.

There's a rap on the door and Eloise bugles at me.

"Cecilia! I do de*clare*, girl! Have you tumbled into the commode?"

We ride back to Beaufort in silence. I want to ask her about Simon and the letter she'd waved at me that first day, but it seems so long ago. Almost as if we were different people back then.

On the bridge into town, I see church spires gleaming white against the midnight-blue sky. All along the downtown Riverwalk, streetlights pour halos on the sidewalk. And, lordy, how the river itself drinks up the moonlight. What a winsome village I have chosen.

Eloise stares out the window. I look at her profile and see that she is lost in thought. When I pull up in front of her house, she turns.

"I have a daughter," she declares, *à propos* of nothing. "Simone. Named for her daddy."

I know I should say more, but I am tired. So very tired. I can't get over the feeling that I'm play-acting — dinner out, the simple dropping of a friend at home. What an imposter I am!

"We're estranged, Simone and I. But I called her today —" she turns from me, embarrassed, groping for the door handle — "I'm not sure why, but it seemed important."

She looks back at me, eyes squinty, lips pursed, as if seeking confirmation that it was, or is, important, and I am framing a response when her face suddenly relaxes as if she had passed from one room to another or turned around at a cocktail party to talk to the person behind her.

"Promise me you'll consider the psychic?"

Could I promise? Even the *thought* of a psychic is miles out of my comfort zone. Perhaps if it were a distraction, a lark on a girls' night-out, perhaps then I could have promised. Maybe if my bracelet was missing, I could have promised. But my *dog*? A living, breathing being. A companion, capable of loyalty and understanding and fear and loneliness. Capable of loving and being loved. Finding Wink is too serious a matter to relegate to voodoo magic or smoke and mirrors. Nonetheless, I nod and Eloise gets out. I've put the car in gear to drive the 20 feet to my house when she turns and motions for me to lower the window. She leans in.

"Remember, CiCi," she says, "every step is a direction."

"A what? A *decision*?"

"That, too," she says.

twenty seven

Before Wink disappeared, I'd always been comfortable with the unknown. Enamored even. Cannonballing into a new experience doesn't frighten me. I often find it exhilarating. Plus, I've always made room for doubt. More room, actually, as I age, which is probably wise because without room for doubt, there's no room for possibility.

That said, seeing a psychic about Wink strikes me as a bridge too far. The more I think about it, the more improbable it seems. What, after all, is the likelihood that Eloise's gypsy can offer true insight, a realistic lead? My rational brain answers: Slim-to-none. Still, how could it hurt?

But, of course, it *could* hurt. It could hurt by distracting me from other avenues. I need to follow every logical lead that may present itself, although there have been precious few so far. Still, I've seen friends tear, hell-bent, down rabbit holes without the remotest chance of success. My dear friend Francine thought her husband was having an affair. There were unexplained absences and she once saw him enter an apartment building where, as far as she knew, they knew no one. When confronted, Kurt insisted he'd rented a loft so he could work on his music compositions. I knew Kurt didn't have a musical bone in his body, but Franny was delighted. She started preparing musically themed dinners to welcome him home from his long weekends in what they took to calling the "Ludwig Von Loft." She secretly took up the violin, practicing long hours during Kurt's absences, planning the big surprise of making music together when his masterpiece was finished. Oh, Francine.

I wanted to help her see reality but walking that fine line without hurting her was difficult. I remember one conversation over wine at a local bistro. I mentioned how doctors use differential diagnosis to get to the bottom of a problem. Ruling out the most-likely explanations first — be it belly pain or a spouse's increasingly long absences from home — was only logical, I said. But Francine disagreed. I had an excessively rational nature, she said. Which is true. Eventually, Kurt's affair with his secretary was revealed. He admitted the whole thing, that it had been going on for years. He cried and begged and protested that he had done it only to save their marriage.

"Oh, Franny," I said when she told me. "What did you say?"

"I said, 'So, what am I supposed to do with this fucking fiddle?'"

And she kicked him to the curb.

Thinking about Francine and her fiddle, I vow to rule out the more plausible explanations for Wink's disappearance before tumbling down the rabbit hole of Eloise's psychic.

The more I think about Zeke, the more convinced I am that he knows what happened to Wink. If that sounds like classic confirmation bias, it's because it is. Science has long known that humans search for, recall, and interpret information in ways that support, that *confirm,* their beliefs. I know how crucial it is to test my beliefs against the principle of confirmation bias. On one hand, Zeke's involvement seems only logical: his bizarre responses about dog-fighting and his anger when I asked to speak to Wade can hardly be ignored. On the other hand, though, a connection between these reactions and the imprisonment of his brother for dog-fighting seems logical, and could explain the man's defense of his nephew. Still, I'm not yet ready to discount my gut feeling about Zeke. If Wink's disappearance is benign as him escaping through a hole in the fence, thinking I'd abandoned him or fleeing a strange place to try to find me, why would Zeke be so unwilling to help? Whether terrible accident or something nefarious, I can't shake my suspicion that he is hiding something.

I know what I must do. The bedside clock reads 2:48 a.m., but this cannot wait. I must write a letter to Zeke Johnson, putting him on notice of my suspicions. I must expose him. Seek charges for negligence, at the very least. And . . . at the most? Certainly, it is criminal to sell a dog for dog-fighting — Wink is little, but scrappy as hell — or, maybe, for medical research? Is that kind of thing still going on? Experiments with primates were outlawed long ago, but perhaps dogs are still used in drug-therapy or auto-crash testing or another type of experiment that requires a warm, blood-flowing body?

With this urgency upon me, I throw off my comforter, dash to the living room, and pull a yellow legal pad out of my computer bag. Yet, when I sit, pen-in-hand, I'm paralyzed. Timidity grips me. I'm not fierce enough to say what I want, what I *need*, to say. I simply am not up to the task. For a half-hour, all I can do is stare at the blank paper. Then, the words begin to flow:

Mr. Zeke Johnson:

It has come to our attention that a canine under your care and responsibility has gone missing. Said canine, Wink, a brown and white Jack Russell mix, approximately 20 pounds, is the lawful property of Ms. Cecilia Genevieve Gilbert, a resident of Beaufort, South Carolina. Licensing regulations in the State of South Carolina for operating an animal kennel/boarding facility require a basic standard of care, which you have breached. The disappearance of Ms. Gilbert's canine is prima facia evidence of your negligence and that of any employees/agents who had involvement with the aforementioned property. Your willful refusal to mitigate these negligent actions, or inactions, is actionable.

I sit back and look at the clock on the microwave. At first, the numerals — 3:26 — don't compute. Is it afternoon or the middle of the night? The long, lonely night.

I walk to the living room, pull the curtains aside, and look up and down the street. Then again. And again. It has become a compulsion. How many times do I perform this ritual? Fifty times a day? One hundred? Do I expect to see Wink trotting down the street? No, but he *is* out there somewhere. The view from my window is so still it resembles a black-and-white snapshot. Not a leaf is stirring. Streetlights throw perfect coronas down on the sidewalk. The streetlamp on Newcastle glows yellow through the Spanish moss that drapes my oak like a funeral cloak.

In the next moment, my phone pings with a text. It's from Eloise and all it says is:

Madam T. Bigelow (finder of lost things)
Regency Park Senior Residence

Oh, my. What is the dear woman doing up at this time of night? But I will do it, damn it! It may be miles outside my comfort zone, but I will ask Madam Bigelow's stars or whatever divining medium she uses to help me find my dog.

I retrieve the letter to Zeke. Re-reading it, I discover more than a few minor issues. I have no idea, for example, what, if any, state or city regulations apply to the licensing of dog kennels and boarding facilities. But surely, I could assume some bedrock principles, right? Nevertheless, the phrase "basic

standard of care" strikes me as so tepid as to be
laughable. If the goal is to grab Zeke's attention, I
should have citations to specific regulations, governing
codes, and paragraphs within codes. "Prima facia" is
good, though — that should stay. And the expression
"lawful property?" Good grief. An elementary-school
kid could come up with that. I hoped that strategically
placed legalese would add some gravity, but seriously,
what do I mean by "aforementioned property?" Let
me be clear and direct. I mean, Wink! Just say it! And,
lordy, "mitigate?!" The only mitigation I'm interested
in is the truth. And the reference to "employees or
agents?" I mean Zeke's brother, Harold Smithson, if he's
back in town, but I also mean Wade. I still think there
could be something there. When I asked to speak to
Wade, Zeke had narrowed his eyes to knife-like slits,
capable of excising my heart. I must be direct. Why
pussyfoot around? I return to the dining-room table,
make the necessary changes and add this sentence:

>**Please have your nephew call me immediately
>to discuss his knowledge regarding the
>last-known whereabouts of my dog.**

I type the letter, address and stamp the
envelope, then sit on my couch, scrolling through
websites until the sun rises. My plan is to send the
letter by certified mail, but a few hours later as I'm
driving to the post office, I don't stop. I keep on driving
in the gray wash of morning light. Out of town and
down to Shug Lane. Apparently, I cannot wait for
the U.S. Mail to deliver the letter. It must be in Zeke

Nancy Ritter

Johnson's hands today. Yes, he'll know I've been on his property again when he finds the letter in his mailbox, stamped, but bearing no cancellation or date-stamp or other evidence of having been mailed. But I don't care. I open Zeke Johnson's mailbox and place it inside.

As I drive home, I review where things stand. I've struck out with Zeke and have little faith that the letter will knock anything loose out of him. Plus, a tiny part of me believes he really might not know anything. Although he seems to be hiding something — or, at least, overreacting to my perseverance — it might, as J.P. suggests, have nothing to do with Wink. I couldn't seem to get Wade out of my mind, but I might have to give up on that. I believe Brenda Lee Hoenecker is doing everything she can. But all of my hours of online searching have yielded nothing. Would the Beaufort Police come up with anything? Although I can't rule that out, I'm not optimistic. Clearly, nothing is giving me hope. Or, rather, my only hope is Wink himself. I know that little dude. If he can get back to me, he will. But if he hasn't in six days, why might day 7 or 8 be any different? But isn't that what hope is? A notion that exists against all odds?

twenty eight

The sign for Regency Park Senior Residence is not large. I might easily have missed it. On the second line, in those small, movable letters that slide into a ready-made groove, it says: *Where you want to be*. When I walk into the lobby, a young man at the reception desk looks up from the book he's reading and beams at me. In one fluid motion, he turns an old-fashioned sign-in ledger towards me and slides it across the desk.

"Welcome to Regency Park," he says. "I'm Loon."

He gestures to his name tag, which, indeed, says "Loon."

"I know, I know," he sighs. "What were my parents *thinking*? Never gave me a straight answer on that and now they're gone. Whadderya gonna do?"

I sign my name where Loon points. I hear a plea in his voice and he furrows his brow and, for all the world, looks like he's hoping for an answer. Needless to say, I have no idea *what* his parents were thinking, and, as to 'whadderya gonna do?' I have no idea what *I* am doing, let alone what this young man should do.

"It's *sad*, right?" he says, his expression becoming even more child-like.

I'm suddenly confused. How had I gotten here? I've been up since 3 a.m. and, standing now in the lobby of this strange place, flashes from the dog-fighting dream come back to me. In between that dream and now, I'd dashed off a semi-threatening letter to the man who ostensibly is responsible for Wink's disappearance and, perhaps, his return. And trespassed on his property. Now, I'm being asked an unfathomable question by a complete stranger on my way to visit a psychic? I truly might be losing it. But the young man seems so earnest and in need of a kind word.

"Well, now . . . Loon," I say, pronouncing his name with tenderness. "I'm sorry you've lost your parents. That *is* sad. Did they love you very much?"

I'm not sure where the question comes from, but, in that moment, it seems important to know that Loon was well-loved. He rests his elbows on the desk, clasps his hands in supplication, and props his chin thereon. His gaze is so expectant, so hopeful, that it nearly breaks my heart.

"Oh, yes," he says. "They loved me a lot."

"Then, I don't find it sad that they named you Loon. Should I?"

His eyes fill with tears.

"No," he whispers. "What's your name?"

And, at that, he giggles and turns the sign-in

book around. He uses his index finger to track down my entry.

"Cecilia Gilbert," he reads. "Now *that's* a funny name."

He looks up and winks.

"And you're here to see?"

"Madam T. Bigelow."

"Friend? Relative?"

"Well—"

"Ah," he says, returning the pen to its holder after writing 'T. Bigelow' in the column next to my name. "What have you lost?"

My heart clenches. But, before I can stammer a response, he continues.

"Oh, forgive me. Please do. It's none of my business."

Loon seems genuinely chagrined. He stands and nearly knocks over his chair. Then, he offers an odd little bow and, in a sweeping gesture, extends his arm toward what appears to be a large common room.

"Please. Madam is in room 320."

The room has a double-sided fireplace and conversational groupings of settees and armchairs. In one area, a middle-aged woman sits on the floor surrounded by six or seven elderly folks in folding chairs. They lean in to see what she's holding up. I step closer, too. The younger woman looks up, smiles, then returns to what I now see is a newspaper. The conversation is lively. A couple of the nicely dressed seniors sport the requisite Southern pearls, and they're all talking at the same time. The only male in the group stares off into space, his liver-spotted hands perched atop a cane.

Two hallways with private rooms spoke off the
main common area. I take the one to the left, but
the room numbers start at 300 and get smaller, so I
venture down the other hall. I walk slowly, sauntering
really, because most of the doors are ajar and I'm
mesmerized by the small, self-contained worlds
within. In many, an old woman sits in front of a TV
with the volume turned up loud. In a few, I discern
the small bump of a human form under blankets and
quilts. I know some regard such scenes as lonely and,
in one respect, I suppose they are. But Wink and I
volunteered in a senior residence not unlike this one,
and I find the close, over-heated smells and snapshots
of slow, simple life comforting.

Oh, those memories flood back and nearly
swamp me. Wink was certified by the Pets on Wheels
program, which allowed us to visit nursing homes or
hospitalized children. Needless to say, Wink was the
decider: If he didn't like visiting older folks who might
smell a bit off, have vacant eyes, or exhibit erratic
behavior, we would switch to kids. But as it turned out,
Wink loved the oldsters, so that's what we did every
Saturday morning. He was a natural at intuiting who
needed what. One man who always wore a plaid flannel
shirt wanted Wink to stay three feet away so he could
simply look at him. Wink divined this and obliged.
Another — it comes back to me now, her name was
Evelyn — was blind. Rather than jumping up on her
lap and scaring her, Wink hopped onto the chair next
to her, extended his long body even longer, and lightly
touched his nose to her cheek. The first time he did

that, Evelyn smiled.

"Oh," she said. "A wet whisper."

After that, she knew it was Wink and would hold him in her lap, stroking his little body and speaking words — or sounds? — that I couldn't decipher. I had no doubt, though, that Wink knew precisely what she was saying.

The door to room 320 is slightly ajar and I see only a slice. I tiptoe nearer — why I tiptoe, I don't know — and hear a low muttering. A radio? No. Then, a voice, kind but with an insistent edge.

"Come in, dear."

I ease the door open, and there, cocooned in an overstuffed chair, is a tiny, crumple-faced bald person of indeterminate gender.

"Madam Bigelow?"

"She is I."

She sounds a wee impatient. Enough so that I might have apologized and made my escape, but for her captivating appearance. She's wearing a purple sleeveless tee shirt, and the skin on the underside of her arms hangs in pleats. Her shoulders are achingly narrow. Her bald pate reminds me of a baby bird, not yet fledged, and, nestled as she is in her roost of cushions and quilts, appears wholly opposed to ever doing so.

She gazes at me for a good long while and I begin to fidget. Once again, I contemplate fleeing, but then, she speaks.

"Sit on the bed, child, but do not say anything."

I sit and look in her eyes, as she does mine. Still, she doesn't speak. My eyes wander around the room. There's no dresser, but in one corner, I see a tall narrow bookcase stuffed with neatly folded articles of clothing. On the higher shelves, shelves too high for this gnome-woman to reach, are sheets and towels, all spanning the purple palette.

"Tell me what you see, young lady."

"I see you have no dresser or chest of drawers."

"And?"

"I see your admiration for the color purple."

"One correct, one incorrect. Turn around."

There, behind me, is a low dresser. I smile at her in surrender.

"Sometimes, Miss—?"

"Gilbert. Cecilia."

"Sometimes, Miss Gilbert Cecilia, we forget that we can't see the thing behind us, the thing in the rearview mirror. Best to keep that in mind."

This she says reprovingly, while still smiling. I'm sure she switched my name on purpose. There's that impishness about her. The room begins to feel too warm and the smell of camphor is strong. I fight the urge to say I've come to the wrong room, but that wouldn't do, as I asked before I entered if she was Madam Bigelow. Stay the course, I counsel myself, stay the course. It occurs to me that, even if Madam has nothing to offer, or, more likely, I am not disposed to accept it, perhaps it is *I* who have something to offer her? I've learned that life is sometimes like that. You want something, but instead, it turns out you have the thing to give.

When Madam finally speaks again, there's a whinge in her tone.

"Oh, dear," she says and exhales dramatically. "I *do* so hope you haven't come to see the future."

I hesitate. 'Yes' is obviously the wrong answer. Yet I *do* want to know if Wink is in my future. And by that, I mean if he is alive and if I will find him.

"Well—"

I draw the word out, trying to gauge her reaction. I sense immediately, however, how ridiculous this is. Even if I had all my wits about me, which I decidedly do not, I suspect I could never out-wit Madam Bigelow. So why even try? I want something from her and, unless this cat-and-mouse game is part of her schtick, it's beginning to feel fruitless. Not to mention, frustrating. Does she want me to just come out and say what I want? She's not yet asked, so I decide to let her drive the boat.

"I only ask," she continues, "because the future is not in high demand around here."

At that, she chuckles.

"So," she says, "not the future and surely not the past . . . which leaves us with?"

Dare I venture a guess? I barely recognize my seesawing heart. Mere hours ago, I scoffed at the idea of a psychic helping me find Wink. Now, here I am, never wanting anything so desperately in my life. I must give Madam Bigelow the precise response that will unlock her heart. Or her brain or her minds-eye. I will give Madam Bigelow anything she asks for. Anything.

"The present," I say, my voice ringing out. "That leaves the present."

"Precisely," she says. "Now, without telling me

why you're here — although I assume it's because you've lost something — I want you to pick three words that describe your feelings. Now. In the *present*. How do you *presently* feel? Three words and, I beg you, please don't overthink it."

This is not difficult. I know precisely how I feel. It's what I've been feeling for six days.

"Desperate. Heartbroken. Guilty."

There's a sharp rap on Madam Bigelow's door and in walks a tall Black woman with a multicolored scarf twisted and knotted on her head like a crown. Her long neck reminds me of drawings I've seen of Queen Nefertiti.

"It's time, Madam-mine, and no guff today, please. Skipped yesterday, you did, and I shan't be leavin' til we complete our mission."

The woman glowers at me, big hands planted on broad hips. She cocks her head, awaiting my departure.

"But I was just—"

"There's no 'just,' girl" — she pronounces it 'gull' — "there is only you skedaddling. Tout suite."

"It's no use, Gilbert Cecilia," Madam says, standing to reveal herself even smaller than I imagined. "This Amazon won't rest until she puts me through the PT-wringer."

"But—"

"Go now, girl. And remember: Look behind."

The nurse shoos me towards the door and eases it closed behind me. Right before it clicks shut, I see Madam Bigelow over her shoulder. She's blowing me a kiss.

My mind reels. Down the hall I go in a daze. I

consider plunking myself on one of the chairs to wait for Madam to finish her physical therapy, but, for some reason, this strikes me as wrong-headed. Why, I don't know. Now that I'm no longer in her presence, I feel increasingly desperate, clinging against all reason to some far-fetched hope. Plus, I'm a bit irritated that Madam seemed to be toying with me. Oh, not maliciously, of course. But she seems to require a lightheartedness that I am incapable of mustering. Waiting for her therapy to conclude is too passive and I'm jumpy now, ready to jump out of my skin.

At the reception desk, Loon is back to his reading. He looks up, but I keep on walking. The automatic door opens with a pneumatic wheeze and I sense his eyes still on me. I know I should make some kind of human connection because he had shown me the same when I first entered. Do I seriously intend to walk out the door with nary a backward glance?

I turn and offer a weak wave.

"My dog," I say. "You asked what I lost. I lost my dog."

I don't know whether Loon hears me or not, but his eyes go soft and he returns my wave.

I sit in my car and ponder what Madam Bigelow said about seeing the thing *behind* me. Is she talking about her dresser again? Or perhaps she's speaking temporally? Something behind me, time-wise. Something in New Jersey, something about Ben? Coming to Beaufort is essentially a new beginning, so everything, in one way or another, is behind me.

And the three adjectives I picked to describe my current state? The first two are obvious, but guilt? The fact of my willful ignorance is now fully upon me. How could I leave Wink at Zeke's? Was I truly blind to the possibility that something bad could happen? Years ago, I saw a TV reality show that profiled girls, and sometimes women, who gave birth without realizing they were pregnant. It exploited that titillating gray area between viewer credulity and incredulity. Every episode concluded, directly or by insinuation, with that question — How could you not know? — as the girl-women were handed their swaddled babes.

How could I not have known, indeed! Worse, how could I *know* — seen the disorder, witnessed the man's strangeness — and still have left my boy to an unknown fate?

The human flaw of blind ignorance is exposed everywhere, from the most individual case — How could you not know your son is failing math — to the most global: How could we not know millions of Jews were being gassed, how could we not know that, in just 100 days in 1994, 800,000 people were being slaughtered in Rwanda?

I wonder what Madam Bigelow would have revealed about the present had we not been interrupted. Would she have detected the stench of my self-indictment, discovered the true nature of my culpability?

All I know is that the present is the most fragile of constructs. For every zig that leads us to the present moment, we could have zagged. It's utterly arbitrary, the present, and exceedingly fragile. But it is, of course, all there is.

twenty-nine

Driving home from Madam Bigelow's, I remind myself to pay attention. As small as Beaufort is, I don't know the town all that well, and I need my wits about me. Plus, it's crucial that I observe *everything*. Wink could be walking down the sidewalk at the end of a stranger's leash and I might miss it completely. Stay vigilant, I command myself.

At the corner of Carteret and Craven, the light turns yellow. Rather than hurrying through, the car ahead of me stops, and I soon see why. A horse-drawn tourist carriage is coming through. The massive Chestnut, bright-blue ribbon braided in her tail, clomps through the intersection on her way to the old historic district. I look up at the sky and see the same heartbreaking shade of cyan blue that Della Robbia used to glaze his sculptures. The color of shallow water over a shady beach.

A couple of blocks later, I turn right on Bay

and lower all the windows. I hear the riggings on the sailboats at the marina clinking against each other, an evocative metallic sound that speaks of distant ports. The breeze blowing off the river carries complex layers of tea olive, gardenia and pluff mud. Sometimes the world is so beautiful that you feel humbled to be in it, and this is one of those moments.

When my phone rings, I nearly let it go, then remember that I can't afford to miss a single call. I answer without looking at the number.

"CiCi, J.P. here. I'm afraid there's been an accident. Eloise — our dear Eloise — has fallen. I'm here now. At Beaufort Memorial. They believe she's suffered some head trauma, although they're trying to rule out a stroke."

"Oh, J.P." My throat thickens and I swallow a sob. "What can I do?"

"Well, my dear, she's asking for Simon's letters. She's quite distraught about it. Keeps saying, 'It's a matter of *love.*' I can't get her to tell me where such letters might be. I'd hunt for them myself, but she won't let go of my hand. I wonder, CiCi, could you possibly assist?"

I'm feeling none-too-able to accomplish any task, let alone search someone else's home for something both hidden and intimate. But I hear the urgency in the Professor's voice. Of course I'll do it.

"I'm five minutes from home, J.P. I'll go to Eloise's right away. If I find them, or *when* I find them, I mean, I'll bring them to—"

"Room 324."

As I'm driving home, it occurs to me that 324

is Ben's birthday — March 24 — numbers I have long-used in just about every password requiring numerals. I guess that will have to change. Or not. Suddenly, I miss Ben tremendously. He loved Wink. He'd be by my side as we went through this agonizing time together. Or would he? Ben in the older days, yes. But in the past year? Oh, he'd become so cold, concrete curtains descending whenever his emotions threatened to go off dead-center. That is part of abandonment syndrome, of course. My dear Ben had become expert at castrating his feelings, closing down when faced with impending grief or loss.

I pull up in front of Eloise's. Was it really only yesterday we had dinner together? Intellectually, we humans know that life can change in a heartbeat, but, for most of us, *owning* that reality requires a tragedy. Your partner leaves, your mother dies, your dog disappears. One day, a rosy-cheeked Eloise sips sweet tea . . . and the next?

I retrieve Eloise's key from under the doormat, where J.P. said it would be, and beat back a sense of foreboding as I enter her house. How will I ever be able to find a bunch of old letters? It seems a herculean task. I rule out the kitchen as an unlikely place, yet if anyone would keep personal treasures in a kitchen drawer, it's Eloise. The uncommon, irrepressible, labyrinthic Eloise. "Our Eloise," as the Professor put it.

There are three bedrooms. One, set up as an office, another, a guest room and, in the third, in the back, the master. I start there, going first to the top shelf in her closet, a place I often store memorabilia. But I find only old quilts and half-completed needlepoint projects. It feels wrong to be poking around in her closet, a violation of personal space. Still, the poor woman needs her letters.

I turn to a nightstand with a single drawer, in which I find face cream, a linen handkerchief embroidered in buttercup-yellow thread with the initial "S," and an old beat-up pocket watch. No letters.

Across from the bed is an antique tallboy with inlaid mother of pearl and brass pulls. I ruffle through panties and socks and a couple of girdles, circa 1960, my fingers spider-crawling to the back of each of the eight drawers. Nothing.

I think about the office-bedroom next, but, for some reason, I walk past it to the living room. I stand and close my eyes, as if the house might speak to me. It doesn't — or at least, I don't think it does — but when I open my eyes, they land on a large, three-drawered buffet in the dining room. There, I think, the letters are in there. Or *could* be in there, I admonish myself. Who do you think you are, CiCi, Finder-in-Training of Lost Things?

I tug on the top drawer. It opens five inches, then catches. I jostle it gently, side-to-side, but it becomes even more firmly stuck. At the very front is an old-fashioned jewelry box, the perfect hiding place for precious letters. I haven't seen one like it in years. Much of the thin padded leather, embossed with a gold-stamped *fleur de lis,* has peeled away, leaving the mere ghost of the pattern. Originally, the box was probably ivory-colored, but it has aged to a pallid beige. I ease it out of the drawer and snap the clasp open. But, alas, it contains only pens, most of which

Slack Tide

I assume are dry, and a wasp nest of ancient rubber
bands. With the jewelry box removed, I can see that
the drawer is crammed with a mishmash of napkins
and bamboo placemats and papers, which I pull out
and spill onto the dining room table. I have no idea
if Simon's letters are neatly bundled together or in
readily recognized envelopes, but surely, they'd not be
intermingled with other papers, would they? There's no
way to know, however, so I sift through it all. But, alas,
no. Only bills, old receipts, and notes and sketches for
a garden.

I reach as far back as I can, but the drawer
still will not budge. When I lean down to eye-level, I
spy the culprit. It appears to be a small statue. I can
see and feel the base and, if I turn my torso just so,
I can extend my reach another inch. But my fingers
just graze it and I can't get any purchase. I grab a
candlestick from the top of the buffet and prod at
the thing until my jimmying finally frees it. It turns
out that the statue is not a statue, but an oversized
corkscrew with a bulbous carved-wooden head. Behind
the corkscrew are a half-dozen gray electrical sockets,
the kind that accommodate multiple plugs.

The second drawer also sticks. I swear under my
breath. I'm beginning to panic that it's taking so long
and what if I never find the letters? Then, in the third
drawer, there they are: pages of ivory linen stationery,
folded in thirds, tied with a pink grosgrain ribbon. I
pull out the top one. It's undated and, in the middle of
the page, in big, looping cursive, it reads:

244

Dear Eloise,

Everything is about to change.

Love, Simon

I return the letter to the bundle. On my way out the door, I grab a red boa that is flung over one of the dining room chairs and scrunch it into my bag.

On the short drive to the hospital, I think about the letter. Five words — ominous words — and how strangely they are placed in the middle of the paper. It seems more like a notice, a notice with a silent, prophetic preface: Be forewarned.

I hope the others are love letters. Perhaps written on various anniversaries during their 50-year marriage? Or maybe when Simon was fighting in Vietnam? In the handful of times I've been with Eloise, she talked of their shared passions and devotion to each other. She told me of Simon's pancreatic cancer, how they threw everything they had at that relentless disease, how, as she cared for him, they grew more cherished to each other than she ever thought possible . . . until he succumbed a decade ago.

The elevator doors ease open on the third floor. The nurses' station is directly in front of me. As I step into the big open space, my phone rings.

"Hello?"

A beat, then . . . "This is Simone."

"I'm sorry?"

"Ha!" she barks. "*That's* rich. Friend of my

mother's and you don't even know my name? Ha! Par for the course, I guess."

She sounds incredibly bitter. But bitter as she may be, her mother is lying in a hospital bed and the last thing I will do is judge her. I will not be defensive.

"Do you know about your mother's—"

"Of course, I do. How'd you think I got your number. Professor Ruopp called me."

"Well, I'm at the hospital now. Your mother was asking for letters from your father."

"Of *course* she was."

I don't respond. I have no idea what to say and fear that almost anything would make matters worse. I take a deep breath. Hold it. Release it slowly. I think she's disconnected the call, but then I hear her breathing.

"I'll never forgive her, you know."

"Oh," I respond. "I'm so—"

"Did my mother tell you he died of cancer?"

"Yes."

"My father didn't die of *cancer*."

She says the word with derision, as if it tastes foul in her mouth.

"My father committed suicide."

thirty

I clutch the letters so tightly that my knuckles are white. The door to 324 is ajar and, when J.P. sees me, his face lights up and he rushes to embrace me. Over his shoulder, I see Eloise, saturated in fluorescent light, so sepulchral she might have been dead. She's miniscule in the hospital bed, but who *doesn't* look diminished when nearly naked and plugged into a machine? Wires creep from under her hospital gown, which is stretched out at the neck and washed to near-opacity. An oxygen tube invades her nostrils and another tube snakes from her arm to a drip bag that hangs, flaccid but menacing, from an IV pole. The room smells sour, like damp leaves and chlorine bleach.

"Eloise!" J.P. cries. "Here's CiCi" — he spots the ribbon-tied packet in my hand — "with Simon's letters!"

Eloise's face crumples, as if she's going to sob.
"I don't know this woman."

Her words are raspy, like sludge moving through
a rusty pipe. Her eyes shine with fever . . . or fear.

"What is *she* doing with Simon's letters?"

J.P. nearly falls over himself to arrange chairs
so we can both be close to the head of the bed. The
legs of one chair momentarily catches on a wire that
disappears under Eloise's gown. He's clearly fighting
back tears. Watching everything, able to control
nothing, Eloise is growing wild-eyed and agitated. J.P.
nods that I should sit. He takes Eloise's hand, carefully
avoiding the needle taped to the back of it. Under her
paper-thin skin, her veins are blue and distended.

"Now, Eloise," he says. "You remember Miss
Cecilia Gilbert, your new next-door neighbor."

J.P. and I are so close to the bed that our knees
press into its metal frame. Eloise's rheumy eyes bore
into mine. Finally, her brow softens.

"It's an urgent matter," she whispers. "A matter
of love."

She pronounces it like a supplication, pleading
with me to understand something profound, but
elusive. I touch her arm.

"I understand," I say.

And I do.

"Did you know my Simon?"

I take her hand and, for a moment, both J.P. and
I are holding it.

"No, your Simon died before we met."

J.P. nods again. His eyes hold such tenderness
that I feel nearly swamped by it.

"But I did bring Simon's letters. Would you like the Professor to read them to you?"

"Not *him*," she cries. "*You*. You understand my Simon's thoughts."

It's clear she still doesn't know who I am. But, with childlike innocence, she apparently has decided to trust me.

I unfold the first letter, the one I read in her house.

"Dear Eloise. Everything is about to change. Love, Simon."

I look up. Her eyes are closed and she's smiling.

"What good are they, words?" she purrs. "Flimsy as air."

J.P. looks mystified. I open the next letter. It, too, begins, "Dear Eloise" and is signed "Love, Simon." But, in between . . . the letter is blank. There are no other words. This must be the letter she asked me to interpret my first day in Beaufort, the letter she waved in my face. I show it to J.P., and we turn to Eloise. Except for the complicated geometry of tubes and wires across her body, she looks beatific. I open another, then a fourth. They are identical. Each is undated, each with the same salutation, each signed, Love, Simon. And in between, a vast sea of emptiness. Blank letters.

J.P. ponders them for a long moment, then leans so close that his lips brush my ear.

"The first is Simon's handwriting," he whispers. "The others, Eloise's. I'm quite sure of it."

I pull away in confusion, but then Eloise speaks.

"Read more," she whispers. "The next one is

about Italy."

"Italy?"

I'm stalling, ticking through options. Should we tell her the remaining pages are not letters from Simon? Of course not. But perhaps if I show her the next letter — blank as it is — she'll say something and we can follow her lead? I engage in more stalling tactics, reaching in my bag and pulling out the red boa. Her eyes light up when she sees it, but she's still focused on the letters. More confident now, she exclaims: "Yes, I'm quite sure of it. Simon went to that meeting in Assisi alone, you remember, Professor. I had to stay home with the flu."

Assisi? I'd been there years ago. I realize there is simply no other course of action — no other *humane* course of action — so I open the second letter with great care, as if it's a parchment, fragile and sacred.

"Why, yes," I say. "This one *is* about Assisi."

She nods, confirmed in her memory. "Dear Eloise," I read, and she murmurs a sound of amazed contentment.

"Dear Eloise," I repeat. "Everything we dreamt about Assisi is true. Piazza Commune, the main square where we planned to get gelato and watch kids play in the fountain, is delightful. I felt awful enjoying my gelato (yes, yes, raspberry, as you well know) with you confined to bed. Are you feeling better? Perhaps it will hasten your recovery to know that I had a second cup of gelato in your honor. Can you guess the flavor? Love, Simon."

"Pistachio," Eloise cries and immediately is beset with a coughing fit. I stand to summon a nurse, but J.P.

is out the door ahead of me. I lean over her frail body and gently coax her to a sitting position. She is as light as a child. I tap on her back.

"Do you know what I'm most afraid of, dear?"

Her coughing abates, but she's still wheezing. I continue to rub her back and the little bird wings of her scapula.

"No," I say. "Tell me."

"I'm afraid that if I die, my Simon dies, too. He's already gone, of course—"

I nod.

"—but it's like he'll be dying all over again."

A nurse hustles in and gently scoots Eloise to a more erect position, coos to her, and motions for me to pour a glass of water.

J.P. stands in the doorway as the room bakes in the setting but still torpid Carolina sun. I hear voices from down the hall, the tinny thud of a metal drawer closing, the clatter of a clipboard tossed on a counter. Although I want to talk to J.P. — I've yet to tell him about the call from Eloise's daughter — I am rooted to the moment: the expression on Eloise's face, how the nurse's stethoscope falls away from her chest when she leans over, the thickness of the air, heavy with heat. Finally, the nurse shoos us out.

I slip my arm through J.P.'s and, before the nurse closes the door behind us, we look back at Eloise.

"She seems so insubstantial," he says, his voice quavering. "As if those wires and tubes are the only things tethering her to this world. But can't you see her, CiCi, can't you just see her as a *girl*, vamping around in a pretty little frock as pink as Pepto?"

Slack Tide

The nurse closes the door and I steer J.P. to an alcove near the elevators. There's so much we should talk about: the troubling phone call from Eloise's daughter, the blank letters, my visit to the psychic, and now my complete fabrication of stories for a woman who is suffering significant cognition issues and is, perhaps, dying. We sit in two identical chairs, facing each other. They're upholstered in a blue, nubby fabric. Why I notice this, I don't know. So many things are swirling in my head, yet this insignificant detail, the nubbiness of the fabric, feels as real as any of it.

I look down at my hands and am startled to see that I'm still clutching Eloise's letters. Why are they blank? Does it have something to do with Simon taking his own life? Or with Eloise's attempt to understand, to accept, perhaps, some unknown story behind his death?

I tell J.P. about the phone call from Simone and he asks me to go through our conversation again, as verbatim as possible. I can't tell if he already knows that Simon died by his own hand. He shakes his head, stands, looks out over the river.

"That would explain the blank letters," he says, finally. "And the different handwriting."

We are thinking the same thing: That the first letter, with its blunt declaration, could have been a suicide note? And the blank letters suggesting Eloise's fantasy or other coping mechanism? I picture her again on the day Wink and I arrived in Beaufort, the way she flew at me, waving a blank letter in my face, demanding to know what I made of it. Did I answer her? I don't think so . . . or, rather, I answered her question with a question, requesting more context or some-such. But then events began falling like dominos. The movers called, I brought Wink to Zeke's, and my new life — only just beginning — crumbled.

J.P. leans forward and rests his hands on my shoulders. He is trying to steady me.

"What are we going to do?" I ask.

"Just what we're doing. We will do whatever the situation *requires* of us. Look at me, CiCi. You and me. *Together.* This is the path now. Eloise and Wink. Do you understand?"

Over J.P.'s shoulder, I see the nurse motioning us back to the room. The heels of my shoes clack on the tile floor. J.P. pauses at the door and steps aside for me to go first. As I do, he makes a slight bow, like a knight in King Arthur's court. I sit again at Eloise's side, marveling how, in the space of a single week, my world has become intertwined with these two people. The connection with J.P. is easier to understand. He's gentle and erudite, the kind of person I've always been attracted to. But what is it about Eloise? I brush a strand of hair from her forehead, then rest the back of my hand there. Earlier, she hadn't even known who I was. Yet she had trusted me with her blank letters, she trusted me with Simon's words. Clearly, something in her subconscious recognizes something in mine: That we are both dealing with ambiguous loss.

thirty one

In college, I studied a theory in psychology called ambiguous loss. This particular type of loss —and the grieving that accompanies it — occurs when a person doesn't have all the facts surrounding the loss of a loved one, when there is no clear picture for the survivors to hang onto: Did my son die on impact when his plane was shot down over Laos, for example, or did he live for days, trapped in the cockpit, his dead copilot beside him? Was my missing daughter kidnapped or did she run away? Is she living in some nameless desert town or is she buried in a shallow grave that I pass every week on my way to the supermarket?

Usually with the loss of a loved one, we know what happened. We are at her bedside when she succumbs to cancer. We see his body after a traffic accident. We are able to bury or cremate our beloved's remains. But ambiguous loss is different. It may be experienced by an entire community on a catastrophic scale in a war or genocide, for example, or a natural disaster. And it can be experienced on an individual level when the loss doesn't make sense, such as in some suicides.

Is this, I wonder, what Eloise is experiencing? Does she know why Simon took his own life, or is his death forever shrouded in mystery? I know that the very uncertainty of ambiguous loss can lead to painful symptoms that are often misdiagnosed or missed entirely. And what about what I'm going through? Can it be experienced with a dog? A dog who has vanished?

A sharp ache in my throat signals impending tears. How will I grieve the ambiguous loss of never knowing what happened to Wink? What protocols govern mentioning him when I meet new people? Without raising undue concern about my psychological state, how long could I claim that the cause of my sadness — my distance, my blank stares, my awkward silences — is that my dog disappeared without a trace? Oh, your dog is lost? What does that even *mean*, "missing?"

T.S. Eliot said what you do not know is the *only* thing you know, and that, indeed, is my greatest fear: That everything I never know about Wink will become all I *do* know. If that's the case, I'd rather he be found dead. Even if his corpse is half-devoured, rank with decay, I want his body found. I don't want to believe he's alive if he's dead, and I don't want to believe he's dead if he's alive. How could I ever find a way to live with that heinous duality? Surviving this ambiguous loss, surviving never knowing, could well be beyond my heart's capacity.

How would I live with so many unanswered questions? Every anniversary — of the day I rescued him, of the day he disappeared — would be forever haunted. For the rest of my life, Wink would be the lingering question at the end of each day.

Throughout the afternoon I "read" Eloise's letters to her. Seventeen blank letters, seventeen wholly fabricated stories. Not once does she hint that my inventions ring false. When I finish the last one, she closes her eyes. The Professor and I listen to the suck and wheeze of her breath, and the hours pass. The Professor strokes her hand. I lose myself in amber-trapped memories of Wink: It's March. The skies are white and, outside the living room window, the snow is swirling sideways. Wink is lying in a trapezoid of faint sunlight and shadows of the window panes form a perfect geometry on his white flank. When he rolls onto his back, I put my book down and join him on the floor. As I massage his long, lean body, his legs relax and his ears flop back. When he begins to snore, I stop touching him. His eyes fly open and he looks at me, startled.

And this: It is July and hotter than blazes at a rest stop in Kansas. Wink and I are driving to see Anne in Colorado and I've let him off the leash to romp with another dog whose person's accent drips of Boston Back Bay. Millie, the dog, eats dirt and, from the moment Wink meets her, he becomes a dirt-eater.

It's October. The sky is blue and strings from a Puccini overture fill the house. Wink wants a walk, so we head out. But the neighborhood leaf-blower

brigade is out in force and Wink *hates* leaf blowers.
When I see one up ahead, I call him and he comes
to me, unwillingly, because all he really wants to do
is find the damn leaf-blower — the machine, not the
human — and bark at it. When the gardener sees me,
he turns off the blower and waits for us to pass. He's a
short, barrel-chested man with a flat face like I've seen
in villages around Oaxaca, Mexico. That was the day I
learned you can judge a person's character by the way
he handles a leaf-blower.

Sometime later, a nurse comes in to take Eloise's
vitals. J.P. looks over at me and seems surprised that
I'm still here.

"Go home," he says. "I'll stay."

I'm nearly to my car, dreading another night in
an empty house, when I look up and see the crescent
moon chalked on the navy-blue sky. I stop in my
tracks. What is my Wink seeing at this moment? Is
he safe for the night or do nocturnal predators lurk
nearby? Perhaps he lies, wounded, looking up at the
moon, this moon, as he takes his final breaths? Does
he know he's dying? Is he cognizant of his body's
imminent death? Or he is bewildered?

I pray the only prayer I can think of: Surrender
to the universe, devoted companion, and amidst all
peril, align yourself with the energy of calm. You walk
on still beside me.

thirty-two

As I'm easing into a parking spot in front of my house, I see a man on my porch. He turns. I raise my hand in greeting, but he does not wave back. It's late, I think, too late to be standing on someone's porch. As I approach, he ducks his head in an odd manner and nearly stumbles as he clambers down the steps.

"Cecilia Gilbert?"

"Yes?"

"You've been served," he says, thrusting a manila envelope at me.

On the outside of the envelope, the word "Summons" is typed in an incongruously delicate font. By the time I gather my wits, the man is halfway down the block and I watch, numb, as he rounds the corner, swinging his left leg in an awkward, hobbled motion.

I'm all thumbs locking the door behind me. One would think I'm afraid of a piece of paper. And, of course, I am. The envelope is the old-fashioned kind. I unwind the red string sealing the flap and pull out a one-page document entitled Temporary Cease-and-Desist Order. Unless I appear at the Beaufort municipal court to challenge this temporary order, it will become permanent on June 5, 2018. Two days from today. I'm ordered to stay at least 100 feet away from the property of one, Zacharia Johnson, doing business as Zeke's Paws Spa.

My gut clenches and my throat tightens, but it's not because I'm frightened or deterred. Rather, I regard this as indisputable evidence that Zeke has something to hide. I will never comply if it means giving up my search for Wink. Let the Sheriff handcuff a harmless, middle-aged trespasser, let the local paper run a front-page photo of a deranged-looking me being led to the hoosegow. I can no more let go of Wink than I can let go of myself.

I need time to think, and this — plus Eloise's diminishing toehold on earth — spurs me to unpack the boxes with my kitchen things, a mindless task that leaves me free to think. Within an hour, all my pots and pans and assorted trays and utensils are put away. Everything fills just two cabinets and two drawers, which only slightly surprises me. Ben was the cook in the family, peacock-proud of every yoke separator and julienne peeler he'd acquired over the years. At the beginning of our relationship, he'd hold up a strange-looking gadget, like someone teaching colors to a child, and ask, "Now what is *this*, CiCi," his tone dripping with irony and mock patience. And love.

Once the kitchen is organized, I check found-animal postings on my laptop, disciplining myself to go only as deep as necessary. I checked all the lost-animal sites this morning, so there's no need to scroll beyond the most recently added postings. To delve further would only fuel my feeling of hopelessness. It's almost unbearable to see "Flynn" and "Arya" and "Pippin" drop further and further down the listings as the days pass. For a moment, I think of deleting my original post about Wink and then re-posting so he continues to appear near the top of the page. But I realize how shameful this would be. Do I really think that Wink is more important to me than Xander and Dixie and Buddy are to their people? Occasionally, there's a bold "FOUND" banner at the top of a posting and, for a moment, my heart soars. But then I feel the hole where Wink should be.

When I open my email, I find scores of unopened messages. But I simply can't deal with them now. I can't even *open* them. One of these days, I'll send a group email to friends about Wink, but not today. When friends find out, they'll start calling and I'll feel obliged to detail my search efforts to-date. I'll have to open my heart to words of encouragement and comfort. I'll have to confess my own complicity.

Not talking to friends is contrary to my nature, and, intellectually, I know that shutting off loved ones means *I* am shutting down. It's unhealthy for me and unfair to them. But to cope with their sorrow and empathy in addition to my own grief? It would overwhelm, rather than buoy, me. Perhaps that's why I feel close to J.P. and Eloise and even Brenda Lee? They only know me without Wink, in all my messed-up-ness. With them, I don't have to explain how I'm feeling because they're witness to it.

I close my laptop and my phone rings. It's Brenda Lee. Not with any news about Wink, just calling to see how I'm doing. Just. As if "just" isn't all, as if it isn't . . . everything.

That night, I sleep soundly, which feels like a minor miracle. In the morning, I shower, do my back exercises, and eat a healthy breakfast. Performing such pedestrian tasks makes me feel inordinately accomplished, and there's a lightness in my step as I walk over to J.P.'s. Seagulls wheel overhead and swifts warble from the trees at the top of their lungs. The scent of tea olive teases me. It's there, then gone, then there again. Even when I stand still for a moment, the delicate sweetness with its hint of ripe apricot lingers then vanishes seductively.

The Professor doesn't answer my first or second knock. I try the doorbell even though I know it doesn't work. His car is in the driveway, so I assume he's not still at the hospital. I cup my hands to my eyes and peer in the window, then walk to the back, expecting to see him at the kitchen table, nose buried in a giant tome of Dickens or Joyce. Nothing. I try the back door and, finding it unlocked, step inside. The house is eerily quiet. I don't want to venture too far for fear of startling him, so I call his cell. I hear the ring in stereo: the tinny buzzing in my ear and a fainter, four-note melody from somewhere deep in the house. When he doesn't pick up, I follow the ringing.

I find J.P. sitting up in bed in awkward recline, slumped against the headboard, his torso canted to one side. Although his eyes are closed, I have the sense he knows I'm here. I'm just about to speak when I notice his nightshirt has fallen off a shoulder, exposing a shiny, purplish seam that snakes from behind his ear, down the side of his neck, and disappears into his shirt. I step closer and see the angry gutters of a scar.

"Oh, my dear, I know," he says, quirking a corner of his mouth. "It's horrible to regard, but be assured, it no longer hurts."

His brow creases and his eyes squint open. He's obviously in some kind of pain, and I fear adding to it with my intrusion, entering his home without permission and glimpsing an inadvertently exposed chapter of his life. But he takes pity on me, the dear man, and invites me to sit at the foot of his bed.

"It was the first day of 7th grade," he whispers. "I was relieved to be escaping a gaggle of ruffians who had moved in next-door over the summer. Four brothers who taunted me unmercifully. But I was happy because I was sure they'd be going to the high school, a blessed two miles across town."

I take a deep breath, steeling myself. J.P. trembles slightly and I imagine he's reliving, a half-century later, what happened next.

"Apparently two of the boys were just big for their age or perhaps they'd been held back? But there they were on the first day of school, following me to science class. And, oh, CiCi," he cries, "I was outraged that it happened in that room. My one safe room, my beloved science lab with its microscopes and beakers and magic potions. I'd already been deemed an effete, you know, by children who equated my love of books with femininity, but I did so hope the science lab would become my sanctuary."

He shudders and pats the bed for me to come closer. I'm now mere inches from the horrible scar. And then J.P. does the most amazing thing: He tugs his nightshirt lower, exposing his entire shoulder. I'm stunned by the unnatural shininess of the rivulets and how deeply they're etched into his skin.

"Carbonic acid," he says. "As you see, they missed my face, which, in some warped way upset me. Ha. I guess because it meant my wounds would remain forever invisible. Hidden by turtlenecks, the well-turned collar of a cardigan, and now my fusty old morning coats. But now, *you* know."

His lips pull a smile.

"My migraine is something awful today, Cecilia, and I think the morphine pill will now have its wily way with me. If you would stay until I fall asleep . . . *mumble-mumble* . . . a gift."

I take his hand and hold it. It is peaceful, sitting here with him. As long as I'm here, I think, perhaps I can keep him safe from harm. And maybe myself, too.

When I return home, I search websites. Occasionally, I give my eyes a break and open a moving box. But every time I look inside, I feel light-headed, as if I'm staring into an abyss. The Temporary Restraining Order niggles at the edges of my brain, but I'm unable to grapple with it in any decisive way. Should I contest it? Not doing so would, I fear, signal that I'm abandoning my conviction that Zeke knows something about Wink.

I find my kitchen radio at the bottom of a box

and plug it in next to the coffee maker. I turn the dial slowly until I land on an NPR station with a clear signal. But hearing the familiar teaser-tune for that afternoon's *All Things Considered* nearly makes me weep. Normalcy seems like a betrayal of Wink.

Around 8 p.m., I return to the Professor's. He seems to be sleeping or floating in a netherworld of opiates. But his bedroom curtains have been opened and a numinous light floods the room. I sit near the bay window. If I crane my neck, I can see the newly risen moon, a whisper-thin ghost of itself against the darkening sky. I'm still gazing at it when the Professor speaks.

"You make me want to speak of Caravaggio," he says.

"Do I?"

He squinches an eye open.

"It's your luscious body, creamy and substantial in this otherworldly moonlight. Do you know him? Caravaggio, I mean?"

"I do," I say, and move to sit on the bed.

"Your hair," he says, touching a strand, "is the color of chestnuts."

I drop my forehead and rest it on his hand. Tears sting my eyes as he strokes the back of my head. After a moment, a precious, quiet moment, I raise my head.

"You would look rakish, Professor," I say, "if you didn't look so awful."

He grimaces, but there is mischief in his eyes.

"Oh, CiCi, isn't there just something so *La Traviata* about lying in bed with a migraine?"

He brings the back of his hand to his forehead,

and I know the operatic gesture is intended to cheer me. But the seriousness of his tone is unnerving and I pull back. I have no idea where he's going with this, but I resolve to go there with him.

"You know, my dear," he continues, "there's a certain irrevocability to being sick. I don't mean that you give *up,* not precisely. It's more like you give *in* to some inexorable tide, to an inevitability that overtakes you."

He pauses, then waves his hand as if to shoo away some noisome insect.

"It may be temporary. Perhaps the tide takes you only temporarily, like with my migraine. You can hope. But if it's permanent — if the tide fails to give you up — there *is* an essential truth in it."

He closes his eyes and sleeps. I'm not sure how long I sit there, listening to his slow, easy breaths. But when I walk home, the streets are silent. With the exception of two or three homes where the extraterrestrial light of a television glows, the houses are dark. Somewhere, not far away, a Barred owl hoots. Out on the sea islands, baby turtles hatch and make their mad dash to the sea. I crawl into bed without brushing my teeth and sleep until my phone rings at 4:00 a.m.

It's the Professor. Eloise is dead.

thirty-three

Three hours later — three fitful hours that leave my bedsheets rumpled and strewn — J.P. phones again. He has called many of Eloise's friends, both locally and across the country. Apparently, she had prepared him for the task, which he refers to as "my somber honor and privilege." He'd made it through the entire list, he says, not considering the time on the west coast, where Simon has family. Then, as is wont to happen, friends reached out to friends and, by the time J.P. talked to the last person on Eloise's list, word of her death had spread widely, particularly in Beaufort County.

"I already have committals from 30," he says. His voice sounds weary and far away. "Could I prevail upon you, Cecilia?"

"Anything," I say. "Committals for what?"

"Oh, dear, let me back up."

Nancy Ritter

J.P. has decided to host a small gathering in his home today at noon. Beaufortonians are coming and there likely will be a handful from Charleston, Aiken, Columbia, and Savannah.

"I would imagine some of them are already on the road," he says, then asks me to pick up plates from a caterer, Miss Beula Mae Schade, who he intends to contact as soon as we hang up. I'm surprised that things can move so quickly in little Beaufort, but he assures me that this woman will have the perfect fare ready by 11 a.m.

Miss Schade lives out on St. Helena's Island, where Eloise and I had dinner just three days ago. Not confident I can find her place on the rural sea island, I leave early. Also, the Professor's directions seem iffy. He's understandably distraught and can't remember if the turn off MLK Jr. Drive is a right or a left, but it's onto a dirt road, he's sure about that, a mile or so past the Penn Center. Then, a left, definitely a left, where the road forks at an abandoned blue truck. I want to ask, What if the old truck is no longer there, but that seems petty.

As it turns out, though, the Professor's directions are spot-on. When I pull into the driveway-slash-front-yard, I see a skinny Black woman dressed in white from head to toe. She's carrying a long, narrow box onto the porch. A couple of floppy-eared mutts lope over to me, barking with delirious delight.

"Butter Bean! Nita-gal!" the woman cries and the dogs drop like flour sacks to their bellies. When she sees me, she stacks another box on top of the one she's already carrying and, moving with the fluency of a ballerina, quick-steps off the porch and across the yard.

"Ms. Schade?" I say, opening my door so she can put the boxes on the back seat.

"Who *else* would I be, sugar? Carting all these shrimp canapes and cheese biscuits hither and yon in the Carolina sun?"

Beula Mae Schade has the body of a whippet, taut and compact. When she bends to place the boxes on the car seat, I glimpse a white scar that snakes along her spine from above her apron and disappears under her skirt. She stands and turns. I begin to close the car door, but she catches it with one hand and eases it open again.

"Lord, child, don't hurry yourself! I got two more boxes inside. May not be what the Professor wants, but I know Miss Eloise better than him. Back from school days. I know what dat gal want, bless her heart."

Standing close now, I can see Beula Mae's hands are as wrinkled as an apricot pit, although her dark face is remarkably unlined. I can't guess her age, but if she and Eloise were kids together, she'd be close to eighty. I look beyond to her house, a faded turquoise with peeling yellow-trimmed shutters. She follows my gaze and says, "I have no interest in painting her. Might be I should, but I don't. Daddy built her the same year I came along — she's exactly my age! — and I like that she's aging right alongside me."

She walks back towards the house, continuing the monologue over her shoulder.

"Or should say I'm aging *in* her?" She laughs a tinkling windchime melody, and the dogs, prancing on either side of her, bark along. "Would that be more accurate? Ha. Well, let's just say, we're growing old together, and me and the house have the same memories. Same dead kin, same animals, all dem dogs and cats and that chicken Baby Otto got hisself! Can't forget that damn *chicken*!"

She loads two more boxes in my car, shuts the door, and turns.

"How the Professor doin'?"

"Not too well," I say.

"Migraine?"

"Yes."

"He gets 'em somethin' awful," Beula Mae says, matter-of-factly, but I think I see a shimmer of tears in her eyes. "He just got to go through them, is all, and we just have to let him."

The dogs come over and snuffle my hands from behind. Wet, cool noses against my palms. I reach back, not wanting to break eye contact with Beula Mae. There's something deeply compelling about her. I have a dog's head now under each hand, nuzzling me. The moment lasts for seconds, or perhaps forever, which is how it can be when you're truly in it. Then, Beula Mae waves me off with a shoo.

"Get a move on, girl! See you in 'bout an hour."

I creep back towards MLK Jr. Drive on dirt roads dusted with fine, white Carolina sand. I'm delighted I'll see Beula Mae Schade again, but the four big boxes on my back seat make me wonder if the Professor's estimate of thirty is off by a factor of two or three.

As soon as I hit the macadam again, I snap back to the present. Picking up the food has been a distraction, and I'm surprised to realize I haven't thought about Wink a single time. But here I am, back in the now. A different now than a half-hour ago, but also the same. Wink is still gone.

I look out over the tidal marsh. As far as the eye can see, sparkling waterways thread through swaths of grassland, then disappear. It pains me to think of Wink wandering in the same topography I inhabit. Half the time, I imagine him in some kind of otherworld, but that's probably my psyche's attempt to detach from what this once beautiful, benignly mysterious landscape has now become.

I park in the Professor's drive. The trill of red-winged black birds comes from the magnolia canopy, and I look up. The tree is heavy with oversized bowls of white flowers, so tender and plushy they make me dizzy. When I lift the top box from the back seat, I'm surprised how heavy it is and that Miss Beula Mae carried two at a time with apparent ease. My back is likely to protest any attempt to do likewise, so I carry the first and hope J.P. can assist with the rest. But that hope vanishes when he greets me at the back door still in his dressing gown and looking frazzled and bewildered. I set the box on the counter and he nudges me aside with a gentle bump of the hip.

"What Gullah magic have we here?" he purrs, tipping the lid back. His eyes are squinty against the light and I can tell he's still hurting, struggling to muster some enthusiasm. Canapes and roasted asparagus tips lie on a field of paper doilies atop a gorgeous beveled-crystal platter.

I ooo and aah, and J.P. says, "She's a magician. Of

the highest order."

When I tell him there are three more boxes, he raises an eyebrow.

"She did so love our Eloise, dear Beula. Our dear Beula Mae."

The Professor says he must dress and would I mind carrying in the other boxes and putting the platters in the dining room? He'll bring me a glass of wine — is a Petit Verdot okay? — and join me as soon as he can. On his way back to his bedroom, he cranks up the music. Bob Marley.

By the time I arrange the trays, remove and polish thirty wineglasses from the breakfront, and locate a stash of white-linen napkins, J.P. has yet to reappear. I pour myself a glass of wine and sit on the couch opposite a painting I'd seen, but not really studied. The dry red wine trickles pleasingly over my midpalate as I study the portrait. A Renaissance prince, perhaps, with dark, broody eyes. His shirt has a lace collar, white and delicate. It's a perfect moment. Sad, of course, but perfect in its poignancy, with the old painting to admire and Marley rhythms in the background. Thoughts of Wink fade a bit as I bring Eloise to mind, a woman who I knew all of nine days but who touched me profoundly.

My meditation is cut short by a sharp rap on the front door. I stand to open it and greet the first guest, but the door swings open and a short, stooped woman peeks in. Her skin is mottled and wrinkled as a Shar-pei. Easily in her nineties, she's immaculately groomed with a corsage of cloth mini-roses on her lapel and a tiny circus hat, netted and perched at a jaunty angle atop her head. "Miss Mabel Schilling," she introduces herself. I look past her to the street and see a boat-sized Pontiac parked askew, its fin-adorned rear-end intruding well into the lane of traffic.

I think quick.

"Why don't I pull your car a little closer, Miss Mabel, while you make sure the table is okay?"

Obviously, I underestimate her nimbleness because she lateral-passes her keys with a perfect toss and says over her shoulder as she scurries to the dining room, "Beula Mae's doing, I presume? They were lovers, you know."

Wait. *Lovers?* She couldn't be talking about Beula Mae and Eloise, I think, but who else? Unless she's confused or suffering some form of dementia, which, at her age, is possible. Then, I quickly censure myself for discounting Beula Mae and Eloise as a couple. And why not? Perhaps they had been lovers — if indeed she was referring to them — when they were teenagers? Or after Simon died?

The next thing I know, people are streaming through the front door. I go to J.P.'s bedroom and knock.

"Yes?"

"Guests are arriving, J.P. Is there anything I can do?"

A rustling within, then his voice vibrates against the door, as if his lips are pressed against it.

"No, my dear. I'm having a moment is all. I'll be out . . ."

I miss the last words. I stand for a long thirty seconds, then return to the living room, where I watch a man introduce himself to another as Reverend Larkin, the preacher from Eloise's church. I recognize our postwoman, Takisha, and there are a few other familiar faces, undoubtedly from the neighborhood.

The front door opens again and in walks Darius with a woman, not yet middle-aged, who must be his mother, and I wonder if my heart is strong enough to take all this love in one place. It might crowd out my pain over Wink and I'm not sure I want that.

Darius and the woman stand against a wall. When he sees me approaching, he grins from ear to ear.

"Miz CiCi," he says, with a solemnity befitting the occasion. "Please meet my mother, Miz Jolene Devoe."

Darius's mother is lovely in blue tweed and pearls. She shakes my hand and bites her lower lip. I recognize the habit from Darius and am beset by a great tenderness for this woman. I place my other hand on top of hers, and she, in turn, swaddles both of mine with hers. I turn to Darius.

"Your hair is especially fine today, young man."

"That would be Mama," he says. "She braided it special this mornin,' owing to Miz LaFitte's passing and all. She always pretends to lose her fingers in it, don't you, Mama? 'Where'd they go, boy?' she says, and I say, 'What, Mama?' and she says — like she always does — 'oh, my *fingers*, I think they be lost in this bountiful hair,' and then she gives it a tug."

It's the longest speech I've ever heard from Darius. He's nearly incandescent with pride, swiveling his head from his mother to me and back again.

Someone touches my shoulder. I turn and come face-to-face with the woman who chastised me about putting Wink's posters up around the neighborhood the day after he disappeared. She's still wearing her pearls.

"Dear?"

Her voice is kind. She's hanging onto the sleeve of a man who surveils the room, then waves in the direction of the kitchen.

"Dear, I'd like you to meet my Earl—"

I offer my hand. Earl takes it and extends sympathy for my loss. I'm ready to protest that I didn't know Eloise all that well or that I've been in town for only a week, but I catch myself. Who's to say how long or well one must know another before feeling their loss? I thank Earl for his condolences and direct my attention to the woman who admonished me about notice-posting "rules."

"And you are?" I say, extending my hand.

"Posh," she responds, or something like that, then, with both arms, sweeps me to her bosom and rocks me side-to-side.

"I'm Margaret Balk," she mumbles into my hair. "And I apologize for speaking to you like I did before. I didn't know, I just didn't know."

In another situation, I might have inquired what, precisely, Margaret Balk didn't know. My mind clicks through several possibilities: Didn't know she'd ever see me again? Didn't know I was the kind of person who would make friends with J.P. and Eloise? But then, Hamilton Reeve, the lost piano-playing soul, walks by and touches the back of his hand to my cheek.

"Would you please excuse me, Miss Margaret?"
I say, adding the "Miss" by way of forgiveness and
respect because I've just seen Beula Mae Schade walk
in. She's wearing a show-stopping church hat, wide-
brimmed with a black silk ribbon and an organza bow
the color of honey. I think it may be the most beautiful
thing I've ever seen.

Before I can get to her, though, she is ambushed
by two older women, also dressed to the nines. I glance
at my watch. Just noon. Only eight hours since J.P.
called to tell me of Eloise's death. It is breathtaking. All
of it. Everything.

A hand grabs my elbow. I flinch and try to twist
away without causing a commotion, but the grip is
tight. The suddenness and violence of it shocks me.
As soon as I see the raven-black hair and baby-hawk
of a nose, I recognize Simone from a photo on Eloise's
piano.

"So, you're the famous Cecilia," she says.
"Charmed, I'm sure."

Good grief. I resist a clever retort, perhaps, 'Well,
I never. . .' but this is not the time to try to out-smarm
Eloise's daughter. Plus, I have a strong suspicion I'd
lose.

I try to take a step back, but I'm unsuccessful
and now she glowers, her face close — too close — to
mine. She's still clamped onto my elbow, as if expecting
me to flee.

"Hello, Simone," I say, aware of the stammer in
my voice. "How are you doing?"

She flaps her hand at me, but continues to
glare, as if I've posed a trick question. I smell her

perfume, a potent floral. I lean back, stifle a sneeze, and finally extricate myself, ungracefully, from her hold. I resent her belligerence. What have I ever done to her? Still, I know I shouldn't take it personally. This woman has just lost her mother and regardless of their relationship — or perhaps *because* of their relationship — kindness is in order.

"I'm sorry for your loss, Simone. Please let me know if there's anything I can do."

Something flashes across her face, perhaps a darkening of the eyes, but I have no time to decipher it because she half-pushes me into the hallway.

"I was going to wait until after," she pouts, as if she's sincerely sorry to raise whatever issue she's about to raise. "But since you brought it up, there *is* something you can do. I simply don't have the time — there's my new job and, well, if you knew me, you'd know that patience is not my strong suit. Not like *you* . . . with your endless search for that missing animal—"

She stops and cuts her eyes. She must sense how cruel her remark is, but it's as if she can't help herself. She neither apologizes nor softens her mien, and continues to hulk over me with her rapacious perfume and raptor-like beak.

"What I *mean* is, you're the *perfect* person. Mama liked you so much and, with you living next-door and all, you could spend a couple of hours a day over there without interfering with your own activities too much."

I shift on my feet. In my peripheral vision, I see Beula Mae holding court in the kitchen.

"Over where?" I'm not following her. Plus, I'm increasingly worried about where J.P. is. I glance toward his bedroom door.

"Why, at *Mama's*, of course. I was going to hire a professional company. Sort through her things, you know — decide what to sell, what to give away, what to . . . oh, I don't know, just *toss*. But now I see you are the *perfect* solution."

What the hell does she mean, perfect solution? The cheapest option? The easiest way to assuage her guilt? Someone calls her name, and I take advantage of the distraction to twist away. It's abrupt, but, really, I'm beginning to lose whatever minimal cool I possess. I go to the Professor's door again and knock. I think I hear a moan, although it could have been the wind. All day, it's been threatening to rain. If it starts, the gathering will last longer, as people dally and settle in to wait it out. It occurs to me that this would — or could — be the first day where my focus would not be entirely on Wink, and I don't feel good about that. As much as I liked Eloise, I hope the gathering does not go on and on. I'm not ready to give up on Wink. I may be closer to accepting that I may never know what happened to him, but not yet.

J.P. cracks his door. I see half his face. One eye, a slice of nose, a segment of chin.

"Oh, CiCi," he says. He looks relieved to see me, and I expect him to invite me in, but he doesn't. "What's happening out there?"

"Are you okay?"

"No. No, I am decidedly *not* okay, darling one. I've been vomiting. Awful migraine. Worst in ages."

I speak to one eye.

"I'm so sorry, J.P. What can I do?"

He winces and offers a lopsided grin.

"Was that Simone?"

Yes, I say, to which he says, I can't bear to see her, she'll break my heart, to which I respond, I understand . . . she's already broken mine.

"J.P.," I say, "You need to take care of *you*. What can I do?"

"Do you mean that?" His voice quavers. His eyes are glazed.

I say I do. Then he asks me to do the nearly impossible.

thirty four

E very neuron in my brain fires the same
message: No! How could I possibly make
J.P.'s apologies to everyone and say a few
words in his stead? I'd known Eloise for barely a week
and we'd spent, what, ten or twelve hours together?
It seems inappropriate, sacrilege even, for a stranger
to bear witness in front of these good people, many of
whom had known Eloise their entire lives. I am wholly
inadequate to the task. Terrified. What do I really *know*
about her? What, for that matter, do the folks here
know about her? Do they know how haunted she was
about her Simon's suicide? So haunted that she penned
letters to herself that said . . . *nothing.*

"Cecilia Gilbert," J.P. says, "my newest and
dearest. Don't be too sad about Eloise. It's nature, is
all. And don't worry about telling folks about Eloise
because they know her. Say something about you. Say
something about your feelings. *Please?*"

How could I decline such a request? J.P. is simply asking me to speak my heart, and I do know how to do that. I have no idea what words might come out, but I know they will be true. Awkward, perhaps. But heartfelt, absolutely.

I nod my agreement.

"One more thing?" he whispers. "Simone. Don't let her get to you, dear. She lacks awe. It's something you're deeply blessed with, but she, the poor thing, has none. And she doesn't even know it. Be gentle with her."

I thread through the living room and dining room, where most of the people are congregated, and stand in the archway to the kitchen. I clear my throat, beg forgiveness for the interruption, and say that the Professor is not well and has asked me to say a few words. A wave of shushing moves through the crowd — at least 40 or 50 folks, I estimate. And then Miss Beula Mae Schade plants herself next to me.

"Quiet, now," she says. "This fine gal has requested our attention."

Clearly, Beula Mae is a woman accustomed to being listened to. I mouth a 'thank you' and take a deep breath.

"Friends of Eloise. Family. One and all, beloved by Eloise. I'm Cecilia Gilbert. I've been Eloise's next-door neighbor for nine days. Just nine days. Yet in that time, this kind, crazy, whirlwind of a woman touched me greatly" — a titter of approval here, a nod there — "and counseled and consoled me about my dog, who went missing" — more murmurs and one woman clasps a handkerchief to her mouth — "and I was honored to share some of her last hours with her."

Beula Mae snakes an arm around my waist. I turn to her. Her eyes widen.

"You did, child?"

I lower my eyes in affirmation and, when I look up, she is beaming.

"Eloise," I continue, "had a contentious relationship with the English language."

Scattered tittering and a few raised eyebrows.

"Once, she said to me, 'I don't listen to all the things I could hear.' At first, I thought she was confused, but I came to see that Eloise knew *precisely* what she was saying. I also came to see — just by the way her eyes held mine — that it would behoove me to locate the wisdom in her words."

I pause, wanting to really be in this moment.

"Oh," I add. "And about Eloise LaFitte's eyes?"

People lean in. They're with me.

"That woman's eyes could *bite*. Usually, just a nip, mind you, but I never met anyone whose eyes you could *feel*."

"True *dat*!" Beula Mae cries in call-and-response fashion. There are a few guffaws and a few 'amens.'

"Sometimes," I continue, "I'd look at Eloise and think she was off wool-gathering. Maybe thinking about her beloved Simon? Or maybe" — here, I glance at Eloise's prodigal daughter — "about Simone? You never knew if Eloise was pondering life on another planet or what she was going to have for lunch. Both were possible, as our Eloise had a robust inner life."

Our Eloise? I note how easily I've adopted the Professor's colloquialism.

Slack Tide

"Eloise thrived in that magical space between reality and . . . well, what would you call it? Wonder?"

I look around the room, focus on individual faces. One woman arches an eyebrow, like she's unsure where I'm going with this and, truthfully, so am I.

"In the short time we knew each other, Eloise gave me a precious gift."

Perhaps it's an optical illusion because my eyes are brimming with tears, but it seems a collective breath is being held. I think of her blank letters and how she wanted me to read them to her. I swallow a sob.

"She trusted me with her story," I say. "That's the gift she gave me. And it's the gift J.P. also gave me when he asked me to say a few words to y'all on his behalf."

I sweep my hand around the room and breathe in all the sorrow and compassion and tenderness.

"By accepting me in your community, I think all of you are trusting me with *your* stories."

Suddenly, I become self-conscious. Perhaps I have assumed too much? Am I making any sense at all? I honestly don't know, so I do a truly brave thing: I ask.

"Does that make sense?"

There's some foot-shuffling and murmuring. Someone blows his nose. A couple of people look at the person next to them and a few look at the floor. Then a voice booms, lusty and confident.

"Well, as Eloise would say, *Lots* of things don't make sense! That's what *she'd* say."

There are more titters, as if a message is being whispered down the line. Then, another voice rings out.

"She'd say, 'Girl, get *over* your fool self!'"

Heads nod, then Miss Mabel, she of the questionably parked Pontiac, sings out, true and clear as a bell.

"More like, she'd say, Get over your damn lack-of-*wonder* self!"

It's a magical moment. I've never experienced anything quite like it. These are not testimonials of what Eloise meant to them; rather, these folks are using her words, as if she is speaking through them. Telling her story.

I look over at Simone. Her lip is quivering. It breaks my heart, how hard she's trying not to cry, and my instinct is to go to her. But I know I have to let this moment play out. It is not mine to control.

There is a pause in the room. A space. Perhaps that liminal space I'd referred to earlier — where Eloise danced between reality and illusion. Someone actually says, 'ahem,' and all heads turn toward an older man in a checkered shirt.

"If I knew Eloise — and I *did* — she would say, We do not see things as they are . . . we see them as *we* are."

The woman next to him puts her hand on his arm. Then, something brushes my side, and Beula Mae takes a step forward.

"Y'all know how much E loved Bob Marley," she says. The murmuring grows louder. Even I knew of her admiration for the great Rastafarian. Marley posters cover her walls and, in the hospital, the Professor pulled up one of his songs on his phone and laid it by her ear.

"My Eloise," Beula Mae says, "dat girl *live* by the words of Mr. Marley. The truth, he say, is this: Everyone's gonna hurt you . . . you just gotta find the ones worth suffering for."

Beula Mae steps back. I turn to her and she rests her hands on the sides of my face and looks me square in the eye.

"I believe you home, child."

thirty five

Shortly before 5 p.m., I tap on J.P.'s door. "I'm leaving, Professor," I whisper, and, as I turn to leave, the door opens. He's fully dressed and he beckons me in, taking me by the hand and guiding me to sit next to him on the bed. The bedsheets are tighter than a drum under the chenille spread.

"I heard what you said, CiCi. Beula Mae told me. She had some tears to get out, so we cried together. Did you know that she and Eloise were lovers? Oh, many years ago now. After Simon's suicide. Yes, dear, I knew. Eloise blamed herself, although there was no reason to. Simone blamed her mother, but the truth is, Simon was a troubled soul. Beula Mae offered Eloise the tenderness she desperately needed."

"That's nice," I say.

J.P. reaches over and pats my hand. It makes me

think of Wink and I stand abruptly. For some reason, I feel I must leave immediately. I say my goodbyes and drive home.

Darius is sitting on my porch steps. I see him before he sees me and I watch one of his legs bounce up and down, as if he's keeping time to some scatologic jazz run in his head. His head swivels down the street in one direction, then the other, with the nervous energy of a colt. He seems ready to bolt at a moment's notice.

When he hears my car door, he shoots up. I haven't made it half way down the walk when he blurts out.

"A weird thing happened today."

"At the Professor's?"

"No, after. At the courts. Me and some kids were shootin' hoops. This kid was asking about you."

He hesitates. I walk up the steps and lean against the porch railing.

"Oh? What was he asking?"

"I'm not supposed to say."

Darius begins to hop from one foot to the other. His eyes flit from me to the street and his hands fidget in his pants pockets. I sit on one of the rocking chairs, hoping he'll take the other, but he retreats to the far end of the porch.

"I mean, he's a *sophomore* and, you know, I'm only in 6th. So, that was kind of weird in the first place."

"Hmmm," I commiserate. "That *would* seem weird."

My mouth goes dry, as I struggle to remain calm.

I'm determined to let Darius tell the story at his own pace, but there's a fluttering in my chest that won't be easy to ignore for long. Still, I must stay focused because Darius seems quite undone, and, if I push too hard, he may shut down.

"What's the kid's name, Darius? Can you tell me that?"

"Well, I guess that'd be all right. His name's Wade. Don't know the other name."

Zeke's nephew! How many Wades could there be? Asking about me?

"Darius, would you like a cold Coke?"

"Yes, ma'am. I'd like that a lot."

Darius is a good kid and I know he wants to do the right thing. But it may take some patience to help him see what, in this case, the right thing is. I invite him to sit. I return with a cold can and pull my rocker closer, trying to create a more intimate, more confidential space. I rock a few times, then speak with as much nonchalance as I can muster.

"I met a Wade when I first moved here, you know?"

I have no doubt Darius sees through the charade. Perhaps he's too young to put a name to it, but he's a bright kid and knows when an adult is being solicitous. He must sense my desire to spring on him like a cat. Shout, grab his shoulders, shake him. When there's that kind of energy in the air, it's nearly impossible to avoid.

"I've always wondered — and I know, as my friend, you'll tell me if this is a little crazy — but I've always wondered if Wade knows something about my dog."

287

Darius narrows his eyes and starts the chair rocking, all herky-jerky. He swigs down half his Coke in a couple of gulps, spilling some on his shirt.

"Wink?" he says, barely above a whisper.

I let a full thirty seconds pass, hoping my silence throws the absurdity of his question into high relief. The poor kid is in agony. But he'll have to determine his allegiance — to me or to Wade — on his own.

"This is really hard, isn't it, Darius? I mean, for you and for me . . . and probably even for Wade. But you know who this is hardest for?"

"Ma'am?"

"Wink. It's hardest for Wink. Unless he's dead . . . ?"

Darius gasps. Horror contorts his sweet face. Perhaps I shouldn't be staring at him so intently, but I can't look away. Am I pushing too hard? Am I bullying a child into telling me something he's been warned not to tell? Threatened, even. But what other path is there? Poor Darius.

Tears well in his eyes. I reach over and touch his hand. He pulls away and drops the Coke can. A dribble slops out. It's nothing.

"Oh, I'm *sorry*, Miss CiCi!"

The next thing I know, he's down on his knees, using his shirt-tail to wipe up the spill. I sit on the porch boards next to him, which shifts the dynamic between us. We sit for a few moments. Two dejected souls, watching the amoebic spread of a cola puddle.

"Do you know if Wink is dead, Darius?"

"No. I mean, I don't *think* he's dead."

"What did Wade say?"

"He asked if I knew you and I said yes and he

said, Did I know about your dog? and I said, Yes, I knew about him because I helped you put up the posters, remember?"

"I remember. You were a big help, Darius, and you barely even knew me."

"And then he said, 'She shouldn't be sad,' and he grabbed me here" — Darius touches my upper arm — "and squeezed and told me not to tell anybody."

I smile. A pained smile, no doubt, but it seems to reassure him.

"That's all he said? That I shouldn't be sad?"

He cocks his head. Looks at the street, considering, then looks back at me.

"*Something* like that."

I sit with my eyes downcast and my mind racing. Finally, I speak.

"What did you *make* of that, Darius? I mean, what do you think he meant by me not being sad?"

"That Wink is alive?"

He says it like a question, and I wonder if he's just saying what he thinks I want to hear.

"That's what you thought when he said it?"

"Well, yeah. That's what he *meant*."

This time, it's a statement.

I feel a glimmer of hope. A glimmer without any empirical evidence, granted, but more hope than I've felt in days. If Darius had reported what Wade said to him in a court of law, a judge would toss it out in a heartbeat. Clearly hearsay. But if one were still in the investigative stage of a case, as was I, what Darius just told me would constitute a solid lead.

I need a plan. And fast. If Wade is beginning to

crack, and I'm convinced he is, I'll have to find a way to slip into that crack before it seals up.

"Ma'am?"

Darius is sitting next to me on the floor of my porch. How did we get down here? I'm so lost in a fog of possibilities that it takes a moment to resurrect what just happened.

"Darius," I say, scrambling to my feet. He pops up with the wiry spring of the eleven-year-old that he is. All attention and hyper-sincerity, poised to do my bidding.

"Darius," I repeat, taking his shoulders and squaring him to me. I look him hard in the eyes.

"You've done the right thing. I want you to know that, okay?"

"Yes, ma'am."

"Here's what I think. I think Wade *wants* me to know something about Wink. I don't know what, but it's something that will help me not feel so sad."

He nods. I think he's come over to my side.

"What I need to do, or what *we* need to do, if you're with me" — he nods again — "is find a way for me to talk to Wade."

I sit in a rocker, projecting a composure I don't feel. Darius backs up a few feet, his eyes on me the entire time, as if I have him under some kind of spell. He nearly falls into the other chair.

"I'm wondering, Darius, if you have any ideas how I might do that?"

"Ma'am?"

"For instance, do you know if Wade has a cell phone?"

"Um . . . "

"Or, you know, know where he goes after school?"

His expression changes. It's just a flash, not long enough for me to interpret, but there *is* something.

"Darius?"

"Yes, ma'am. Wade has a job at the auto place, you know the one out on PIG, but I don't know if it's every day. I mean, I only know cuz that's where my mom takes our car."

"Pig?"

"Parris Island Gateway? I don't know how to get there, though."

"That's okay. Can you wait a sec, Darius . . . let's see if we can find it."

I dash inside and grab my cell, searching for auto-repair shops on Parris Island Gateway. There's only one, The Auto Care Center, and it's just nine miles away. I click on the website. Open until 6 p.m. Of course, I have no idea if Wade is working today, but, if I leave now, I can make it by 5:45. I grab my keys. Darius looks panicked.

"What ha-a-a-ppens next?"

I put a hand on his shoulder.

"One thing about life, Darius, is that a person never *knows* what happens next."

This seems to reassure him, although I'm not sure why. Maybe he sees it as a sign that nothing more is expected of him, that there's nothing more he can do.

"But you won't tell him I told you, right, Miss Cecilia?"

"No, I won't Darius, but he might figure it out, you know? He might realize it's more than a coincidence."

Again, the kid looks relieved.

"Oh, I think coincidences are fine," he says, then turns and runs down the sidewalk.

As I break every speed limit on the way to The Auto Care Center, I think, yes, Darius, coincidences are very fine, indeed.

thirty six

In New Jersey, an establishment called The Auto Care Center would be a sprawling, two-story emporium of new and used cars with an immaculate multi-bayed work area and a "guest lobby" with padded chairs and magazine-strewn coffee tables. There'd probably be a big-screen TV, free coffee and tea, and even a basket of wrapped Danishes. Not so in rural South Carolina. Which is part of what drew me here after spending my life in hubs of sophistication and privilege.

The Auto Care Center on Parris Island Gateway, PIG to the locals, is a single-story cement bunker, tattooed by time and the brutish heat and humidity of Southern summers. Although I'm not sure Wade would recognize me — we'd spent no more than an hour in each other's company the night Wink vanished — I don't want to scare him off, so I park on the far side of the building. One of the bay doors is open and I hear a metallic, pounding sound from within. Still, I think it best to enter through the front door.

I stand at the high-top reception counter. My gorge rises at the sharp, cloying odor of grease and oil. There's no bell to ring, so I holler, "Hello, hello," but the hammering in the bay area continues.

I walk outside again and see a slight, coveralled man under the hood of an SUV. He's standing on a wooden crate that looks none-too-sturdy and I'm concerned about startling him to such a degree that he clunks his head on the hood of the car and falls off the crate. But there's no other way to alert him to my presence, so I step back and, in a high-pitched, insipidly feminine voice that actually startles me, say, "Hello, sir?"

The banging stops, there's some unintelligible muttering, then a torso and head emerge from under the hood. One cheek is slashed with grease, like war-paint, and he's wearing a MAGA baseball cap.

"Oh, hey," he says. "Didn't hear you."

At that, he, well, she, pulls off the cap and out tumbles a cascade of auburn curls. She looks at the bill of the hat as if it surprises her and tosses it onto a work bench.

"Good grief," she says. "Don't mind the hat. Unless you *like* the hat, I mean . . . in which case, join most of my customers."

She wipes her hands on her coveralls and, still talking, walks towards me.

"I, myself, am a card-carrying progressive, but sometimes I wear that damn hat because it seems to minimize discussion with a certain Ford pick-up crowd that is currently funding my daughter's education."

I step forward and we shake hands. I don't know if I should respond to her soliloquy, but I'm nearly jumping out of my skin. It seems pretty clear Wade isn't here. I'm unsure what tack to take and am so flustered that I know I'll never pull off a clever subterfuge. So, the truth, then.

"I was hoping to see Wade," I say.

She pulls a kerchief out of her back pocket and swipes it around her neck.

"Wade? Sent him home a few minutes ago. Mind if I ask what you want with him? Hey, join me for a ginger ale? I'm *dying* for a ginger ale."

"Sure," I say, following her through a side door to the lobby.

"Be right back," she calls over her shoulder and disappears in the back. I look around, feeling more hopeless and dejected than any time in these past days. For the life of me, I can't say why that would be, but, perhaps, it's because I'm closer to the truth than I've been. And the truth is not likely to be pretty.

I sit, rigidly, in one of the lobby chairs. The woman comes around the reception counter and hands me a cold can. She pulls another chair around so we're facing each other. Pops the top and takes a long pull.

"Now," she says, as if we're conducting important business. "Where were we?"

"Wade," I say. "I'd like to ask him a few questions."

"About?"

She says this so tenderly, so empathetically, that tears sting my eyes.

"My dog."

She doesn't respond.

"My dog," I continue. "My dog went missing—"

"—from Zeke's?"

I gasp.

"Gosh, I guessed only cuz you want to talk to Wade."

"Oh."

"If your dog—"

"—Wink—"

"—Wink, is missing, you must have talked to my sister?"

"Your sister?"

"Brenda Lee?"

That was all it took. I burst into tears. With Eloise's death, the trip to Beula Mae's and the gathering at J.P.'s, the day has been long and emotional. My heart races at how close I might be, a hair's breadth, to discovering the truth about Wink.

"Oh, dear one, don't cry. We're going to figure this out. I promise."

She pulls a box of Kleenex from the other side of the counter. I blow my nose and wipe my eyes, thanking her copiously, as people do when a stranger bestows kindness.

"I'm Tammy Lee Hoenecker," she says, tapping the nametag on her coveralls. "See? Same as Brenda Lee's. Neither of us took our husbands' names. The SOBs."

"Cecilia Gilbert," I say, and proceed to tell Tammy Lee the entire story from beginning to end. Or, if not the end, at least until this moment. She remains perched on the edge of her chair, ready to spring into action. When I finish, she does just that. Doesn't even say what she intends to do . . . simply stands, turns her back to me, and puts her cell to her ear.

"Tammy Lee here. Is that you, Wade?"

"Uh-hunh. Well, good. Listen, I need you to come back to the shop. Yes, now. Can you do that?"

She turns and nods at me.

"Well, I was going to give you your paycheck early because I need to go up to Charleston tomorrow" — a pause, then — "Okay, great. Park and come inside, k? See you in? Okay, see you in 20."

While Tammy Lee and I wait, we make small talk. It's awkward, for both of us, I think, but that's what you do when you're biding time, when you're on the cusp of a potentially life-changing event. She was born and bred in Beaufort, she says, and wouldn't live any other place. I say that's nice to hear, especially for a Northerner who's barely unpacked and isn't sure she can stay, depending on what Wade says.

"First," she says, confidentially, "be advised that folks may still call you a Yankee, not a Northerner, but they won't mean anything by it."

"Duly noted," I respond. "And second?"

"Second. If leaving or staying depends on Wade, we gotta get the truth out of that boy. We worry about Wade, you know. Zeke's been drinking a lot lately. To folks who say he's all Wade *has*, I say that's even *worse* than nothing. I don't mean that he's a *bad* man, he tries and all. But Zeke Johnson was dealt a bad hand in life. He tries, he slips, he tries some more, like all of us, I guess."

We hear gravel crunching out front. A car door slams.

"Get in the back room!" she yell-whispers. "I need to corral him 'fore he spooks."

I do as I'm told.

"Hey, Wade. Sit down, would you?"

"Ma'am?"

"I'm saying I got you here under false pretenses. But it's mighty important, what I got you here for, so I want us to be looking each other eye-to-eye. Sit down, son."

"Cecilia?"

She calls to me and I come around the corner. Wade looks like he can't believe his eyes. He clutches the edge of his chair with both hands, and I'm not sure if he's ready to propel himself up and out the door or, like a lost soul on rough seas in a rudderless boat, is holding on for dear life.

Tammy Lee pulls another chair over and I sit next to her. Wade is facing an interrogation and he knows it.

"I believe you know who this is, Wade."

Her tone is no-nonsense.

"Wade," I say.

"Ma'am," he responds.

Any fear I had that he'd dig in, lash out against Darius, indignantly recite his uncle's party-line and deny any knowledge of Wink, dissolves instantly. He hangs his head and buries his face in his hands. His shoulders begin to shake. Tammy Lee and I say nothing.

After a minute, he raises his head. His face is red

and mottled and he speaks in hiccoughs, struggling to hold back tears.

"My uncle shouldn't have done what he did," he says. "That legal paper and all. Wasn't right."

I scooch forward in my chair. I don't want to engage in a conversation about the temporary restraining order. I want the bottom line and I want it now. I clench my teeth so hard I feel woozy. I don't dare speak, however, and Tammy Lee either agrees with my strategy or simply follows my lead. Our mini-tribunal faces him down, our silence demands the truth.

"I sold your dog to a man."

It's everything I can do to not scream or break down. When Wade sees my resolve, he caves.

"See, I was bedding down the dogs for the night, putting 'em in the shed, you know, and this guy comes out of nowhere — scared the beejeebers out of me — and your dog runs right over to him. Acted crazy-excited to see him."

I look at Tammy Lee. She looks at me and we turn back to Wade.

"So, like, this guy says, 'This is my dog and I want to surprise my girlfriend and bring him home early, and I'd like to pay you for not saying anything about it, cuz it's a big surprise and all.'"

"And did he pay you?"

This from Tammy Lee, not me. In that moment, I'm not sure I could have spoken if my life depended on it.

"Yeah. A hunnert bucks."

"And?"

Tammy Lee again. She's getting mad.

"And, I figured it was okay. I mean, I knew it wasn't, *really*. But this guy knew the dog! Then, like a few minutes later, or I don't know, a while later, you came" — finally, he looks at me — "and obviously something's wrong, I mean, I *know* I did wrong, but I didn't say anything because . . . I needed that money. I wanted it and I don't know what I was thinking. I was scared, I guess. Mostly scared of Uncle Zeke, and then everything happened so fast and the next thing I know, Uncle Zeke did those legal papers and I knew that was wrong, specially 'cuz you was just trying to find out about your dog and that was pretty understandable—"

He stops mid-sentence. I think he's simply run out of steam. I pull out my phone. Scroll through photos.

"Is this the man who paid you?"

I turn the phone and hold it in front of his face.

"Yes, ma'am."

thirty seven

Ben.

thirty eight

Those next moments feel suspended, unstressed, motionless. Nothing happens. But *everything* happens. I levitate outside my body, and images of every imaginable and unimaginable scenario flash in my mind's eye like a flip book. Wink dead. Wink taking his last gasp in a ditch on the side of the road. Wink safe on the prairie after a Minnesota family found him wandering on Highway 21. Wink starving, collapsing in a bed of pine needles. All those scenarios, all those possibilities. But never in all my tree-branching nightmares did I think Ben had kidnapped him.

After Wade identifies Ben, my mouth goes dry and chemicals flood my already-wracked body: Endorphins, oxytocin, dopamine. Relief, followed by disbelief. Horror, followed by anger. I'm dimly aware that Tammy Lee and Wade are talking, but their words are removed, as if spoken in an underground echo chamber. If I focus beyond the sweat prickling my scalp and the blood thrumming in my ears, I can generally decipher what they're saying.

Wade sobs how sorry he is. Tammy Lee says she's not sure she can keep him on at the shop, she's that disappointed. She trusted him, she was trying to help him. But to discover that he is capable of such cruelty? Such abject disregard for another human being? She just doesn't know. Wade pledges to find a way to repay me to which Tammy Lee responds, "There's no repaying this lady! It wasn't *her* money. *Plus*, nothing can repay the pain you've caused."

I hear the words, but all I can think is: Wink is alive. He's *alive*!

My brain grapples with how Ben could have known about Zeke's. How did he even know about my move to Beaufort? Had he followed me? Had me tailed? I find it incomprehensible that he is capable of this. Yes, he had hurt me. Yes, he'd been unwilling to make the slightest effort to salvage our relationship. But evil? Sadistic? *Felonious*?

I know I say something to Tammy Lee as I stumble out of The Auto Care Center, but what, I don't know. I race down Parris Island Gateway at 20 miles over the speed limit. I toss a few things in my backpack and am on the road by 7 p.m. It's a 12-hour drive to Jersey and I may need a few hours' sleep along the way, but it's more important that I arrive when Ben — and Wink — are likely to be home.

I tick through people I should call: J.P., Becca, Anne, and Carol. Talking to Darius, reassuring him that he's done the right thing, would have to wait until I get back home. I have no idea what to do about Wade.

Many would say it's not my business. Let his uncle deal with him or his own conscience or the justice system. Surely, he'd broken a law or two. But I'm interested in redemption, not retribution. Could I help Wade come to terms with what he'd done? Perhaps. All I know, in my heart of hearts, is that this is not the end with Wade. I'd have to find a way to forgive him if I want to forgive myself.

Whether I could ever forgive Ben is an entirely different matter.

Into the darkening night I drive, crossing the border into North Carolina shortly before 10 p.m. I do not play the radio. I don't want to be distracted or entertained by an oldies station or a dead-of-night talk show. All I want to do, all I *need* to do, is think about Ben.

Do I think about calling him? Of course. I'm enraged, on fire with anger so pure it's like a burning coal in my gut. But I won't call him because I don't want to alert him. And, frankly, I don't trust myself. I'm unaccustomed to this kind of anger. It's fierce and I'm afraid of the words that might pour out of my mouth like molten lava. Inflamed, inciting words that might drive Ben to another act of desperation. One like throwing himself and Wink off the pier into the Atlantic.

Ben's feelings of hopelessness and desperation were always there, but I never thought they were capable of galvanizing this kind of act. Still, peel away the man's remarkable grey matter and nimble humor and you'd find a scared little boy. A boy disdainful of hope. It wasn't a useful tool, he argued, comparing hope to Marx's bromide about religion being an opiate for the masses.

I remember a conversation we had, maybe five or six years ago, when he said, "Whoever referred to hope as a virtue was crazy." I was at the piano when he said this, working through some tricky stanzas of a Chopin etude. Ben was on the couch reading, Wink snuggled against his thigh. I'd been playing the same bars over and over, and it was becoming tiresome. It took me a moment to register what he'd said.

"Hmmmm? Are you saying my piano-playing is *hopeless*?"

"I'm serious, Cees," he said, wagging his book at me. "Only a sociopath would hold out this sort of hope."

I couldn't see what he was reading, which was fine with me. I didn't want to be drawn into an excursus on the topic of hope. What I wanted was to master the damn Chopin with its tempo changes and sudden introduction of sharps. Which is not to say I didn't usually love exploring sociological phenomenon with Ben. His brain is a miraculous thing. But I could see his thumb marking a page in the book, so I knew he didn't really want to talk. He only wanted to spar for a minute, then return to his reading. I was willing to oblige.

"I agree, Ben. Hope is a terrible thing."

"Miserable," he said. "A deceitful charlatan."

"*Worse* than a charlatan," I insisted. "A gnat on the hairy *backside* of a charlatan."

"My sentiments precisely," he said, then returned to his book, and I to my Chopin.

Slack Tide

North Carolina morphs into Virginia as the clock on my dashboard clicks onto a new day. 12:01 a.m. I approach the bridge over the Roanoke River and open the windows to hear the rapids, but all I hear is the thrumming of my tires on the bridge's expansion joints. What does it say about me, I wonder, that I chose to love a hopeless man? Maybe I thought I had enough hope for both of us? That's how hopeful I was. But I certainly can't plead ignorance because there were always signs of Ben's unhappiness. Of his self-doubt and fear. And, in truth, he told me as much from the very beginning.

I'll bet you were popular in high school, he said over a pre-dinner martini on one of our first dates. I'll bet you had lots of sleepovers with girlfriends when you were a kid.

I allowed that I did.

He flashed a smile, then his face clouded over.

"I don't really like people," he said.

I'll never forget that moment because time stopped. Everything went still, including my heartbeat. Even now, seven years later, as I approach the glowing dome of light above Washington, D.C., I remember there was a brief pause in the action, as if the universe, or something inside me, was giving me a moment to carefully consider my response.

"That can't be true," I said, choosing the easiest path.

"No, really," he responded.

"We'll see about that," I purred, popped the olive in my mouth, and reached across the white, linen tablecloth to sweep my fingers across the back of his hand.

I remember the conversation like it was yesterday, as one is wont to do with first dates. Why didn't I ask more questions? Why didn't I say, 'What do you *mean*, you don't like people?' Why didn't I press? Ben had told me a truth about himself and what did I do? I ignored it. I completely disregarded his confession. I butterfly-waved it away with a touch of my hand. I chose not to believe him.

But can either of us, I wonder, be blamed for failing to ask — or offer — more? We believed in our better angels back then. Who, after all, *doesn't* believe the best about themselves and their beloved when they're falling in love? That self-delusion, that blind hope, may be the only thing that gives us the courage to fall in love in the first place.

At the root of it all, of course, was Ben's abandonment. Still, does knowing about that make it easier to understand why Ben followed me to South Carolina? That he stalked me, as he must have, that he was capable of stealing Wink? Was I to view even *this* through a more sympathetic lens?

Somewhere north of D.C., I stop at a rest stop to pee and stretch. I consider, but reject, a short nap. The gravitational pull of Wink is that strong. I drive miles and miles without seeing another car. I drive through Delaware, grateful for the sparse traffic on I-95, remembering a conversation I had with Ben's father. Raymond called late one night, but Ben was on a business trip, so Ray and I talked for hours. I think he was a little drunk by the time he told me about the birthday card. The story haunted me for years and, as the Interstate's reflective mile-posts tick by, I realize that it haunts me still.

On Ben's tenth birthday, his mother sent him a birthday card. It was the first communication from her since she disappeared after leaving him at the orphanage. Ben took the card as a sign that she was coming back. For days, Ray said, Ben planned for her return. He rearranged the den to turn it into her bedroom, taping his drawings on the walls as artwork. He wrote poems and hid them in places she'd be sure to find them. When Ray asked Ben why he was doing all that, Ben explained he was making things "more interesting" for his mother so she wouldn't leave again. Every afternoon after school, Ben baked what he thought would be her favorite desserts. In short, he held out hope.

She never came.

So, yes, I understand that Ben's loss, never knowing why his mother left, was an ambiguous loss. But does understanding make it easier to accept? Should it make it easier to forgive?

I cross the mighty Delaware River into New Jersey, feeling the exhaustion deep in my bones. I think about Raymond's losses: His wife leaving, the loss of some elemental thing in himself that kept him from retrieving his orphanage-dumped son for nearly three years. And Ben's mother? What must she have suffered both before and after abandoning her son?

At 5 a.m., I'm just shy of Philadelphia and traffic is picking up. South-bound headlights pool in a dawn so pale-green I'm reminded of cucumber flesh. Half-an-hour later, I take an exit off the Interstate and head due east into the sunrise. A billboard for a personal-injury lawyer whizzes by on my right. Two police cars pass me, lights flashing. I feel a little rummy and my body is tingling all over. I'm not sure I'll be able to straighten my poor spine when I get out of the car or if bolts of searing pain will shoot down my legs and hobble me. Should I stop before I get to Ben's and walk around a bit, just to make sure I can stand erect?

My catacomb-brain wanders to Eloise and I wish — oh, how I wish — she'd known I would find Wink. I squint hard against the rising sun as a theory crystallizes in my exhausted brain about Eloise's blank letters: If words on paper are not required to recite a poem "by heart" — or notes on sheet music to play a piece by heart — why would Eloise need words to "read" a letter from her dead husband? Are her letters any different than the pause Barber wrote near the end of his "Adagio" movement? If the great Samuel Barber could let his composition's naked emotion simply hang in the silence of that poignant pause, couldn't the great Eloise LaFitte do the same with her blank letters? Both simply created an empty space for hearts to fill. My lips begin to tremble when I realize that, in her final hours, Eloise asked me to help her fill her heart's blank spaces.

Twenty miles to go. I pass the grocery store where Ben and I shopped, the elementary school where I tutored third graders, the vet clinic where Wink had his annual physicals. It is just shy of 7 a.m. when I pull up at the side of the house. I wait for a wave of painful recollections to scuttle me, but it doesn't come. The morning air is crisp and sunlight stipples the sidewalk where Wink and I had walked a thousand times. I see no visible activity in the house, but that doesn't mean anything. Ben is an early riser and I know he's up. In his office checking email, perhaps, or in the kitchen frying an egg for breakfast. It's possible he's taken Wink on a morning walk. We liked to do this, Ben and I. We'd walk to the ocean and, if it was early enough and no other folks were around, we let Wink run off-leash and he'd tear up the sand with his joyful abandon.

I take a few steps towards the back gate and nearly stumble where the roots of an old oak buckle the sidewalk. But, at the last moment, muscle memory kicks in and I sidestep it. I hear music from the house. The *Nachtgesang* from "Tristan and Isolde." Ben's favorite opera. Mine, too.

I see Wink a split-second before he sees, or smells, me. He's in the backyard, sniffing along the fence line. When he looks up, I feel a sudden swelling in my suprasternal notch. As much as I had hoped for this moment, I'm not sure I believed it would actually come. Of course, that's the thing about hope. As ethereal as it is, we still try to grab hold because to do otherwise might kill us.

I don't want to alert Ben before I decide what to do. I'm fairly sure Wink won't bark, but it's all in his paws now. His tail begins to wag, then his muscular little body wriggles in every direction at once. Ben opens the back door. He's wearing a ratty, untucked flannel shirt and his too-long hair is matted on one side of his head. He has a slightly feral look. When he sees me, he smiles a wan smile and raises a hand as if to wave, but halfway up, his arm drops feebly to his side.

I open the gate and step into the backyard. The flower beds are choked with weeds, but the hydrangea we planted three years ago valiantly pushes through. Ben takes a few steps towards me, then stops.

"Oh, CiCi."

"Benjamin."

"I fucked up."

"You did."

thirty nine

I squat and Wink runs into my arms.

Ben drops his head to his chest.

"The store didn't happen," he mumbles.

"I'm sorry, Ben."

"I gave it my *all*. And it wasn't enough. Don't you *understand*, Ci? Even my *all* is not enough!"

"Things fail, Ben. People fail."

Anger sparks in his eyes, then vanishes.

"You always were so forgiving, Cecilia. Even of yourself."

It's an odd thing to say, but true.

"You'll forgive me," he says.

"Will I, Ben?"

Truthfully, I'm not so sure. I've always put a high premium on forgiveness. When you love, you forgive, and when you forgive, you love. But this? This stalking, this theft of what is most dear to me, this duplicity? Ben opens his arms as if he wants me to step into them. I stand and back up. Wink scoots behind me and sits.

"How did you find me?"

"I never lost you," he says, which pisses me off.

"Enough of the riddles, Ben. Seriously, *enough*. Did you follow me? To South Carolina? To my house? Did you trail me to the dog kennel, for Chrissake?"

I take a deep breath. One question at a time, CiCi. Make him answer one question at a time. Do not give him the opportunity to pick which question to answer. I look down at Wink. He's glued to me. This dog is not going anywhere.

"I used our phones," he says. "That program we downloaded when you were working late, remember?"

"I remember."

I remember, but am stunned. I'd forgotten about the joint GPS-tracker, a tool that allowed me to see where Ben, or Ben's phone, was at all times and vice-versa. When I was editor of the newspaper, I often worked late into the night and Ben worried about my safety, so we bought the tracer app. I'd forgotten it was still on my phone.

"That is *creepy*, Ben."

I sound like a teenager. I can't afford to go easy on Ben now that I know what he is capable of. I admonish myself to toughen up.

"Why, Ben? What did you think would happen?"

"Oh, CiCi, I don't *know*. Can't you understand that it all just seemed to happen? Maybe happening to someone else, but not to *me*, you know? I've been completely untethered. I didn't think about what was next. It all just happened so fast—"

"Passive voice, Ben!" I snap. "There's no 'it' that happens fast. It was *you*. Every step of the way, *you* made the decisions!"

He cringes.

"Okay, true. When I saw you traveling so far south, I wanted to know where you were going. So, I just got in my car. Caught up when you stayed that night in Virginia and from there, it was easy. I saw your new place and, oh, Ci, I *knew* you'd be happy — and I knew *I* wouldn't. Then, when I saw where you were leaving *Wink*?! Our Wink? I mean, *seriously*, Cecilia, it was not very nice."

I stare at him. I'm not going to engage because it's crazy. Crazy . . . and sad.

"I don't *know*, Cecilia," he says when he realizes I'm not going to rescue him. "Maybe I thought I was saving him? I mean, I know, I know, not *really*, but the fact is, I simply was not *thinking*. I was on auto pilot. But I swear, Ci, I *swear*, I was going to call you. Every day, I woke up with the intention of calling you. I punched in your number a hundred times, but then the day would go by and the next . . . and it was like it was the same. The same except I didn't have you, of course. But I had Wink."

I struggle to maintain my composure.

"Remove the application from your phone immediately," I say. "Right *now*, Ben!"

"I did. This morning. When I saw you driving here."

I nod, but I'm gutted. We stand, staring at each other in heartbroken silence. Finally, he speaks.

"I just want to live a life of consequence."

Oh, Ben. How the hell am I supposed to respond

to *that*? There are so many words that should have preceded such a statement. Not words that would matter now, but over the years. Still, here we are, in this goddamn moment. I truly don't want to add to his pain, but I feel compelled to remind him that he does not live in a bubble.

"You . . . and the *rest* of the world, Benjamin."

Bells from the old Methodist church sound eight o'clock. A school bus rattles by on Jackson Street and hits a pothole with a thunk. The air is beginning to feel soupy.

"May I say goodbye to Wink?"

I agree to walk around the block so he can say his goodbyes, but before I even round the corner, I panic. When I turn, I see Wink focused on me like a laser beam, his little snout poking through the fence slats. I can't see Ben, and I realize I'm being insanely trusting or insanely stupid, and this is not the time to be either. I pivot on my heels and dash back to the house. Ben is sitting on the ground, trying to coax Wink to him. I recognize the expression on his face. When Ben wants to ward off emotions, he goes to another place, the place I now see in his eyes.

I open the gate and call Wink. He doesn't hesitate. He runs to me, looks up, awaits further instructions. He never looks back.

I close the gate. I want to say something more. I want to warn Ben off from ever interfering with my life again. I want to wail and scream about the pain he's caused me. I want to tell him to get help before he spirals completely out of control. But I do none of this.

I simply turn and walk away.

forty

I tap my thigh once and Wink heels. When I look back, Ben is gone. My first thought is that he's getting Wink's leash, then I realize that the leash is probably still at Zeke's where I left it. I can't imagine Wade taking the time to retrieve it, nor would Ben have thought to ask for it. The whole sordid transaction was probably conducted in less than five minutes.

I put Wink in his car seat, strap him in, and pull away from the curb. When I turn onto Jackson, I catch a glimpse of Ben standing in the middle of the street. Or maybe I don't. It's just a flash in my rearview mirror, and I can't imagine him enduring the heartache of watching us drive away. Except that Ben courts heartache. He expects it from life. It's his baseline, his propensity, the karmic seed planted by his mother. It didn't really matter who did the leaving.

Nancy Ritter

Whether Ben is watching my tail-lights recede or back in his favorite chair, drowning his Wagnerian sorrow in a Wagnerian opus, only one person is always leaving. His mother.

I think of the lacuna in his heart where his mother should have been and, in that moment, I forgive him.

Not that I approve of his actions. Forgiveness doesn't mean that, and it certainly doesn't mean I'm being passive. I am simply letting go of blame — the blaming armor around my heart — so I can live with more clarity and freedom. I'm choosing to engage the world with an undefended heart, and, yes, I do understand how vulnerable that makes me. But I *chose* to be vulnerable, so I can love more freely.

Six blocks down the road, I pull into an old Texaco station. It's vintage Art Deco, old red gas pumps topped with white globes. I get out of the car and scan the three iconic stripes that wrap around the roof and, above them, the widely spaced letters, T E X A C O, in red. Wink follows my every move.

I find and delete the tracking app on my phone, then unstrap Wink's car seat and move it to the front. When I strap him back in, his body tenses, and who could blame him? I stroke his back and haunches, and he relaxes under my touch. He puts his head out the window, calm now. I lean in close and he touches my face with his nose.

J.P. answers on the first ring.

"Mission accomplished," I say.

He allows a long silence to pass between us. It contains a thousand words, none of which needs to be said. Then, just this: "Bring him home, Cecilia."

One-story strip malls line the road leading to the Interstate. Most of the stores have long since fallen into disrepair, but every hundred feet or so, there's a hanging basket overflowing with flowers. Oh, I think, this humanity. This sad, beautiful struggle of being human.

Up ahead, a green neon sign for I-95 marks the way home. Beyond the sign, potbellied clouds pile up on the horizon. I depress my turn signal and pull into the left-turn lane, heading south. South, where osprey and heron and hermit crabs will inhabit Wink's dreams for the rest of his days. South, where disappearing waterways flow off the map and into my veins. The light turns green and I look over at my dog and into his fathomless eyes.

fin

A Note from the Author

This is a work of fiction. I took literary license with my portrayal of the Beaufort animal shelter to present Cecilia with another challenge in her search for Wink; the entity I've created in *"Slack Tide"* bears no resemblance to the real Beaufort County Animal Services, which is top-notch and makes me proud to live in Beaufort.

What is true is this: With few exceptions, animal shelters and rescue organizations across the United States are underfunded and understaffed, and they do the best they can to provide care and sanctuary for lost, abused, abandoned, exploited and neglected animals.

A randomly controlled study of lost dogs found that, during a five-year period (2005–2010), nearly 11 million dogs would have been lost in the U.S.; seven percent — or 766,360 dogs — would not have been reunited with their owners. (See National Institutes of Health, National Library of Medicine: "Frequency of Lost Dogs and Cats in the United States and the Methods Used to Locate Them," www.ncbi.nlm.nih.gov/pmc/articles/pmc4494319.)

Mahatma Gandhi said, "The greatness of a nation and its moral progress can be judged by the way its animals are treated." If you were touched or inspired by *"Slack Tide,"* please consider a donation to your local shelter or rescue group.

To contact Nancy: slacktideanovel@gmail.com

Acknowledgments

Two stunningly talented people pushed my writing to places I didn't even know I wanted to go. Jonathan Haupt, executive director of the Pat Conroy Literary Center, and Fay Sandven, college roommate, poet and reader-extraordinaire, shared their expertise and hearts, rendering me both awed and (in the very best way) terrified.

Thank you to my early readers whose guidance in matters of plot, character, and writing exceeded my every expectation: Becky Bruff, the only other member of the Can-You-Believe Writing Club besides me; Lee Weimer, lover of dogs and No. 2 pencils; Susan Schilling, who could have looked the other way the day we met, but didn't; Carolyn Jirousek, Nature Girl and poet (the poem at the beginning of the novel is hers, the last stanza of a longer poem); the creative, curious Carolyn Mason, who asks the best 'What if?' questions; and Kathy Dratch, Guru Queen of Motivation and Meaning — mine and my characters.

To my later readers who offered counsel on the 101st draft (but who's counting?): Mary Eggert, soul sister and marrow-sharer; Rosalie Gross and Jolene Hernon, editors in my former life, who taught me more about writing than they'll ever own up to; Beaufort buddies Mary Flynn, Suzie Parker Devoe, Patrice Andrews, and Lynn and Cele Seldon; and, finally, Teresa Bigelow, who convinced me 35 years ago that I could — and should — write fiction.

My wicked-smart niece, Michelle Reid, earns her own paragraph of gratitude just because she does; her deconstruction of plot developments and psychoanalysis of characters made this a better book. Plus, she designed *"Slack Tide's"* cover; with Michelle's vision — and Beth Williams' glorious painting — this book should fly off the shelves, right?

My rescue dog, Otis, witnessed every drop of blood, sweat and tears that went into this novel. Thanks for your patience, O-Boy . . . NOW we can go for a walk.

Finally, to Carolyn and Jeff Mason, who shared their story with me. The disappearance of their dog Hank haunted and inspired every word herein.

About the Author

Author photos by Michelle Reid

Nancy has been writing her entire life, including long letters to her English professor grandfather and notes passed surreptitiously to her best friend in junior high. In her professional career, she worked as a paralegal, a reporter, and an editor. She has received numerous awards for her writing, culminating in a Service to America Medal for her work at the U.S. Department of Justice on the nation's missing persons crisis, where she first learned about "ambiguous loss," an issue she explores in *"Slack Tide"*.

Born in New Mexico, Nancy grew up in Minnesota, receiving her B.S. in English Education from the University of Minnesota. When she realized she didn't possess the temperament to survive classroom teaching or Minnesota winters, she moved to Seattle, where she worked as a paralegal. Other jobs took her across the country to New Jersey, then down to Washington, D.C., before she followed the siren call of the South and landed in Beaufort, South Carolina.

A vocal advocate of community service, Nancy has tutored and mentored kids, worked with elderly folks in nursing homes, and, most recently, served on a citizen task force investigating issues of racial equity and civic rights justice. She volunteers with the Pat Conroy Literary Center, a nonprofit organization that nurtures a diverse community of readers and writers. An avid reader and lapsed musician, Nancy spends as much time as possible exploring Hunting Island and other South Carolina treasures with her [fifth] rescue dog, Otis.

To contact Nancy: slacktideanovel@gmail.com

About the Artist

Beth Tockey Williams — whose work graces the cover of this novel — is a Beaufort, SC, oil painter and pastelist whose work focuses on the diverse sea island landscapes that surround her home studio. Beth achieved her Master Circle Status with the International Association of Pastel Societies in 2021. Her work has been featured in numerous publications, including *Pastel Journal*. You can find her work at Charleston Artist Collective, or her studio at Atelier on Bay in downtown Beaufort.

Learn more at Beth's website:
bethwilliamspastels.squarespace.com

Discussion Questions

1. One of the novel's themes is the canine-human relationship. In your personal experience, how would you describe this type of reciprocal/symbiotic bond? If your pet disappeared, how long would you look for him/her/them? To what lengths would you go?

2. How did you feel about Cecilia when she left Wink at Zeke's Paws Spa? Did those feelings change as the novel progressed?

3. Discuss the human trait of willful or "blind" ignorance. Have you ever ignored your gut feelings about something and later regretted it?

4. The author explores the psychological concept of "ambiguous loss." Have you ever experienced this? When, in the absence of any evidence, do you think you would accept that you might never know what happened to someone or something you love? What tools might you employ in achieving that acceptance?

5. Did the story unfold the way you expected? If not, what surprised you?

6. "*Slack Tide*" uses the literary themes of "stranger-in-a-strange land" and "found community." What other books have you read that employ these themes?

7. How do you think the obstacle of Wink's disappearance impacted the development of Ceclia's relationships throughout the book? Did it leave her determined and short-sighted? Did it make her more vulnerable to the influence of others? What ways did you see Cecilia becoming increasingly undone as the days went by?

8. Cecilia imagines an "explanation," or meaning, for Eloise's letters. Do you agree? What do you make of Eloise's letters?

9. The author — who was in her 70's when she wrote "*Slack Tide*" — wanted to explore the concepts of mercy and grace. For example, when CiCi realizes that the Professor has hooked up her stereo speakers, she says, "Oh, the unexpected mercies of people." What is your definition of grace? Do you think one's experience of mercy or grace (both bestowed and received) changes as we age? When you're reading a novel, do you ever think about the age of the author? Do you think age affects how a story is told — and, if so, how?

10. In forgiving a character at the end of the novel, CiCi says she feels "clarity" and "freedom." What do you think she means by that?

11. The literary concept of "place as character" describes when the setting/place of a novel functions as a catalyst for the characters or, in and of itself, becomes dynamic, changes, or perhaps serves as a metaphor. How does the author use the Lowcountry as a "character" in the story? What, if any, feelings did you develop about the Carolina Lowcountry as a "character" in *Slack Tide*? What does the term "slack tide" mean to you in the story?